A Legend in the Baking

ALSO BY JAMIE WESLEY

Fake It Till You Bake It

Body and Soul: Those Jones Boys Series
Make the Play

Camp Firefly Falls Series
The Time of His Life
Her Dream Come True

The Exclusive! Series
This Is True Love
The Trouble with Love

The One-on-One Series
Tell Me Something Good
Slamdunked by Love
The Deal with Love

A Legend in the Baking

Jamie Wesley

ST. MARTIN'S GRIFFIN
NEW YORK

First published in the United States by St. Martin's Griffin, an imprint of St. Martin's Publishing Group

A LEGEND IN THE BAKING. Copyright © 2024 by Jamie Wesley. All rights reserved. Printed in the United States of America. For information, address St. Martin's Publishing Group, 120 Broadway, New York, NY 10271.

www.stmartins.com

Designed by Jen Edwards

The Library of Congress Cataloging-in-Publication Data is available upon request.

ISBN 978-1-250-80187-6 (trade paperback)
ISBN 978-1-250-80188-3 (ebook)

Our books may be purchased in bulk for promotional, educational, or business use. Please contact your local bookseller or the Macmillan Corporate and Premium Sales Department at 1-800-221-7945, extension 5442, or by email at MacmillanSpecialMarkets@macmillan.com.

First Edition: 2024

10 9 8 7 6 5 4 3 2 1

To Cheris Hodges. May reading about your play cousin August finding true love brighten your day.

A Legend in the Baking

Chapter One

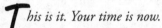

This is it. Your time is now.

Sloane Dell beamed at Candace, her boss and the director of marketing at Organic Chemistry, who was seated across the glass desk from her. Sloane had put in the hours, the less-than-desirable assignments (which sometimes included literally scooping up dog poop) as a social media assistant at the organic pet food company for the last three years. But it was all for a good cause. The promotion to social media manager was about to be hers. Finally.

Candace's head was bent down as she reviewed Sloane's work file, no doubt cataloging all the metaphorical gold stars Sloane had received from colleagues over the years.

Sloane is the best! Sloane is such a team player! Sloane comes up with the best, most innovative ideas! We couldn't survive without her!

Okay, maybe that last one wouldn't be in there, even though it was true. She wasn't cocky, but she loved her job and was good at it.

Sloane's smile spread as Candace lifted her head, her eyes narrowing slightly. Her bright pink lipstick had started to bleed in the right corner.

Concentrate, Sloane! Now's not the time.

Candace cleared her throat and adjusted the black frames that always seemed to be slipping down her nose. "Thanks for coming to see me, Sloane. I wanted to let you know we enjoy having you here at Organic Chemistry."

Here it came. The big promotion. Sloane's chest swelled with hope and excitement. She was already starting to think of all the ideas she wanted to implement to further the company's goals, the student loan payments she could increase . . .

". . . believe you still need more experience before you can move up to the manager position."

"Tha—" The rest of that word petered out as Candace's words sank through Sloane's body like a lead stone, anchoring her to the stiff leather chair.

What the fuck?

Only the self-control she'd learned to assert over herself even through the most trying of times stopped her from blurting out that way-too-real question. Instead, she went with the much more sedate, more "professional" "Excuse me? Could you repeat that, please?"

Candace sighed and pushed up her glasses again. "Yes, it's true. We agonized over this decision, but don't feel putting you in a position you're not quite ready for is the right move. It can only hurt your career."

Such bullshit. Over the past two years, she'd put in countless hours for this company, come up with several campaigns that went viral, tripling their social media followers and directly correlating to an increase in sales, only for her immediate supervisor, the assistant director, Daniel, to take the credit. She'd let him get away with it because Sloane was a team player. And now her generosity had officially blown up in her face.

What a bunch of horseshit. Cow shit. Bear shit. Whatever excretions from whatever animal you could think of.

But she had to play the game.

After all, this was corporate America, where fakeness ruled and Black women were often punished for having the unmitigated gall to be both Black and female, so she was going to smile and play the game with the sunshiney-est smile possible. It was the only way to reach her ultimate goal of receiving the promotion she most definitely deserved. "I appreciate you looking out for me."

Candace pressed a hand to her chest, the pink shade of her polish perfectly matching her lipstick, because appearances were always important. Her beady little green eyes gave off earnest vibes. "Thank you so much for understanding that this was such a tough decision for us. We agonized, but truly think this is the best for you."

"I quit."

Sloane froze. Wait. Who said that? The voice sounded familiar. Wait. She, Sloane Renee Dell, had said that. Sloane's chest filled, not with panic, as she'd initially assumed, but a sense of rightness. Damn right she quit.

Candace's mouth had fallen open in pure shock, her eyes bugging out behind her very tasteful, yet very expensive frames.

Sloane rose as a sense of purpose surged throughout her entire body. "I deserved that promotion. You know it. I know it. Everyone in this office knows it, and I'm not going to let you gaslight me into thinking it's my fault you didn't offer it to me. Consider this my resignation letter. I won't need two weeks."

Sloane whirled and strode confidently out of the office. With laser focus, she headed to her little cube—because offices were reserved for managers and directors and the like and not little pesky assistants who apparently didn't deserve promotions. She quickly collected the few personal items she kept on her desk—the framed photo of her mom and siblings, her lucky shamrock plushy—and headed for the elevator.

Bethany, who worked in accounting, blinked when she saw Sloane. "Where are you going, Sloane?"

"I quit!"

Perhaps she'd said that a little too loudly, because heads began popping over the top of cubicle walls like the creatures in the Whac-A-Mole arcade game. She regally nodded at them all and gave them her best Duchess Meghan wave as she glided down the hall.

Her best friend, Felicia, the admin assistant, gave her a questioning look as she passed the front desk. Sloane shook her head but didn't stop. Later. She would explain later. If she stopped now, she'd end up screaming at the top of her lungs about the injustice of it all and wind up being escorted off the property by building security.

Reality didn't hit her until she was behind the wheel of her Mazda. Her vision went hazy for a second as she sucked in unsteady breaths.

Oh, God. What had she done? She had bills to pay. Student loans to whittle away at. She couldn't quit a good job without another one lined up. But she had. She pressed a shaky hand to her abdomen. That mocha latte she'd treated herself to as a midday snack and pre-promotion celebration was now curdling in her stomach with the fury of sour milk.

But if the powers-that-be didn't have her back, did she really want to work there?

No. She. Did. Not.

Anger surged in her anew. She hit the steering wheel with a balled-up fist. "How fucking dare they?"

Sloane screwed her eyes shut and let out her best primal scream, stretching her vocal cords to their limits as she poured out her frustration.

A few seconds later, her eyes fluttered open. Damn, that felt good. She loosened her grip on the steering wheel and put the car in reverse.

Time to get as far away as she possibly could from the job she'd poured blood, sweat, and way too many tears into. Next stop was home, to wallow in peace. Eat ice cream, binge some good old-fashioned reality TV that didn't require much thinking on her part other than judging the decisions people made. Perfect.

At a red light, she pulled the car to a stop and stared unseeing out the windshield, her brain still trying to process the last fifteen minutes. And failing. How could they do this to her? In an instant, she'd gone from being next in line for a promotion to no-go, because she supposedly hadn't hacked it. Maybe she'd add a nice bottle of wine to her ice cream and TV plans.

Buzz.

Sloane glanced at the screen on the dashboard. Her older sister, Shana, was calling. No surprise. It was like Shana had a sixth sense when her baby sister was in distress. Sloane pressed the icon on the screen to send the call to voicemail. While she loved her sister dearly, she couldn't talk to her right now. Not when she was vacillating between succumbing to a blubbering crying jag or another thunderous roar. Both were worthy options she would most likely indulge in when she got home.

The light turned green. Sloane took her foot off the brake . . . and jerked the steering wheel to the right. Actually, she had a better idea. Well, the wallowing with ice cream and wine was still on the table. After all, she no longer had a job. She now had all the time in the world to wallow. But first, she needed sugar in another form. And she knew the best place in San Diego to get some.

Sugar Blitz Cupcakes, owned, or rather co-owned, by her older brother, Donovan.

The shop made the biggest and best cupcakes in California and she needed to stuff her face with one *right now*. And maybe get some advice from her brother. While Shana would go storming into Organic Chemistry on her behalf to demand they give her younger sibling that promotion, Donovan was a bit more pragmatic.

Only a year older than her, he was always a rock, always there with some sensible advice. And since the only thought ping-ponging through her brain was *You quit a decent job. You quit a decent job,* maybe he could convince her that this was not the worst thing in the world. He was great at advice. Always ready with the "when one door closes, another one opens, we'll figure this out, blah blah blah" stuff. She was ready to eat that cliché shit up.

Ten minutes later, she entered the cupcakery and scanned the bright, open space for her brother. The place was packed with customers, laughing and enjoying themselves. Maybe the patrons all had the day off. Or maybe they were on vacation. Hell, maybe they were independently wealthy and didn't have to worry about pesky things like jobs and rent.

Panic sank its sharp claws into her stomach lining again.

Okay, enough of that. Sloane took a deep breath, counted to five, and scanned the room again. No, her brother wasn't here. Neither were his two partners, August and Nicholas. She nodded at Ella, a part-time worker who was manning the front counter.

Donovan and his partners had done a great job over the past year of establishing the cupcakery as a vital part of the surrounding community. The shop's yellow walls were adorned with photos of her brother and his partners and some of the regulars. It was a warm, welcoming space.

Which was great, but not why she was here. Maybe her brother was in his office. He loved sitting in there and poring over numbers when he wasn't wreaking havoc on a football field as a member of the San Diego Knights.

She weaved her way through the tables and down the hall to his office. She briskly knocked on the closed door. When no answer was forthcoming from inside, she tried the knob. It turned easily in her hand.

The office was empty. Crap.

No job, no brother, no cupcakes as of yet. Could this day get any worse?

Wait. No. No need to put that thought into the universe and tempt fate. Things could *always* get worse.

Sloane squared her shoulders. Okay, then. One last place to check—the kitchen. If Donovan wasn't there, maybe she'd find Nicholas, the head baker, creating the bakery's soon-to-be newest sensation. She could charm one of his delicacies out of him. Her lips crooked. Not that he would need much charming. The man had a black belt in flirting.

Her mouth watered as she neared the kitchen in the back of the building. Baking was definitely happening inside. The fresh, warm scents of sugar, vanilla, and lemon floated through the air. Lemon meringue cupcakes? Also known as her favorite? Yes, please.

She pushed the door open and hurried inside. But again, she was disappointed. No brother, no Nicholas, no cupcakes cooling on the counter waiting for her to devour, er—*taste test*—them.

The good news was the aroma of cupcakes was stronger here. She was one step closer to heaven. Her eyes locked on the oven across the room. It was on. Her much-needed reward waited inside. Drawn to the oven like bees to nectar, she marched across the room.

Until a butt entered her line of vision. An exceptional butt. Extraordinary, really. Perfectly rounded and muscular. Biteable.

Sloane halted. Suddenly, finding her brother or getting to cupcakes were no longer her top priorities. Time to appease a different type of hunger. One she didn't allow herself to indulge in much because embarrassing the shit out of herself once was more than enough times to last a lifetime. Yeah . . . but this was different. The owner of the butt couldn't see her, so ogling was allowed.

He was on his knees, his head underneath a sink as he reached, unsuccessfully based on his colorful curses, for something deep inside.

"Shitdamnfuck," he muttered.

"You okay there?" she called out, biting her lip to stop a giggle from escaping.

Thwack! His upper body jerked upward, making an unpleasant sound.

More colorful curses followed as August Hodges, the third co-owner of Sugar Blitz, scooted back, patting the spot on his head where he'd bashed it against the counter.

Sloane grimaced in equal measures of sympathy and guilt. "Ouch. Sorry. I didn't mean to startle you."

He cocked his head to the side and glared up at her. "Sloane."

All growly and annoyed. And panty-melting. If one was interested in having one's panties melted off, and she most certainly was not. Not by him, anyway.

Not anymore.

He wiped away water dripping down his impressive cheekbones. With grace that belied his large frame, he rose to his feet. Well, almost. His right foot slipped on a small puddle of water—maybe that was the reason for the cursing—and he fell romantically, like a damsel in distress in every romcom known to mankind, into her waiting arms. Well, sorta.

More like stumbled into her like a runaway bowling ball. And given that she was five-five and he outweighed her by many, many pounds, it didn't go well for her. She staggered back and, OMG, he came with her, the firmness of his chest pressing into hers, his arms caging her against the counter behind her. His body was shockingly warm. And unshockingly, deliciously hard.

Her eyes sought his of their own volition. Once upon a time she'd thought he'd had the most beautiful pair of eyes she'd ever seen. They were the color of a deep maple. She'd spent way too much time as a besotted teen trying to pinpoint the exact color. Molasses was too light, chocolate too dark. Once upon a time. They'd darkened. Just a tad, like he too felt the electric currents darting through her system.

Her breath hitched as it dawned on her that with their bodies pressed together like this they were the closest they'd been since . . .

He jumped back like she was infected with *cooties* and crossed his arms, both roped with thick muscle, over the impressive chest she'd just gotten reacquainted with. "What are you doing here?"

Yeah, he still wasn't pleased to see her. Nothing new there.

She lifted an eyebrow. She wasn't offended. Not really. August didn't talk much, and when he did, he didn't mince words. "Looking for my brother."

"He's taking his engagement photos today." Again, straight no chaser.

Sloane snapped her fingers. "Oh, that's right."

In the misery of her day, she'd forgotten that there were actual happy people in the world, looking forward to things. Her sibling and his fiancée, Jada, were too cute for words, and if she hadn't sworn off love for the foreseeable future, she might have been jealous of their happiness.

His eyebrows snapped together. "You were looking for Donovan in the kitchen?"

Slapping a hand to her chest, Sloane gasped in mock indignation. "He could've been back here. He bakes."

August didn't say anything. He didn't have to.

Donovan did bake, but he was more likely to be found in his

office, especially now, when they were about to open a second location. Donovan lived to make sure all i's were dotted and t's crossed. And they both knew it.

August leaned against the counter and crossed his arms again. She wouldn't notice how the movement highlighted biceps that needed no help in being showstoppers and forearms lightly dusted with hair. What was it about the veins in forearms that did it for her? Probably because she wanted to trace the veins with her tongue, then continue the exploration of the rest of his body. Wait. No.

She controlled her wayward thoughts, especially when it came to him, not the other way around. Acknowledging that he was an attractive man was *not* the same as being attracted to him. She'd been down that road once and had the skid marks to prove it. There was no way she was taking that route again.

Sloane mimicked his position to prove she was as relaxed as he was. No fidgeting or any other hints that she was antsy or uncomfortable. Not that he made it easy. He focused his whole attention on her like she was an opposing defensive back he'd been tasked to block. Those beautiful eyes seemed to look deep into her soul, determined to wrest every secret she hoarded like Halloween candy. But she wasn't going to give him any. She'd perfected the skill as a child who'd had to hide how her parents' unhappy relationship affected her. Only once—with him—had she let down her guard and caused a rift in their relationship they'd never recovered from. That decision had cost her dearly.

So she held her ground.

"What are you doing here, Sloane?" He refused to let her look away. Not that she would. That would denote weakness. Sloane Dell was never weak.

She shrugged. "I already told you. I came to see my brother."

His eyes narrowed. "In the middle of the day? You're a workaholic."

Was a workaholic.

All of a sudden, the loss of her job overwhelmed her with the finality of it all. Every pore in her body filled with failure. Her eyesight blurred for a moment. All her dreams, her plans for the future gone like balloons released to a scattering wind.

Her gaze skidded away. Damn it. She'd blinked first. He stepped toward her, bringing the smell of lemons and the soft, alluring scent of his cologne closer. He'd changed brands about two years ago. She hated that she knew that. She hated that she had a preference, and whatever he wore now won in a landslide. She hated that, on one particularly dark day, she'd spent time in the cologne section of a department store, trying to determine which fragrance it was. But only so she could buy all the bottles, leaving him with none, which would potentially give her peace. At least that's what she'd told herself.

"Sloane." August reached out like he was going to touch her, possibly offer comfort, but remembered at the last moment that he was August and she was Sloane, and by silent decree, they never touched. She tracked the movement of the large hand he used to both battle guys on the football field and bake delicate cupcakes as it fell harmlessly to his side. She would not be sad that he hadn't made contact.

She lifted her gaze. A mistake. Those beautiful eyes that had only a few seconds ago been filled with annoyance now conveyed concern, worry. Compassion.

But she would be okay. She would make sure of it. One job, one loss of a job, did not define her. Sloane held up a hand to prevent him from coming closer. "I'm fine. I quit my job, okay."

His brows drew together in a deep V. "Why? Did something happen?"

She lifted her chin. "I didn't get the promotion I assumed I was going to get."

"Oh, Sloane, I'm sorry."

The sympathy in his eyes, in his voice, pierced her heart, which had already been slowly bleeding since she'd marched out of Candace's office.

"I don't need sympathy. I'm fine. I'll be fine. I have a plan." Points to her for the conviction and courage in her tone. She didn't have a plan—well, other than cupcakes, ice cream, and wine. Not yet. The wound was still too fresh. But she'd been knocked down before and always rose, stronger, more resilient, more sure of her purpose. This would be no different. As soon as she figured out her next step.

He continued to study her, like he could penetrate her armor if he stared long enough. But she'd already blinked once. It wasn't going to happen again.

Finally, he nodded. "Okay. But just so you know, it's okay not to be okay."

The loud buzz of the oven timer saved her from having to respond. He crossed the room and pulled out the lemon meringue cupcakes and placed them on the counter. Sloane tried not to drool. They were her faves, and she was weak. And hungry. And unemployed.

They were perfect. A nice golden color. Fat and plentiful. Heavenly smell. A small moan, tiny really, slipped past her lips.

He looked back over his shoulder. "Did you say something?"

He saw and heard far too much.

Sloane swallowed hard. "No."

"I have cupcakes." Again with the sympathy and understanding that she couldn't handle right now. Not from him.

"Thanks, but since my brother isn't anywhere on the premises, I'm gonna leave. I'm probably violating five different health codes being here in the kitchen anyway."

She beat a hasty retreat without too much trouble. Well, if one didn't count stumbling away like a baby giraffe just learning to walk. Which she totally didn't.

"There should still be a few lemon meringue cupcakes at the front counter," he called as she slipped through the door.

She didn't even look back. Because she was a badass bitch.

Chapter Two

Twelve years ago . . .

August answered the phone. "Hello."

"Donovan?" a female voice responded. "Wait. No, this isn't Donovan. Who is this? And what have you done with my brother?"

August found himself smiling. Donovan had often talked of his outspoken baby sister, Sloane. "This is August, his roommate, and as far as I know, I've done nothing with him."

Her sniff came through the phone. "Then why are you answering his phone?"

"You've been blowing up his phone."

"No, I haven't. I only called three times."

"And texted three times."

"Whatever. Why doesn't my brother have a lock on his phone like normal people?"

His smile spread. "Can't answer that, sorry."

"Hmmph. Some help you are. Where is my brother, by the way? Why do you have his phone, anyway?"

"Your brother was running late to class and ran out without

it. I answered in case something had happened to you or your mom."

August didn't know all the details about Donovan and Sloane's parents' relationship, but Donovan was still apprehensive about leaving them in Oakland, although he was only a few hours away in Los Angeles.

"Oh. Well, I guess that was nice of you, Month of the Year."

She didn't sound thrilled to be making that admission. His grin widened. "August means impressive and respected, and not just the month of the year."

"Hmm. I'll try to remember that," she said, still clearly unimpressed and not willing to offer him any respect just yet. "Why aren't you in class?"

"Because your brother and I don't have the same class schedule. He's a business major."

"What are you?"

He hesitated before answering. He often saw people's confusion when they learned his major. But he couldn't see her, could he? "English."

"Oh, that's cool, but not really helpful to me in the moment."

"How come?" August settled against his bed's headboard.

"My brother is good in math. He likes numbers and stuff. My older sister, too, but she's busy. I'm the family weirdo."

"Anything I can help with?"

August blinked. He stared at the phone before bringing it back to his ear. Why the hell had he said that? Maybe because talking to her on the phone was easier and less pressure-filled than trying to carry on a conversation in person. Also, because she didn't expect anything from him. There was no pressure to impress someone who didn't seem to get impressed as a rule.

She sighed. "Only if you know something about quadratic equations and AP Calculus."

"I muddled my way through that class. Let's see if I remember anything."

She groaned. "You're an English major. What do you know about AP Calculus?"

"I know I passed the class, which is more than you can say at this point."

Sloane laughed, a light musical sound that flowed through the phone and straight into his soul. "Touché, sir, touché. Then I accept your help, but if I end up failing this test, I'm going to come down to campus and kick your butt somehow. I don't care that you play football. I'll watch some YouTube videos first or something."

He laughed harder than he had in a long time.

Chapter Three

August Hodges blew out a breath as soon as the door shut behind Sloane. Maybe his heart rate could return to normal now. Maybe. He gripped the counter and let out another breath.

His day wasn't going bad—at least it hadn't been until he noticed the small leak in the pipe under the sink. He had no reason to complain. His careers—as the starting fullback for the San Diego Knights and one of the co-owners of the cupcake shop—were going well. And even a minor leak wasn't that big of a problem. He'd fixed similar issues with no problems since he was a kid. But this little fucker wanted to be stubborn. No matter how much he cursed and yanked, a bit of water trickled out.

He hadn't wanted to believe it, but he needed a new repair clamp. It didn't matter that he'd replaced it last month. To make matters worse, just when he'd thought he'd asserted his dominance over the inanimate object, he'd heard it.

It being the magical voice. The voice sure to lead any man interested in women to doom.

And he'd responded by embarrassing himself, smashing his head against the underside of the sink. And he hadn't even gotten to the part where a puddle of water spelled doom for him and his twelve-year-old promise to never commit the folly of touching Sloane again. As her breasts contoured against his chest, as their stomachs pressed against each other, the air had seized in his throat, and his skin began tingling. The desire to wrap his arms around her killer body and draw her closer nearly overwhelmed him. But then common sense returned.

Sloane didn't feel that way about him, which was fine and expected. Totally. He'd moved on. So had she.

Fuck.

August scrubbed a hand across his face. So yeah, his day was no longer going okay. But the day wasn't over yet. Time to get back to work.

He shook out his arms and turned his attention to the cupcakes on the counter. They weren't going to decorate themselves. Although, truth to be told, they were so good they didn't need frosting or any other ornamentation to make them appealing. As Sloane often liked to say. His lips quirked as he recalled the many times she turned cupcakes upside down and ate the desserts from the bottom because she didn't give two damns about hand-whipped buttercream frosting.

August shook his head.

No more thinking about Sloane. *For now, anyway,* an annoying inner voice whispered.

Anyway . . . he liked decorating. Giving the cupcakes that final touch before they were presented to an eager public that would *ooh* and *aah* over them before devouring them in the next breath. He liked the repetitive action that never led to uniform results. Each cupcake, though decorated in the same way, was its own unique, beautiful creation. He got to work, his eyes narrowing as he concentrated on the task at hand.

A few minutes later, his phone chimed. August picked it up from the counter and sighed. His father was calling. He gave a moment's thought to not answering. Actually, two moments, but the phone kept ringing and the man was his father, and maybe unicorns would start flying and this conversation would go better than their other, infrequent talks. Not likely, but again the man was his father. Stifling another sigh, he answered. "Hey, Dad."

"August," the esteemed Dale Hodges boomed. "How's it going? Training for the upcoming season?"

"I'm at Sugar Blitz."

A beat of silence followed, then a slight chuckle. "Good, good, but you're not slacking on your training, are you?"

Football was okay. Not great, but acceptable. The sport had made him a lot of money and he was on TV every week. His father got to claim he was the father of a pro athlete. Cupcakes, on the other hand . . .

"No, I work out every day."

"Right, right."

His father was already losing interest. Someone was talking to him in the background. The familiar pang, now mostly a dull ache, zinged inside August's chest.

"What's up with you?" August asked, the need to respect his father and garner his attention never really leaving him.

"Business as usual. About to close another deal. Paula said I should call."

Right. Paula. His father's latest in a long string of lady friends, as Dale referred to them. August hadn't met Paula. He'd long ago lost any desire to meet the women who flitted in and then out of his father's life when they realized the suave, debonair Dale would never give them or their relationship the attention or care each deserved.

August could have told them that from jump. He knew firsthand his father's shortcomings. The internal scars from childhood never fully healed, did they?

"We're on our way to San Francisco and wine country for a weekend away." Dale sounded aggrieved. The trip had undoubtedly been Paula's idea.

"Sounds fun."

Dale grunted. Someone was still talking to his father. August made out "meeting" and "contract."

"Son, I gotta go. Make sure you keep working out. Cupcakes? I don't know why you're wasting time with that. My son making cupcakes. So silly. If you wanted to cook, you could have trained under me. Do something respectful. Important. Women make cupcakes."

After one final sniff of disdain, the phone went dead. Not that August needed to hear much else. He'd heard it all before. Baking cupcakes wasn't manly enough. Owing a shop wasn't ambitious enough. Not when he could be a Michelin-starred chef like his father and own several world-renowned restaurants. Be a *New York Times* bestselling author of a series of cookbooks. All bullshit. He'd tried, a time or two, to correct his father—respectfully, of course, thanks to the lessons drummed into him by his grandfather, who'd essentially raised him. All to no avail.

His father was self-centered. His father was a chauvinist. Facts August repeated to himself on a regular basis. And yet it still hurt that he couldn't gain his father's approval.

But that was nothing new. And he had work to do. A few short feet away, customers eagerly awaited the shop's products. He returned to work, even as his conversation with his father and all the things left unsaid gnawed at him in the recesses of his brain.

When he was done, he stepped back to study his efforts. Pretty good, if he did say so himself. Nicholas would probably have something to say about the exact level of imprecision, but his ass wasn't here, was he? They were running out of the day's special, lemon meringue cupcakes, and August had done what needed to be done to get them through the pre-dinner rush, when people stopped by on their way home from work.

He checked the clock on the wall. He'd been in here over an hour. He needed to take the cupcakes to the front of the store before their current supply ran out.

August scrubbed a hand across his face. He also needed to check on the customers. The part of the job he hated most. He loved Sugar Blitz's clientele, but he preferred to stay in the background and let his more gregarious partners deal with the limelight. Talking was not the way. Neither was being the center of attention. The exact opposite of how his father operated. August blinked. He'd never thought about it before, but hell, maybe being quiet was his way of rebelling against his father, who loved to talk and have all eyes on him.

In any case, Nicholas had left for the day, and Donovan was off with his fiancée. Which left August with the responsibility of representing ownership.

They had a full-time manager, Marissa, who ran the place when they were off doing the football thing, but she was taking a much-needed vacation now that football season was over and the owners could spend more time at the shop. Being at Sugar Blitz was A-OK with August. The offseason meant downtime, and he hated downtime. Downtime gave him too much time to think about how quiet his house was. Too much time to think about the aching loneliness that sometimes ate at his soul until he managed to push it to the far recesses of his brain. Besides, he loved being here, building a legacy with his best friends and teammates, and contributing to it all.

He picked up the rack of desserts and headed to the front of the store.

As he rounded the corner, he came to an abrupt halt. Apparently, Sloane hadn't left like she'd said she was going to. She'd taken up residence at a table in the back of the shop. Not that he needed much to sense her presence. She'd taken his advice and gotten a cupcake. He bit back a smile. The wrapper was empty. The only thing left on the plate the cupcake came on was a wide smear of frosting. She still had no use for it.

Because he was a masochist, he took the opportunity to surreptitiously study her. She'd gotten a tablet from somewhere, probably from that bottomless pit she called a purse. Her eyes were glued to the screen. Whatever she was reading commanded her full attention. But not necessarily in a good way. She'd said she was fine quitting her job, but he didn't believe her. A worry line creased the usually smooth line of her forehead. Not that it marred her appearance in any way.

Facts were facts. Sloane Dell was beautiful.

Lush, perfectly formed lips and sharp cheekbones highlighted a gorgeous face. Any lipstick she'd worn had lost the battle long ago. A fact that only underscored how pink and soft her lips were. His eyes slid down as she worked the thin silver chain of her necklace between her thumb and index finger. Her throat was smooth, skin the color of freshly brewed mocha, a perfect brown. Her expressive, deep brown eyes always glittered, usually mocking him. Except for that one time . . .

She released the necklace and reached up to twirl one of her two-strand Senegalese twist braids around her finger.

She swiped at the screen a few times with her other hand, her lips muttering something. What held her enthralled like that?

A waving hand in his periphery caught his attention. He turned. Ella was frantically waving him toward the front counter. Oh right, he held the holy grail in his hands.

He rushed over, maneuvering between a rowdy crowd that tried to swipe the treats straight off the tray. Before they opened the shop, he never would have guessed his blocking skills, honed over two decades as a fullback, would come in so handy. A few precarious seconds later, he made it behind the counter and successfully delivered the cupcakes to the case. He let out a breath. There was only one sad and lonely lemon meringue cupcake left.

He ducked his head at the cheers from the customers who had been not-so-patiently waiting for the cupcakes. He didn't like attention, never courted it. But he liked serving, and feeling like he contributed to a team effort.

He rang up orders, while Ella packaged the goods. His eyes only skidded once, okay twice, to the back of the room where Sloane was still engrossed in her tablet.

"I've got it from here," Ella said when the line that had stretched all the way to the front door dwindled to only a woman and the guy she was with, who both looked like they'd just come from the gym.

August nodded. "Right." He had no more excuses.

Time to mingle. Check on the customers. Try to make casual conversation.

Logically, he knew it wasn't that big of a deal. That most people didn't want to talk to him. They'd rather stuff cupcakes in their mouths, but still. He always felt flat-footed, unsure of the right thing to say. He didn't have Nicholas's charm or Donovan's business sense. But he was a hard worker and he took pride in Sugar Blitz and its offerings, no matter what his father said. Making sure customers were happy and had everything they needed was his responsibility as a business owner. He could smile and nod with the best of them.

So that's what he did. He smiled and nodded. Took a selfie with a San Diego Knights fan, who didn't require much other than a high five and an autograph.

"August, August!" At the sound of the high-pitched yell, August's shoulders relaxed.

Kids were easier. They assumed your goodness and expected less from you than adults. He turned to find a whirling dervish heading straight for him.

Young Chad was a five-year-old regular, and a regular menace. His parents placated him with cupcakes if he did well at school. August couldn't fault them. If bribes were what it took, then so be it. He crouched down and held out his arms as Chad, missing his two front teeth, came careening toward him. He braced himself for the contact. He only winced slightly when he saw Chad's hands covered in frosting. "August, August, you're here!"

Since he was here pretty much every time Chad showed up for his weekly treat, August could only smile. Chad patted his cheeks with his tiny, messy hands. The little boy leaned closer. "I've got a secret," he whispered. "I got a crush."

He then pointed across the room to Sloane. All August could do was laugh. He understood all too well the allure of that woman.

Sloane, of course, chose that moment to look up from her tablet like she sensed his regard. Her eyebrows lifted in query. Her gorgeous eyes punched him in the gut yet again. Chad's mom, Theresa, groaned. Thankful for the interruption, August turned back to the smitten kindergartner.

"You might be a little young for her, buddy," August said.

Chad shrugged, then went into a monologue about his favorite

YouTube shows. August listened attentively for a few minutes, then handed him back to his mother, who thanked him for indulging her son.

"No need for thanks. Chad's my dude." August grabbed a napkin from a dispenser on the next table and wiped the sticky residue off his face, then resumed his patented smiling and nodding with the customers. Yes, he felt ridiculous, but everybody smiled back before returning to their cupcakes and drinks.

He headed back to the front counter, where business had picked up again. He easily fell into the rhythm of boxing cupcakes as Ella rang up the sales.

"This place is so girly. Football players run this place? Yeah, right."

August lifted his head. Three guys, who looked to be in their early to mid-twenties, had joined the line. One of them was running his mouth. Had they stumbled in here by mistake?

"Why are we here?" the second one said, obviously reading August's mind.

Dude One made a face. "My girl likes their cupcakes. I want to get laid tonight, so you know . . ."

Dude Two raised his hand for a high five. "That's what I'm talking about."

Awesome. August mentally rolled his eyes as the Dudes stepped up to the counter. Who cared what some assholes were saying? They'd be gone in a few minutes and hopefully would never step foot in this establishment again, since cupcakes and cupcakeries were obviously beneath them. He kept his mouth shut, his preferred way of being, while Ella took their orders. All three bought cupcakes, since according to Dude Three, "They were there. Might as well."

Who could ever resist such a compliment?

"Go, go." Ella shooed him away again after they were done with the Dudes. She was like the little sister he'd never asked for. She thought he needed to come out of his shell. He liked his shell, thank you very much. His shell protected him, while allowing him to safely observe the world around him. If, sometimes, in the quiet of night, he felt like that wasn't enough, well, that was his problem to deal with.

With a sigh, he rounded the counter and wandered through the tables, picking up an errant napkin, smiling and nodding there. He did the same to the Dudes who'd taken up a table in the middle of the store.

Dude One stood, blocking August's path. "Yo, let me ask you a question."

August's brows rose. "Sure."

"Isn't this beneath you?"

August decided to be magnanimous. "Is what beneath me?"

"Baking cupcakes. That's what room moms do to celebrate little Susie's birthday. It's stupid. What kind of man opens a cupcake shop, especially when he's a badass football player?"

A question his father had lobbed his way when he told him his plans during one of their infrequent conversations. His dad was full of shit. So was this jackass.

August fixed a hard stare on him. "So baking cupcakes is un-masculine?"

"Yeah."

"But you respect the fact that I play football."

"Yeah, which is why I don't understand why you'd open this froufrou place."

Another page from his father's handbook. The vein in his temple began to throb.

"You don't?" His voice had quieted, but even August could hear how lethal he sounded.

"Uh . . . no." The dude backed up a step, his voice catching on the word.

August was too mad to care. "According to you, I'm manly because I play football, but I'm unmanly because I own a cupcake shop. Which is it? I'm the same person."

Dude's mouth flopped open like a guppy's.

August still didn't care. "Also, according to you, baking is women's work, which means it's beneath a man to do. Did you know cupcakes is a three-billion-dollar industry? You know who made that happen? Women. Women who knew that bringing joy to people's lives was a worthy endeavor."

He unleashed all the words he bottled up every time he spoke to his dad.

"You think men have to live up to this ridiculous, harmful definition of what being a man is. Heaven forbid people be happy and do what they love. My partners—also manly football players, by the way—and I decided to open a shop because the women in our lives shared the joy of baking with us, and in our small way we're continuing and honoring their legacy. We are doing our damnedest to be men the women in our lives can be proud of. So I suggest you go and try to do the same. All of you. Now."

He wasn't one to use his size to intimidate, but he also believed in using the resources available to him. He stared them down until they all scuttled toward the door. A swell of satisfaction filled him when they were on the other side.

It was only then that he realized the shop, usually full of lively chatter, had gone ominously quiet. Worse, everyone was staring at him, some with their phones up like they were taking photos. Or video. Fuck. Sweat beaded on his forehead. His hands curled into fists, which only served to underscore how clammy his palms had become.

His stomach churned, with the cupcake he'd consumed earlier backing up in his throat.

Someone, a dad with two preteen kids, started clapping. One by one, the other patrons joined in until the slap of hands rang like a three-bell alarm in his ears. They all beamed at him. It was the teen romcom movie scene from his nightmares. Over their heads, he met Sloane's wide eyes. At least she wasn't applauding. Her eyes offered sympathy. Somehow that was worse.

He couldn't even summon a half-hearted smile and nod to the customers gathering around him. He pushed through the crowd and escaped down the hall. They didn't know he didn't have an office. Donovan wasn't here. His office would do. As the door closed behind him, only one thought rang in his head.

Oh, shit. This is going to be bad.

Chapter Four

Two days later, Sloane sank into her big brother's welcoming hug. Donovan's solid presence never failed to calm her.

He was the logical one. She was the tenacious, go-for-what-she-wanted-no-matter-what one. Until her job at Organic Chemistry. She'd stayed there longer than she should have. It was her first job after returning to San Diego. She'd always been appreciative of the opportunity and remained loyal, no matter what they threw at her. That decision had ultimately cost her. But no matter. A good lemon meringue cupcake had ended up giving her the boost she needed. Fortified by sugar and cream, she'd opened her tablet and started scouring job posting sites for her next potential gig.

She was okay. Mostly. She was still unemployed, and the swirling in her stomach hadn't ceased entirely. She'd been thrilled to get a call from her brother last night, inviting her to the shop. He had some family business he wanted to discuss with her. She'd leaped at the opportunity to get out of her apartment and away from her personal turmoil.

Donovan stepped back. "Thanks for coming. How you doing?"

Peachy keen. Gainfully unemployed. But she wasn't ready to say that out loud just yet. Then, it would be real. Really real. She'd quit a decent job with no backup plan in place. And although she'd come seeking some "here's the plan" advice from Donovan a few days ago, she'd ultimately decided to figure things out on her own. Besides, hopefully, she'd have a new job soon, and this moment of unemployment would just be a little blip in her plan for world domination.

"I'm good. What about you?" She sounded normal, cheerful even.

"Busy, but good." Her brother walked around his desk and sank into his leather chair. "Did you see what happened with August a couple of days ago?"

Sloane sat in one of the chairs in front of the desk and dropped her purse at her feet. "Yeah, I was here, actually."

Donovan's head cocked to the side, his brow furrowing. "You were? August didn't mention it."

Like she would be surprised by that. Sloane's lips quirked. "When does August mention things?"

Donovan's expression cleared. "Good point." His eyes narrowed. "Wait. Why were you here in the middle of the day?"

Prepared for the question, she had her answer ready. "I got off early and decided to come see my brother, but *someone* was off getting his engagement photos taken."

A gloriously goofy grin bloomed across his face, which was hilarious, because "goofy" was a word that would have never applied to her brother before he met his now-fiancée, Jada. A sickeningly sweet expression took up residence on his face as he reached out to trace a picture frame on his desk. Sloane didn't have to crane her neck to know the photo was of Jada. She loved that her brother had found love, but she still had her role to play as the little sister, so she rolled her eyes and made a gagging noise.

He cleared his throat and sat up straighter. "Back to why I asked you to come down here."

A serious expression settled on his face, while his voice deepened, which only made her roll her eyes harder. They'd lived in the same house too long for her to be intimidated by his business owner persona.

He side-eyed her.

She grinned harder.

He shook his head. "Did you happen to notice the line when you walked in?"

Her eyes widened. "Uh, yeah. It's crazy out there."

Every table was filled, and the line was out the door. She'd had to use the skills she'd honed in ballet classes as a kid to wind her way through the rambunctious crowd.

He chuckled. "I presume you know why."

She could play dumb, but one, that was nonsensical, and two, she was already lying to her brother. No need to add anything to her apologize-for-this-later list. "August went viral."

An understatement.

She loved social media, and she saw in real time how the videos of August blew up on the app still known as Twitter, Instagram, and TikTok. Because the store had been full, there'd been several videos to choose from, from all around the store. And like the fool she was, she'd watched them all. The man did not have a bad angle. His voice was pure velvet, his words pure poetry.

But hey, she didn't have a job to worry about. She had nothing but time to watch and catalog every minute movement of his handsome features. The right eyebrow that went up slightly higher than the left while he ranted. The pinkness of his tongue. His biteable Adam's apple that bobbed up and down. The flex of his shoulders under a polo that barely seemed up to the task of holding the wide body parts inside.

They were calling him SugarBae, and really, she couldn't blame them. His passionate response to those dweebs was panty-melting. What woman attracted to men wouldn't find another man passionately defending women and railing against toxic masculinity attractive? That inner fire and innate sense of good is what had attracted her to August so many years ago. Back then, August had decimated all her defenses, and she'd had to work overtime to rebuild the walls around her heart after that whole situation blew up in her face.

As she sat there, undoubtedly odes to his goodness and hotness were being written and recorded about him. Yes, she'd watched some of those videos and had tracked the #SugarBae hashtag before she'd come to her senses and stopped. She was not a smitten seventeen-year-old anymore. She was an adult and knew idolizing men was a recipe for disaster. Her last relationship was testament to that. After that relationship met its demise three years ago, she'd returned to San Diego.

Her brother's laughter brought her back to the present. "He did, much to his dismay. I'm surprised you didn't bring it up as soon as you walked in."

"Well, I was here when all that went down, and you're right. In real time, he was definitely horrified when the place erupted in applause. He bolted to your office." She'd waffled on whether or not to go after him. After all, they didn't have that kind of relationship, not anymore. But he'd been concerned about her earlier, so she'd gone after him.

She'd slipped inside the office. He'd been sitting at the desk with his head in his hands.

"Hey," she said softly. "You okay?"

He looked up. "I'm fine." His voice sounded fine, but his beautiful eyes told a different story.

"Okay, but . . ."

"I'm fine, Sloane." His lips twisted into a faint resemblance of a smile. "They'll forget about me in five minutes."

She wasn't so sure, but she said "okay" after a moment's hesitation, and left him alone. What else was she supposed to do?

After all, they weren't close. Not anymore. Even when they were, he was very good at keeping his thoughts to himself.

Returning to the present, she focused on her brother. "He said he was fine, so I decided to keep my two cents to myself and let y'all handle it."

And because she was a marketing professional, she asked, "So what did y'all decide to do about it?"

Donovan grimaced. "That's the thing. We haven't done much beyond coaxing him out to the front to take selfies with his new fans. He does it, and then goes back into hiding."

Sloane groaned. "Seriously? What are you paying that marketing company money for? Y'all have to capitalize on the moment. You can't buy advertising like that."

"I'm aware, Sloane."

Sloane waited to see if he would add to his statement. When he didn't, she threw her hands up. "That's all you have to say? Donovan, have I taught you nothing? He went viral and you guys did nothing? Did you even look at social media?"

"Briefly." He continued when she groaned. "In my defense, I've been busy. When it all went down, I was taking engagement photos. I'm planning a wedding, running a business, and making sure I stay in somewhat decent shape during the offseason."

"Blah, blah, blah." She loved her brother, but really. "Part of running a successful business is courting potential customers, and when you're handed a golden opportunity like this, you can't let it slip through your fingers. You let the public do the work with you and Jada last year, but y'all should really up your game and do some work yourself. Aren't you about to open a second location?"

"Yes, Sloane. Any other aspersions you'd like to cast against my character?"

She rolled her eyes. "Stop being dramatic. And didactic. You're not the only one in the family who knows big words." Education had been drummed into their heads by their parents. "Anyway, I digress. You have to take advantage of this opportunity. Give me your phone."

"Sloane . . ."

"Give me the phone. Don't worry. I'm not going to sext Jada or whatever you're worrying about. I'm just going to show you how social media is done."

Donovan groaned. "Really, Sloane?" But he handed over the phone.

Her brother might not put much stock in social media, but he was also a control freak and would be logged in to all of the store's accounts to monitor them and delete anything the marketing company posted he didn't like. Sloane opened Instagram and went to Sugar Blitz's page. She scrolled through a few posts. Gross. Nothing but generic tripe that didn't reflect the personalities of any of the three owners. Yay, they made cupcakes. Big whoop. So did a million other companies in San Diego. She could do better in her sleep.

She scrolled through her brother's photo album. He was very organized. She very carefully avoided any folder that could even be remotely related to his fiancée. No brother dick pics for her. Actually, no dick pics for her no matter who was sending them. Why did men think the sexual organ was so visually appealing or that women were dying to being confronted with images of them before they had their first coffee of the day?

She stopped at a photo of August and Nicholas standing in Sugar Blitz, the natural sunshine streaming in through the window bathing them in perfect light. He and Nicholas were laughing. That really was too much handsome in one photo, even if only one of them made her heart race like she'd been running in the hundred-meter dash, something she'd never willingly participate in. Exercise was a necessary evil, according to all the medical experts, so she reluctantly put in her time in the gym, but she hated every second of it.

She opened a photo editing app on the phone, adjusted the lighting in the shot, and after a moment's hesitation cropped Nicholas out of the picture. *Sorry,* she mentally apologized to her friend. He could get his own post later, but today was all about August.

The all-important caption was next. "August is here, right?" When Donovan nodded, she quickly typed. Spontaneity and authenticity were important.

WE SEE ALL THOSE POSTS ABOUT #SUGARBAE AND WE LOVE THEM. TO SHOW HOW MUCH WE APPRECIATE THEM, WE THOUGHT WE'D LET Y'ALL KNOW AUGUST IS HERE NOW! Come meet your feminist king and get 15% off your order when you show this post.

She reread the post to make sure there were no typos, stared at his photo a second longer than was strictly necessary, and pressed Send. She cross-posted to Twitter.

She quickly checked the stats on Instagram and handed the phone back. "There. One thousand likes in two minutes. See how easy that was."

Donovan shook his head. "August isn't going to like this."

"August isn't going to like what?" The voice of the man in question filled the room.

Sloane twisted in her seat. She'd tried to prepare herself, but fine was fine, and could a woman ever really prepare herself for all this? She'd been around August and Nicholas countless times over the years, but it still never failed to hit her how good-looking they were. Photos didn't do them justice.

They came in, all pure athletic grace, and took seats at the small conference table a few feet away.

"Hey, if it isn't my favorite Dell, who also happens to be the prettiest and smartest member of the family," Nicholas said, with a flirtatious wink. He'd flirt with a fish if he thought he'd get a reaction. He was a pretty man, there was no doubt, but he'd never made her heart go pitter-patter. Not like . . .

Sloane rolled her eyes. "How was last night's date, Nicholas?"

"Great, but I'd drop her in a minute if only you'd give me a chance."

Sloane snorted. He was kidding. They both knew it. Everyone in the room knew it. Donovan was barely paying attention, his head buried in something fascinating on his computer.

August only briefly met her eyes. He nodded but remained quiet. She would not acknowledge the shiver the quick glance sent through her.

"Thanks for joining us," Nicholas said.

Us? She shifted a suspicious gaze to her brother. "No offense, guys, but what are they doing here?"

"Well, they do co-own the business with me," Donovan said.

She shot him a look. "I'm aware, but you said you needed to talk to me. You said it was very important family business, and I couldn't say no, remember?"

"Yes, and it is about family business. This business."

Was it illegal to kill your sibling if you had just cause? Surely no jury would convict her. She worked her jaw side to side, in search of calm, before responding. "What do you want, Donovan?"

"I want to offer you a job."

"You told him you quit your job?" August asked.

"You quit your job?" Big-brother tone had made an appearance.

Sloane winced. Shit. She should have been prepared for that, but she didn't expect to see August today, given that he usually avoided her like the plague. Double homicide was going to be the charge, a little harder to get out of, but she wasn't going to let that stop her. She glared at August, who was already whispering "fuck" to himself. Yeah, well, join the party. She'd been fucked over at her last place of employment. "Yes, I quit a couple of days ago."

"Why didn't you tell me? And how does August know?" Bewilderment spread across Donovan's face.

"Well, I did come by the store to talk to you about it, but you were out shooting your engagement photos."

"I called you last night." Add hurt to the list of her brother's emotional whiplash.

"Yes, but back to the day I quit. That was the day August made his speech."

"And?" Donovan crossed his arms. Uh-oh. Overprotective big-brother mode had been activated.

"Right. Well, as it so happens, I was inspired by what he said and decided to take control of my own destiny, so to speak. I went home and made a plan. Hopefully, this is temporary unemployment, a small blip that we'll laugh about in the future." Her brother didn't look convinced. Maybe because she was still trying to convince herself. But she made sure her gaze didn't waver. Her brother would smell weakness in an instant and start putting together an action plan before she could blink.

He propped his elbows on the desk, steepled his fingers, and tilted his head to the side, just like their mother did when she suspected her children were up to some bullshit. "I see. Like I said, I want to offer you a job, and it looks like it's coming at exactly the right time." He held up a hand. "Let me get it all out before you object. As you know, we employ an outside company to handle our social media. However, I haven't been happy with their performance in a while. It's very rudimentary, nothing that's going to move the needle. Now is the time to devote more time to growing our following, as we prepare to open a second location. Courting viral moments rarely works out in anyone's favor, but luckily for us, we recently had one drop into our laps, and we need to take advantage of it."

August groaned. Donovan continued like he hadn't heard him. "Which you yourself admitted and demonstrated less than ten minutes ago, dear sister."

Oops. A miscalculation on her part. She hadn't thought her brother was going to offer her a job, if only because they'd been down this road several times before. She loved her brother to pieces, but she didn't want to rely on him. She didn't want to rely on any man. That hadn't worked for her mom with her dad, and she'd vowed as a young girl to never find herself in the same position.

No, Donovan would never do her wrong, but she also didn't want to ride the coattails of her famous and successful brother. She wanted to earn everything she did on her own, through her own merits. The last time he'd asked, she'd told him if he offered her a job again she'd replace all the sugar in Sugar Blitz's coffers with salt. He hadn't asked again. Until now.

Donovan continued speaking. "This is the perfect time for you and me. I've already relieved the company of their duties. You need a job."

While her big brother was correct, she had some tricks up the ol' sleeve, as well. "Yes, I need a job, but I have several prospects already. I have an interview tomorrow, and I'm not lying about that."

Her brother sighed. "Is there anything we can do to get you to change your mind?"

Again, her gaze caught on the silent man sitting a few feet away. "Nope."

Chapter Five

Sloane stood to exit the room a few minutes later. Thank God. Being across from her had rendered him more silent than he usually was.

If she hadn't forgotten what happened between them all those years ago, she'd clearly moved on. As she should have. If every now and then he wondered about what could have been, well, he was taking it to the grave. When she lived in Chicago, it had been easier to forget their friendship. But she'd been back for three years. And they both deserved Emmys for pretending the past had never happened. She teased him, threw out droll comments. Slowly but surely, over the past three years, that attraction had snuck up on him and sunk its unforgiving claws into him. Today, it was at an all-time high.

As she took the few steps to the door, he tracked the long length of her legs, her pants emphasizing her noteworthy butt and the smooth curve of her hips. The way her braids swayed across her back. The door closed behind her.

"August? August?"

He started, and turned his attention to Donovan. "Sorry. What did you say?"

"I asked how you were doing." Donovan's eyes probed his for the truth.

"And don't shrug," Donovan and Nicholas said simultaneously as August shrugged.

Having best friends who knew you as well as they did sucked sometimes. Donovan and Nicholas exchanged a glance before turning back to him. He refused to flinch. "Why are we talking about this now?"

Nicholas lifted a shoulder. "We were trying to be nice and give you some space to process everything, but you're still as surly as ever."

August's eyes narrowed. "Thanks."

Donovan held up a hand. "Look, we were thinking that maybe your, uhh . . . speech might have had something to do with your dad."

Damn it. August forced a casual shrug. "He called. Said some shitty things right before those guys showed up. I'm fine. It's over."

They wanted him to say more. He could see it on their faces. But he'd said all he intended to say. Still, their concern warmed the cold, hard cockles of his heart. They were his brothers in every way that counted, but he had no desire to relive that conversation, or any conversation really, that involved his father.

"Well, it's not quite over," Nicholas said.

"Right. And since you say you're fine—" Donovan paused like he was giving August time to contradict him. When no response was forthcoming, he continued. "We have to talk about the aftermath. Do you have any ideas on how to handle our latest viral moment? We need to do something to capitalize on the extra attention we're receiving, especially with the new location opening soon."

Guilt burrowed under August's skin. Donovan wasn't wrong. He had no desire to be the face of their franchise, but that didn't mean he wasn't invested in making Sugar Blitz a success. "You can't find someone else to fake-date? Worked the last time."

Donovan side-eyed him. "An idea that has some merit, but I have a feeling Jada might object. Besides, I'm not the one trending on social media."

"Yeah, SugarBae," Nicholas chimed in with a wiggle of his eyebrows.

August recoiled at the nickname. What had he been thinking, going on that rant? He'd asked himself that question a billion times in the past forty-eight hours. While he wholeheartedly believed everything he'd said, he never courted attention to himself.

All he'd done was tell the truth because some jackasses had pissed him off with their nonsense. He sure as hell hadn't said it with the goal of earning *fans*. But in his desire to knock some sense into those knuckleheads, he'd forgotten they were now living in the Time of Camera Phones and Social Media.

And now his anonymity was blown to hell and back. Fuck.

He'd turned off all notifications on his phone and basically gone into hibernation mode, only coming out because of his loyalty to his partners and best friends. Though he might have an opening for one of those positions soon. August glared at his other best friend. "Why don't you find someone to fake-date since you're throwing out ideas?"

Nicholas's shit-eating grin spread wider. "We all know I only do the real thing, and I do it so well, we'd have a rebellion on our hands if I let down the ladies by taking myself out of the dating pool for a scheme."

August met Donovan's gaze and they rolled their eyes in unison.

They were back on familiar ground. The tension in his shoulders loosened ever so slightly.

"You are a fool," Donovan said, shaking his head.

August looked around for something to chuck at Nicholas's head, the heavier the better, but a knock sounded on the door before he found a suitable object.

Ella popped her head inside. "Y'all have to come out here right now. Especially you, August."

August exchanged glances with his friends before hurrying out of the room, with Donovan and Nicholas hot on his heels. When he turned the corner into the store, he came to a screeching halt. He barely registered someone—Nicholas, based on the sound of his bellow—plowing into his back.

Holy shit. The room was packed with women. And, as if sensing new helpless prey nearby, they all turned in unison. To face him. And descended on him like a pack of rabid wildebeests.

"Oh, my God, it's him!" A lady in a hot pink romper yelled about three inches away from his face.

"SugarBae!" yelled an older woman in jeans and sneakers.

"I can't believe you said all that," a lady in tight yoga pants and a crop top whispered breathlessly in his ear, as she pressed her boob into his arm. Maybe that part was unintentional. Then she pinched his butt. Maybe not.

Her lips landed on his right cheek. The one on his face. Thank God for small favors.

"How did you get to be so amazing?" someone else shrieked in his other ear.

"I've watched your speech a million times," Butt Pincher said.

Romper clasped her hands together at chest level. "It was so empowering. That's what true allyship looks like."

The hero worship in the woman's voice and on her face was freaking weird. No one ever wanted to hear from him. He was the team fullback, the one who hit the hole first to block for Nicholas, who would then hopefully speed through the opening, run down the field, and score a touchdown as the crowd roared their approval and adoration.

Donovan and Nicholas were the ones the press went to after the game for their thoughts. August was the worker bee, and he liked it that way. Contribute in the background. Do his part to make the team go. Expect no praise for it. Desire no praise for it.

Heat crawled up his throat to his cheeks like the tentacles of scary robots in sci-fi horror movies. His face was going to burst into flames at any second. They were all staring at him, waiting for him to say something insightful. Something illuminating. Something meme-worthy. He gave them . . . "Thanks."

A breathless collective moment of silence descended on the room, like they were waiting for him to continue, but that's all he had to give. They were lucky they got that. Performing for a crowd wasn't his thing.

Butt Pincher broke the quiet first. "We came down as soon as we heard you would be here."

The others nodded, backing up her statement. As one, they inched a little closer, a considerable feat given their faces were only about six inches away from his.

How the hell had they known he would be here *right now*? Nicholas and Donovan had agreed to tell inquiring "fans"—he was going to hurl using that word—that he was out running errands or taking a day off. Okay, yes, he was hiding, but what were words with meaning, really? He voiced aloud the question zipping through his brain. "Who told you?"

Butt Pincher blinked, clearly surprised by the question. "You did. I mean, whoever handles Sugar Blitz's social media. It was on Instagram. Great post, by the way."

What Instagram post? Who would post it? *Why* would they post it? Who was *they*?

"You're like the best man ever."

The others nodded. "Total dream man," the kisser said.

Not a dream man. Just a man who had his foibles like every other man on earth. A position Sloane undoubtedly would endorse. Hell, someone else—his ex-wife, Melinda—had already let him know, in no uncertain terms, that he was no longer her dream man. And while he didn't mourn the relationship anymore, what could have been still stung. The inability to live up to his promise. The inability to be who his ex-wife wanted him to be. Who she needed him to be. That failure had left scars. They'd faded, but they were still there, discolored, jagged lines across his heart.

"Are you dating someone?" Yoga Pants asked.

"He's not married, and that's all that counts," Butt Pincher countered. "No ring, fair game."

"Well . . . umm . . ." He lost his train of thought as he was forced to use one of the footwork drill exercises they practiced during training camp to avoid Butt Pincher's wandering hands.

"So you're dating someone?"

If he said yes, odds were halfway decent they'd leave him alone, but as a general rule, he didn't lie. Nothing good came from telling untruths. You had to remember the lie, and then expound upon it at some point, and yeah, as painful as it sometimes was, telling the truth was the way to go.

He should maybe make an exception in this case. It had worked out, eventually, for Donovan. Exceptions proved the rule, after all. He couldn't smooth-talk and flirt with them like Nicholas or go the no-nonsense route like Donovan.

"Umm, well . . ."

"Excuse me, ladies. We're so happy to have you here, but you're blocking the entryway. It's a fire hazard." Sloane appeared out of nowhere like a fairy godmother and somehow managed to wedge her body in between him and his overzealous fan club.

"Who are you?" Yoga Pants asked, looking Sloane up and down, her lip curled.

"I'm Sloane Dell," Sloane returned confidently, not in the least intimidated. Not for the first time, admiration for her bloomed in his chest. "Donovan Dell is my brother. I'm helping out here today. With that said, August will be happy to sign autographs and take selfies."

He would? Before he could even think about voicing any objections, she continued. "However, we need you to back up and give him a chance to breathe." Her face was pleasant, but a thread of steel underlined her tone. His "fans" heard it, too, and they backed up. Again, August was impressed.

She corralled the group into a back corner, away from people who'd actually come into Sugar Blitz to buy cupcakes. The women seemed content to chatter at him, which meant he didn't have to put his rudimentary conversational skills to the test much. While he'd rather be back in the kitchen fixing the leak that was the bane of his existence or doing inventory, he could smile for pictures and scribble his name on pieces of paper or forearms. He drew the line at boobs, even with Sloane laughing at him.

"We're so happy to have you here," Sloane said, addressing the crowd of women. "If you buy a cupcake, which I have it on good authority August personally baked with his own two hands, then he will sign your receipt and let you know the secret ingredient for the cupcake."

August just stared at her. He could interject and let the women know Sloane was full of shit. She had no clue whether he'd stepped foot in the kitchen that morning. But watching her work was pure magic.

"Really, you baked?" Butt Pincher asked breathlessly.

Sloane nodded emphatically. "He loves showing off his handiwork. Complimenting his baking is the way to his heart."

Some of the women took her at her word, making a beeline for the front counter, where Donovan and Ella were waiting to take their orders.

Yoga Pants hung back and studied Sloane with narrowed eyes. "You seem kinda bossy. Eye on the prize and all. Was that Instagram post your handiwork?"

If he wasn't studying her so closely, he would've missed the guilt flashing in Sloane's eyes a moment before she wiped her expression clear. "One, there's no kinda about it. I am bossy, because I'm a boss, so thank you. Two, my brother and his partners have a company that handles their social media. Three, does it matter? The post was accurate and you're meeting SugarBae, so it's all good."

That wasn't a denial. Sloane was still on some bullshit.

He pinned her with his gaze. To her credit, she didn't wilt under his hard stare. Her smile, though strained, never wavered. He didn't have time to grill her, because the other women returned with cupcakes, receipts, and napkins they'd pilfered from the front counter for him to sign. He signed autographs until his hand cramped and took selfies until his cheeks rebelled against the terrible misuse. But he kept on keeping on, even as more fans arrived, thanks to good ole Instagram.

He did his best "Nicholas as running back" imitation as he weaved and dodged propositions, some made in good fun and others coming in at an OnlyFans level, as best as he could until his reserves reached damn near zero. He sent an SOS to Nicholas with his eyes. Without another word, Nicholas stepped into the fray.

"Ladies, why are we bothering August here when your real dream man is standing right next to him, single and ready to mingle?" Nicholas offered up the dazzling smile that never failed to make women swoon. Today was no exception. August's fan club followed Nicholas like little ducklings while August escaped. But not before snagging Sloane's wrist as she tried to slink away.

August sucked in a breath. Touching her was a terrible mistake. Her skin, so soft, scalded him. A ridiculous notion, but accurate all the same. But he didn't let go.

Donovan was at the front counter, ringing up sales. Good. He opened his partner's office door and wedged his body to block the hall passageway, so she couldn't slide by him and make a break for the exit.

Sloane lifted her chin and swept by him into the office. He followed and locked the door behind him. No interruptions allowed. She swallowed hard, the line of her throat working up and down at the snick, but then she met his gaze defiantly.

That was his Sloane. No, not his Sloane. Never his Sloane.

Endeavoring to ignore the slight ache near his heart, he leaned back against the door. "You know I was going to apologize for blurting out that you'd quit your job."

Sloane's mouth twisted in a grimace. "August—"

He held up a hand. "Actually, I'm still going to do that. It wasn't my place, as unintentional as it was, to tell your personal business. I'm sorry."

"August—"

"However, I can only assume, based on some good context clues, that you are the reason the shop is currently being overrun with women, who are all ready to take a bite out of me, figuratively and maybe literally."

She stepped closer, her gorgeous eyes pleading with him for forgiveness. August steeled himself, well, as best as he could. He would not be moved by the guilt swimming in her beautiful eyes. He was doing good-ish until her hand landed on his arm. The shock to his system was instant and unwelcome. Her hand sliding away as she stepped away was even more unwelcome.

"I'm sorry. I wasn't thinking. I've just been pushing Donovan to do more on the social media side since you opened Sugar Blitz. When he told me y'all hadn't posted since your speech, my instincts took over. He gave me his phone, and it just . . . happened."

"Without thinking how it would affect me."

That was Sloane. She saw a goal and acted to achieve it, not letting anyone or anything stand in her way. He'd always admired her for it—from afar, of course. But now the tables had turned, and he'd inadvertently got caught up in her whirlwind. The truth sent a dart of hurt rushing through him. He ignored it. He'd been hurt worse, much worse, before. He'd always survived. This was no different. He would remain stoic. Unaffected.

Maybe he didn't do a good job of hiding it. She came forward again, her hand outstretched like she intended to offer comfort. He braced himself but didn't step away. When she touched him, the charge through his system was electrifying.

"You're right. I'm sorry. I didn't think about how it would affect you. I was only focused on how to make the shop more successful."

He shook his head, annoyed anew. "But not enough to come work for him. Us." He didn't know why, but it felt like a rejection of him, which was beyond ridiculous. He'd been the one to reject her years ago, and he'd been paying for that decision ever since, in small and gigantic ways. But that was his pain, his confusion to bear. It had been the right decision, and he couldn't change the past. He knew that better than anyone. Obsessing about it solved nothing. He knew *that* better than anyone.

Her eyes skidded away. She seemed to realize she was still touching him because she yanked her hand away, leaving him feeling bereft. Lost.

"You know I can't do that."

"I do?"

Her beautiful eyes pleaded with him. "Of course you do. Better than anyone."

He did. Memories of those long-ago phone calls slipped through the lock he kept on them. She wanted to succeed on her own terms, which he understood, but he also understood his best friend's point of view. She was terrific at what she did and would be an asset to Sugar Blitz. "Donovan respects you."

She nodded. "I know. I just need everyone else to. I don't want anyone to think I can't succeed on my own, especially here in San Diego, where everyone loves my brother."

He nodded. He didn't necessarily agree, but he understood. Sloane was a go-getter, a prideful go-getter. She'd succeed on her own terms, in her own way. "Okay, but the offer still stands."

"I know." She made her way to the door. "Thanks." She turned to face him again, her eyes seeking his. "And I really am sorry about siccing the hordes on you."

And he was sorry about everything.

She slipped through the door, leaving him all alone with his thoughts. Thoughts that were never truly free of Sloane Dell, no matter how hard he tried.

Chapter Six

Twelve years ago . . .

Sloane shut her bedroom door and slid down to the floor with her phone clutched in her trembling hand. She studied her recent calls. Reaching out to her sister or brother was always a viable option. They would always be there for her, but . . . no. Sloane shook her head. She didn't want to worry them. They didn't know how bad things still were, and they had their own lives to worry about. So she called the person she knew who would always listen.

August answered on the second ring. "Hey, Sloane."

Hearing his voice—so friendly and open—freed the emotions she'd tried so hard to keep locked up. A sob escaped. She covered her mouth with her hand like that could stop the flow of tears.

"Sloane."

She tried to answer, but only a watery whimper eked out.

"Sloane, what's wrong? Talk to me."

She squeezed her eyes shut. She wished she could do the same to her ears. Anything to block out the screaming argument her parents were having down the hall.

She sucked in a breath and tried again.

"I'm sorry. I shouldn't have called you." She spoke in a whisper, although there was no need. Her parents couldn't possibly hear her over their yelling. "You're probably with your girlfriend or something."

He'd dropped that bombshell a few conversations ago, all casual-like. "Yeah, Melinda thinks I should take a sociology class next semester." She was totally cool with it because they were just friends.

"Hey, what's going on? I'm by myself." His voice was quiet, yet sure. "You can tell me."

This is why she'd called him. She'd known he would be supportive.

Sloane rubbed her right temple with her free hand like that had a shot in hell of easing the headache that was currently pulsating there. "My parents are fighting about money and my dad's gambling debts again. He can't or won't pay the child support he owes. I don't know what to do."

"Oh, Sloane. I'm sorry."

"And here I thought a divorce would end all of our suffering."

"A logical conclusion. Too bad they couldn't comply. Hmmph."

August's judgment of her parents made her chuckle. It came out a little watery, but it was better than the crying jag she'd almost given in to. "Then I hate myself because . . ."

"They're your parents, and you don't want to be insensitive to their feelings."

Sloane dropped her head back against the door. "Yeah. I should be used to the fights by now, but tonight is different. They're not using their inside voices. I think they forgot I was here."

"Parents are the worst."

The response, stated so matter-of-factly, had more laughter bubbling in her chest. "They are. Speaking of, how is Papa Hodges?"

August's sniff of derision came through loud and clear. "Still running his business empire and uninterested in his only child."

She wished with all her heart that she could reach through the phone and offer him a hug. "August."

"It's okay."

Except it wasn't. She could hear it in his voice. "Do you mind if I ask about your mom?"

During their first call, she'd asked for—okay, more like demanded—he give her his number, so she could call for math help in the future. His vibe was way chiller than her brother's when it came to helping her. Now, they talked at least once a week. Their conversations had morphed from mostly about calculus to the normal everyday highs and lows of life. They were friends. Though August never said much, he said enough for her to know his dad wouldn't be winning any "Father of the Year" awards. But he never talked about his mother. But maybe he needed to.

After a moment of quiet, he sighed. "No, I don't mind. She died when I was seven, and I spent most of my childhood with my grandfather because my dad was off working."

Sloane's hand fisted into a tight ball. She knew August's mom had passed away, but not that it happened so long ago. Her heart ached for that sweet, young boy. "I'm so sorry to hear that. Do you know a lot about her?"

"My dad doesn't like talking about her, so I only got bits and pieces growing up, but I always wondered about her." He paused. "Can I tell you something?"

"Anything." She'd never answered a question so quickly.

"I wonder if I'm making her proud."

"Of course you are." Of that, she had no doubt.

"Well, it's sure as hell not happening with my dad."

"We've already established that parents are the worst."

His chuckle made her smile.

"That we did," he said. "A few months ago, I found some of her journals."

"Oh, that's dope."

His voice lightened with happiness. "Yeah, she was really funny. And she loved cooking all types of food, but baking was her first love."

"Do you bake?"

August scoffed. "Me? No, I'm no good in the kitchen."

"Maybe you should. To honor her memory."

He paused for a second. When he spoke, his voice was soft. "Maybe I should."

Chapter Seven

August's muscles melted in relief as he sank into his couch cushions and let out a gusty sigh. Finally. The day was over, and he was home. Alone. Thank you, sweet baby Jesus.

Thanks to Nicholas and Sloane, he'd survived the first wave of folks stopping by, hoping to catch a glimpse of SugarBae. But then the second wave came. And the third.

He'd escaped to the kitchen, but he could still hear them as they got rowdier and rowdier demanding to see him. So, after giving serious consideration to fleeing out the back door in search of alcohol, he'd girded his loins and put in an appearance. He'd gotten himself into this mess, with an assist from Sloane, and it was up to him to live up to his responsibilities, even as he daydreamed about coming up with a scientific discovery that would allow him to fade into the yellow walls of the shop.

Still, he'd never aspired to be a rock star. After today, he had to pat himself on the back for his good judgment. Being a rock star sucked.

His . . . fans (and he still wanted to hurl at using that term) kept looking to him for wise, aspirational words or something. At least that was the motive of the respectful ones. The not-so-respectful ones? He'd never been propositioned so much in his life. Women were super bold and quick with their hands when they wanted to be. He had no choice but to respect the game, but that's not how he expected his Wednesday to go.

August released a sigh, but really, this was his fault. He'd gone on that rant all by his lonesome.

Tonight, he wanted to do nothing more taxing than watching a basketball game. His social interaction reserves were shot.

August picked up the remote and turned on the TV. MSNBC was on. He wasn't exactly a news junkie, but he liked to stay abreast of what was happening in the world, even if it was often depressing as shit. His finger hovered over the Channel Up button when the anchor said, "Tonight's special guest is Melinda DeJesus, better known as the artist MDJ."

All of August's relaxed muscles tensed up again.

He stared blankly as his ex-wife filled the screen. Logically, it wasn't a surprise to see Melinda, one of New York's most heralded artists/activists, on TV. Fame and accolades had always been inevitable for her, but still he wasn't prepared. He shook his head in bemusement. Her locs, dyed a dark gold, hung midway down her back. August touched his own locs. They'd decided to grow them together one long-ago night during their senior year in high school. Back when they were still each other's biggest support system.

They'd met in middle school, in a youth support group for kids who'd lost parents. By sophomore year in high school, they were dating. By the time they graduated high school, they'd promised to marry and be together forever. They'd married a week after graduating college. Forever had lasted three years.

"MDJ, thank you for joining us tonight," the anchor added.

"Thank you for having me." Melinda nodded, sending her signature dangling turquoise earrings jingling. She'd debated between silver and turquoise for weeks. She'd decided on turquoise because of the mineral's mystical powers or something.

"We wanted to have you on to talk about your new book, *Happiness,* and how it gives voice to the many people across the country, across the world, who are unhappy in their relationships and trying to find their way out of them."

August groaned. Really? They'd been divorced for five years. She'd moved to New York as soon as she'd told him their marriage was no longer working and couldn't be saved. In other words, he hadn't been the person she needed him to be. He hadn't been worth trying for. He hadn't been able to change the mind of the person he'd agreed to love and cherish for the rest of his life. That failure stuck with him to this day.

They hadn't spoken in years. There was no need to. They lived completely different lives.

Was she mining their marriage for inspiration? Why hadn't he changed the channel yet?

Melinda nodded. "Yes, my ex-husband and I were never destined to live the rest of our lives together. We were too different, but too stubborn to admit it."

August let out a deep, heavy sigh. There was no relief in it this time. Only pure, unadulterated exhaustion. Lesson learned. Never ever say the day couldn't get any worse, because it absolutely could.

"Our audience might not know you were married to professional football player August Hodges." A photo of him in his uniform on the sidelines, squinting into the sun, appeared on the screen.

August squeezed his scalp with both hands and groaned.

Fucking A. Yes, info about who he used to be married to was only a Google search away, but bringing it back to the forefront of people's minds was the last thing he needed. He wasn't ashamed to have been married to Melinda, but answering questions about his personal life sounded like the worst form of torture, second only to answering questions about himself.

The anchor leaned forward, a faux concerned tone entering her voice. "What happened? How were you different and unable to overcome those differences?"

Melinda took a deep breath, as though the end of their marriage still hurt. "I'm an artist, and I was being stifled. I had to leave and explore and take risks. My ex-husband was never interested in that. He never took risks, never took the road less traveled to build anything on his own. I had to leave to reach my potential. And I want all the people who feel stuck to reach their potential too."

She meant she hadn't loved him. Or that he hadn't been good enough to love. Not for the long haul, anyway. The story of his life. During their trial separation that turned permanent, he'd often told himself that if he could've been who she needed him to be, then maybe she would've stuck around. Logically, he knew that wasn't the case, but what the hell did logic have to do with feelings? He'd tried, and he'd failed in his marriage. Facts were facts.

August tugged on the collar of his shirt like that would help draw air into his suddenly tight lungs. Damn. Thinking about this shit was the worst. Why hadn't he stopped by the kitchen for a beer or sip of whiskey before heading to the living room? He'd heard all this before. Plenty of times. He thought he'd moved beyond the hurt, the feelings of failure, the feelings of abandonment. Ultimately, their marriage didn't work. Being miserable so you didn't have to say you failed was a losing proposition. Therapy had gotten him to that place. And yet . . . he blew out a breath. Why did it hit different tonight?

Maybe because of what Sloane said. That he needed to step into the spotlight in order for Sugar Blitz to really grow.

"What advice would you offer to those who are afraid to take risks, like your ex-husband?" the anchor asked.

Melinda looked straight into the camera. "You only have one life to live. Don't let fear of being acknowledged for who you are stop you from realizing your full potential. Don't be a passive participant in your own life. Don't be scared to take risks."

Was that it? Was he scared to take risks? Is that how he wanted to live his life?

* * *

Two days later, Sloane stood outside the corporate headquarters of San Diego Today, a media company that focused on all things San Diego. From highlighting those working in the community to make the city the best it could be for its residents to the best new restaurants to exposing corruption at city hall, SDT could be counted on to be there. She loved the positive nature of the website and how they were trying to make a difference in the lives of residents. Working here would be a dream come true. Now, all she had to do was impress the powers-that-be during her interview.

She'd rehearsed her presentation over and over. She'd practiced her answers to typical interview questions. She was ready. The nerves dive-bombing in her stomach would chill once she started her presentation. Hopefully.

Her phone rang. She dug it out of her messenger bag and smiled. Answering was not a problem. "Hey, bestie."

"Let me guess. You're nervous," Felicia answered.

"I am."

Felicia hummed in understanding. "Which is only normal. But you got this. You are a fabulous social media manager who is going to kill this interview."

"You're just saying that because you're my friend." And one of the nicest people Sloane knew.

"No, I'm saying that because I witnessed the miracles you produced and the brilliant ideas you came up with for years. You got this."

Sloane squared her shoulders. "I've got this."

"Yes, you do. Now go before you're late."

Sloane ended the call and strode inside to the receptionist's desk and confidently gave her name. The woman, who introduced herself as Daisy, told her to take a seat. "Would you like some coffee while you wait for Emily?"

"No, thank you," Sloane said. Coffee? That was the last thing she needed. All kinds of calamities were possible with the dark liquid. She could spill it on her dry-cleaned power suit, leaving a big-ass stain and scalding herself in the process. The coffee could upset her already-in-turmoil stomach, and she'd find herself up-chucking all over the blue suede of the chair she was sitting in. Yeah, no coffee for her.

She took a seat and tried to take an undetectable deep breath. She was the only one in the waiting room, but the walls might have eyes or something.

A minute later, a woman came down the hall toward her, her heels clicking on the floor's dark tiles. Emily Chan, the director of marketing. Sloane recognized her from her internet research on SDT. Emily had started with the company eight years ago after earning her MBA from USC. She was a quickly rising star in the world of corporate marketing. Sloane could learn a lot from her, assuming she nailed this interview.

Sloane planted her feet on the floor and rose gracefully, silently thanking her mother for all those dance classes as a kid, even if she'd always been more likely to be cast as Candy Cane #5 rather than the Sugar Plum Fairy in the annual Christmas recital.

"Sloane?" Emily asked. She wore red slacks and a crisp white button-down shirt.

"Yes," she answered, holding out her hand. Emily was about Sloane's height, with her shoulder-length dark brown hair cut into a stylish bob. "It's nice to meet you."

"You as well. I'm Emily. Please follow me."

Sloane caught glimpses of offices and cubicles as they made their way down the hall and through the office suite to the conference room.

"Please, have a seat," Emily said, gesturing to the leather seats around the sleek glass table dominating the middle of the room. Sloane did her bidding, placing her messenger bag at her feet.

"I thought it would be better to meet here instead of my office," Emily said, joining her at the table. "This place is much better equipped for presentations. I was very impressed with your résumé. Why don't you tell me a little about yourself?"

Sloane ran through her prepared remarks, making sure to hesitate here and there, so she didn't sound completely rehearsed. Emily nodded, encouraging her to continue. As she became more comfortable discussing past projects she knew like the back of her hand, the nerves started to slip away.

"Why do you want to work here?" Emily asked when she finished her opening statement.

Because you're hiring and I have bills to pay!

Because that was *so* not an acceptable answer, Sloane went with, "I've been a fan of SDT for years. When I moved to San Diego a few years ago, I used the website to catch up on what was new and exciting in the city. SDT is growing with podcasts and other ventures, and I'd love to contribute to that growth."

Emily nodded, studying her. But Sloane couldn't read her. She wouldn't want to play poker with this woman.

"Why don't you show me your presentation?" Emily finally said.

"I'd love to." Sloane retrieved her tablet from the messenger bag and hooked it up to the audiovisual cables carefully tucked away in a hidden compartment in the table. She picked up a remote off the table and turned on the large-screen TV hanging on the wall at the opposite end of the room. After a few taps on the tablet screen, her presentation deck appeared onscreen.

She'd put together a sample program of how she would use social media to boost the company's fortunes. She'd done her research. Their market share had been on a steady rise over the last decade but had stagnated over the past few years. Social media could change that like no other medium. It was a new day. Commercials and ads wouldn't do it. She had some great ideas, if she did say so herself. Her confidence swelled as she went through the slides. She loved marketing and had a special place in her heart for social media. One day, she wanted to lead her own marketing department. This was her next step.

"That was a great presentation," Emily said at the conclusion.

"Thank you," Sloane said, beaming, adrenaline pumping through her system.

Emily propped her elbows on the table and steepled her fingers together. "However, I'm a little concerned. You've never been the head of a social media department. You've talked about your former company and how you *helped* with some of their most successful campaigns."

"Yes." Sloane bit her tongue before she said anything else. She wanted to yell that they had all been her ideas, that her former boss had taken all the credit, but bad-talking former employers was so not kosher, especially after she'd quit. True or not, it would come across as sour grapes.

Sloane did her best to give off I'm-not-worried vibes as she searched for something more appropriate to say. Did it matter, though? Emily was still silently watching her. Was she about to be told no, she wasn't a good fit, putting her back at square one in her job search? Back to contemplating dipping into her savings, which she guarded like an endangered species? She was there to help the account's population grow, not plunder it for ill-gotten goods.

A knock sounded on the door as the nerves she'd been so confident were gone rose from the dead like the villain in the last act of a slasher flick.

"Come in," Emily called out.

Sloane frowned. Someone else was joining the interview? Her stomach sank. Or maybe the interruption was Emily's out, so she had an excuse not to turn Sloane down in person and could send an impersonal email later? Neither option sounded optimal.

The door opened, and a man entered. Sloane gasped. Not just any man, but Preston Bridges.

Aka, her longtime nemesis.

They'd gone to college together and lived in the same dorm. Which wasn't too terrible except they shared a major and he showed up in all her classes like a bad penny. They'd competed for everything in college—from scholarships to the presidency of their college chapter of Young Marketing Leaders of America to high honors in their classes.

She'd moved into an apartment junior year only to discover he was dating her roommate, Anna. Which again, wasn't too terrible. What was terrible was that he was an ass.

Friendly competition, she could deal with and thrive in. Sabotage and plain doucherty were another matter. Hell, he'd even cheated on Anna and broken her heart. Because he was an ass. Sloane had wiped her roommate's tears and gotten drunk on cheap tequila with her while they conjured up all kinds of torturous ways of ending Preston's life. Sloane had been thrilled to stand up for her former roommate last year at her wedding to a man who treated her like the most precious gold.

Preston still looked the same. Asshole exuded from his pores. His black shoes were so shiny she was surprised he hadn't blinded someone yet.

What the hell was he doing here in San Diego? They'd attended college in Illinois. She'd scoured the company's organizational chart. He wasn't on there. She would have recoiled in horror if he had been, and begun plotting the best way to avoid him at all costs if she was hired.

But maybe she was overreacting. She hadn't seen him in years. Maybe he'd matured. Become a fine, upstanding citizen.

"Well, hey, if it isn't Sloane Bell!" he exclaimed. Sloane's teeth clenched so hard she was surprised the clamping sound didn't reverberate through the room. He knew good and damn well her last name was Dell. He'd tried buttering her up enough when they were undergrads, so he could meet her brother, to make that mistake. Her first instinct had been correct. Once an ass, always an ass.

"Hi, Preston," Emily said. "Thanks for joining us. Why don't you have a seat?" After he smartly took a seat on the other side of the conference table, the better to avoid Sloane's kick in the shin, Emily continued, "Do you two know each other?"

Sloane pasted on a smile. "Yes, we knew each other in college. But it's Dell, Preston, not Bell."

He grimaced and slapped his forehead. "Yes. I'm so sorry about that. Please forgive me."

Sloane struggled not to roll her eyes. Why hadn't he moved to Hollywood and tried his hand at acting? Marketing was obviously not his true calling. "It's okay. It's been a long time. Time flies when you're having fun."

Especially when I don't have to see you every day. Her eyes flashed the warning, even as her smile never wavered because she was a pro, baby.

He got the message. His ubiquitous smirk dimmed a tad.

"You two are probably wondering what's going on," Emily said.

Sloane sent a more gracious smile her way. She wasn't going to let Preston throw her off her game.

"I was impressed with both of you and your presentations," Emily added. "However, in order to make a final decision about who to offer the position to, I need to see a little more from you two."

Sloane sat up straighter. What did that mean? At least she was still in the running for the job. Whatever Emily wanted, Sloane was prepared to give her.

"Sounds like a plan," Preston, that swarmy bastard, said, oozing slime. He was handsome in that bland, no-notable-features way. Medium build. Pale skin, light blond hair slicked back with too much hair gel, and ice-blue eyes.

"You both have worked at high-caliber businesses, but I want to know what you can do. Alone. With that said, I'd like to see you take on a client of your choosing and become the company's de facto social media manager for the next two weeks. Whoever runs the best, most successful, most impressive campaign will be offered the job."

"And I'm prepared to deliver," Preston said. "I've been freelancing for Pedal. You might have noticed they've been getting some press lately."

Emily nodded, while Sloane's teeth clenched harder. Everyone had heard of Pedal, the exercise bike that had taken the at-home exercise equipment world by storm. Its parent company was a small startup that had found success on the West Coast and was poised to expand their success and reach to the rest of the country. Even if people were uninterested in exercise, they'd surely seen the company's social media posts in which they challenged other bike companies to a race and encouraged their followers to join in on the fun. He'd been responsible for those posts? She'd laughed at them, like everyone else. She'd laughed at something *Preston* had come up with? Would she see pigs zooming through the air if she looked out the window?

Of course, there was every possibility in the world Preston was lying. She wanted to ask why he was pursuing an opportunity elsewhere if he was such a social media expert for another company, but that would invite questions about why she was here, and there was no way in hell, purgatory, or heaven she was answering that question in front of him.

Emily nodded. "Great. I'll need to see proof and acknowledgment from Pedal that you are indeed the one in charge of their social media at the end of the period." She turned to Sloane. "What about you, Sloane?"

What about me?

Sloane refused to let the panic grabbing her by the throat choke her. She couldn't say, "I'm currently unemployed, so I won't be able to meet the challenge." Not with Preston sitting right there. Not with her pride on the line. Not with her desire to get this job consuming her. She had to say something, come up with a terrific idea that would counteract the bead of sweat clinging to her forehead. Counteract the arrogant stare coming from Preston.

Sloane balled her hands into tight fists under the table. "My brother co-owns Sugar Blitz, the cupcake shop. I'll be revamping their social media presence and website."

Chapter Eight

*E*mily leaned forward, the first sign she'd been remotely impressed by what Sloane had to say. "Oh, yes. I've been there a time or two. Fantastic cupcakes. I didn't realize you were related to one of the owners."

Which was not a coincidence. She refused to trade on her brother's fame to advance her career. Or at least that had always been her stance. What was she doing?

"Yes, Donovan Dell is my brother."

Preston's chair squeaked as he leaned forward, his eyes narrowing. He knew how much she hated people fawning over her once they found out who her brother was. But they hadn't seen each other in seven years. He couldn't know with certainty she still felt that way. As far as he knew, she could've done a 180 and now dropped her brother's name at every opportunity.

Emily clapped her hands together. "Excellent. It seems you two both have very promising clients. I can't wait to see your results in two weeks."

She had two weeks to prove her worth to Emily and SDT. Two

weeks to prove she was the badass marketing executive she knew she was.

Sloane nodded at Emily and rose. They all said their goodbyes. Preston clearly didn't want to leave until she did, and she sure as hell wouldn't give him the satisfaction of having the last word with Emily, which is how they found themselves standing at the elevator watching the floor numbers light up while they studiously ignored each other by tacit agreement. There were SDT employees walking by. Probably wouldn't do to get into a screaming match in the lobby after a job interview. She was sure that was in an etiquette book some-where. LinkedIn probably had something to say about it, as well.

The elevator light for their floor lit up and the bell dinged as the doors slid open. Like synchronized swimmers, they stepped into the space together and turned to face the closing doors. They were finally alone.

Preston sniffed. "Interesting save back there."

And there went their mutual truce.

She stared straight ahead. The image of his shiny forehead bounced off the mirrored doors. "I have no idea what you're talking about."

"You were taken aback by Emily's curveball. You didn't expect there to be more to getting the job. You pulled that project out of your ass."

Her grip on her messenger bag tightened. "I have no idea what you're talking about."

"I know you're awfully touchy about your brother. If you're dropping his name, you must be desperate to get this job."

She would not curse this fool out. "My brother owns a business. I am doing work for him. She asked. I answered. The end."

She kept her eyes on the floor numbers lighting up. Why hadn't they reached the lobby yet? He was getting on her nerves, yes, but he also wore some cologne that probably cost more than her monthly car payment and was presently clogging up her olfactory senses. It was nothing like August's amazing scent, and oh God, she'd just volunteered to work at his business. Which meant she'd be seeing a lot more of him. Inhaling more of that delicious scent. What had she done?

But she couldn't worry about that right now. She had more pressing concerns. In this enclosed space, standing so close, her sinuses were having a field day. Her head was starting to ache and her eyes were tearing up. She needed to get away from the cologne from hell—and Preston—as soon as possible.

Finally, they reached the ground floor. She took a breath, but not too much because she didn't want to inhale any more of his scent than necessary.

"As nice as this little catch-up session was, I've got to go." Sloane exited the elevator and headed toward her car.

"I'm going to win, you know," Preston called from behind her.

Not if she had anything to say about it. As soon as she told her brother—and August—that they would be seeing a lot more of her.

* * *

For the third time in less than a week, Sloane found herself knocking on her brother's office door at Sugar Blitz. She most certainly had not scoured the storefront to see if August was there. He wasn't, but that wasn't important. Neither was her disappointment when she hadn't spotted him. She was here to see her brother.

At Donovan's "Come in," she walked inside. He blinked in surprise when he spotted her. "Sloane, what are you doing here?"

She settled in one of the chairs in front of the desk. "What? I can't come see my wise older brother?"

He dropped his pen and pinned her with a get-real gaze. "Okay, now I know you're up to something. What's up?"

Sloane lifted her chin. *Get on with it. The ends justify the means. Pride will do nothing but keep you on the unemployment line.* "I've been thinking about your offer, and I've reconsidered. I would like to come work for Sugar Blitz."

His patented big-brother suspicious gaze didn't waver. "Why the change of heart? You've been pretty adamant about doing your own thing."

There was no reason to lie, other than pride, and she'd already concluded she couldn't let her pride hold her back. "I had a job interview earlier. I wasn't lying about that."

"Did it not go well?" Now, worry replaced suspicion on his face. She shouldn't bristle. He was being protective. She wouldn't bristle, but sometimes being the youngest Dell sibling sucked.

"No, it went great. However, my potential boss has some concerns about my work history."

Donovan's chest puffed up. Uh-oh, here came big-brother indignation. "What does that mean? Your work history and work ethic are impeccable. That's why I've tried to hire you several times."

Sloane smiled. Her brother really was the best. "I appreciate the vote of confidence, but she's worried that most of my history has been as an assistant. You and I both know I did the bulk of the social media work for my previous job, but that's hard to prove, especially with a former boss who will deny it to his last breath."

He inclined his head in agreement. He'd heard her complaints plenty of times. "So this new place has concerns. Where does that leave you?"

"She'd like me to lead a social media campaign for a company or product of my choosing." Sloane scrunched up her nose. "I kinda sorta blurted out that I was about to start doing that very thing for my brother's cupcake shop. She's a big fan of Sugar Blitz, by the way."

Donovan's lips quirked in amusement. "Ah, Rash Sloane made an appearance."

She sniffed. "I prefer resolute."

His eyes, so like their father's, twinkled. "I'm sure you do."

Sloane rolled her eyes. "Whatever, Donovan. On to more important things. What do you say about bringing me onboard?"

"There's the focused Sloane who won't let anyone or anything stand in her way of succeeding." He studied her. "But have you really thought this through? Despite repeatedly asking you to come work here, I've always understood why you turn me down."

She nodded. "Well, things have changed. Let's be real. One, I quit my job, and I need a new one. My bills aren't going to pay themselves. And I really want this job. Two, you have a high-profile business in San Diego. There aren't a lot of those beating down my door right now. Your business is in transition. I can and will help make sure your new location is a success. Finally, you need my help. Your social media game is weak."

Donovan's eyebrows lifted. "Tell me how you really feel, Sloane."

"I will. Always. With the latest incident of a Sugar Blitz owner going viral, I have a million ideas on how we can capitalize."

"You do? Can't wait to hear them. But what about the personal reasons you always give every time you tell me to get lost?"

Already prepared for this question, Sloane leaned back in the chair and crossed her legs. "This is only temporary. I plan to use this opportunity to launch me into another fantastic opportunity that has nothing to do with my famous brother. It's a failsafe plan."

He chuckled. "I'm not sure such a thing exists, but I'm game if you are. I'm sure Nicholas and August will be too."

She ignored the little shiver that raced down her spine at the mention of August's name. She asked very, *very* casually, "Speaking of the social media darling, where is he?"

Donovan spread his arms wide. "Off being a social media darling."

Sloane blinked, probably a couple of hundred times, as shock skittered through her entire system like a train going off the tracks. "I'm sorry. What?"

* * *

August twisted in the chair as lights beat down on him in unrelenting waves. He was positive the makeup they'd dabbed on him was melting away like ice cream in ninety-degree weather. Why was he here? Whose big, bright idea was this?

Oh, yeah. His.

Before he could come to his senses last night, he'd replied to an email invitation he'd studiously ignored since the Rant Heard Round the World.

In two minutes, he was going to make his debut on *Good Morning, San Diego.* For the whole city to see and comment. The producers had already assured him that the national network morning show that aired before *Good Morning, San Diego* planned to re-air the segment tomorrow.

Fucking great.

August shifted on the metal stool, seeking a more comfortable position. He usually didn't give his size much thought. He was a big guy. That was one of his best assets as a professional football player. His teammates were mostly the same size or bigger, which meant he was normal in that world. But, in the real world, that wasn't the case.

He didn't doubt the stool looked great on camera, but it was making a suspicious creaking noise under him. Still, the chair was the least of his concerns at the moment. But concentrating on the stool meant he didn't have to think about what was to come. Namely, that he was about to do an actual interview, and not a postgame interview, where he could toss out a few clichés until the media horde left in disgust to find better prey, or if a reporter actually asked a decent question, he could delve deep into the game he loved.

A pesky bead of sweat slithered down his hairline to his cheek. What the hell was he doing here?

Oh, yeah. Being brave or some such bullshit. Taking the road less traveled after preferring the tried-and-true path of never seeking attention for so long. Maybe his ex-wife and father had a point. He'd recited his reasons on a nonstop loop in his head since he woke up that morning. Too bad his stomach didn't care. It was currently doing its best impression of a boat lost at sea during a dangerous storm as it pitched back and forth, never settling down for more than two seconds at a time.

The anchor, Kayla Ruiz, smiled at him in sympathy as though she could sense his turmoil. Hell, she probably didn't have to guess. His distress was probably written all over his face. He forced his lips into a smile that undoubtedly more closely resembled a grimace, but she visibly relaxed.

Kayla smiled into the camera as the producer counted down the return from the commercial break. "We're joined today by August Hodges, who you might know as SugarBae on social media. He's also the star fullback for the San Diego Knights."

Amused by her wording choice, August's smile became a little more natural. Fullbacks weren't usually referred to as stars. Fullbacks did the grunt work that allowed players like Nicholas to get the glory. Which was exactly how August liked it.

"Thanks for stopping by today, August," she said.

He nodded. "Thanks for having me." He sounded almost normal, his voice only wobbling slightly on the last word.

She was staring at him like he was a conquering hero returned home from battle. Usually, he only got that reaction at sports bars when drunk Knights fans spotted him. Which is why he rarely stepped foot in a bar.

"I believe I speak for women all across San Diego, heck, all across the world, when I say I'm thrilled you're here," Kayla said. "I'm thrilled you said what you said. It's not every day that men speak so eloquently on the discrimination women face and advocate for us to receive the recognition we deserve."

August made sure his smile didn't waver. Or he tried to. He didn't know what to say. She was looking at him expectantly. Apparently, a smile wasn't going to cut it. "Thanks."

"You're welcome." Her voice brightened like she could coax a hardier response out of him if she were friendlier. "Did you know you were being filmed?"

"I didn't."

She waited a beat, expecting more. But he'd already answered the question. He didn't know what else to say. Theoretically, if his brain wasn't whirring at a million beats per second, he could've come up with something more. But this is what shyness and nerves did to him. Beads of sweat at both temples slid silently down his face. His hands, clenched together under the table out of sight, were clammy.

Amazingly enough, Kayla's voice brightened even more. "Okay, then. Let's talk about what you said. You were very adamant about respecting women and fighting back against toxic masculinity. You and your partners at Sugar Blitz have done your part to rewrite what masculinity is. Have you all talked about that?"

August shook his head. "We haven't. We had an idea for a business, and we went with it. We all like cupcakes and thought it would be a fun challenge."

"But surely you understand why your speech struck a chord in so many."

August shrugged. "The truth is important to me." One of the core tenets of his life. "Those guys were spewing BS and they needed to hear the truth." He could mention his own upbringing, his life with a father who didn't much value his role as a father, how he'd never really been able to let go of that pain, but there was no way in hell he was opening himself up to that type of scrutiny. "I wasn't looking for attention."

She nodded like he'd spoken some pearl of wisdom that opened her eyes to the true meaning of life. "Speaking of attention, how have the last few days been for you?"

"Crazy."

She chuckled. "I can imagine. When that post went up on Sugar Blitz's Instagram account letting everyone know you were at the store, there were a few people in this studio who cut out early for the day. You must be loving all the attention."

He shrugged. "Not really."

A considering light entered her eyes. "Is there someone special in your life who might object to all this attention? That's what everyone wants to know. We know you're not married."

Unbidden, an image of Sloane flickered in his conscience. She wasn't his. He wasn't hers. And that's how it was going to stay. That ship had sailed years ago, thanks to his actions. She'd moved on. Proved it by dating other men who weren't good enough to breathe the same air as her, let alone touch or kiss her.

He told the truth. "No, there isn't. I'm single."

The anchor turned back to the camera with a brilliant and blinding smile. "Well, there you have it, San Diego. SugarBae is single and ready to mingle."

Wait. What?

Chapter Nine

*T*hirty minutes after leaving the *Good Day, San Diego* studio, August pulled into a parking spot at Sugar Blitz. He'd had the good sense to park in the back when he spotted the throng spilling out the front door when he turned onto the street.

What the hell? Were they there to see him, "single and ready to mingle" SugarBae? Were that many people watching *Good Day, San Diego*? If so, how and why had they made it down here so fast?

August shook his head. Maybe he was being an egomaniac and the crowd had nothing to do with him. Maybe they were there for Nicholas's latest creations. After all, he was getting a lot of buzz about his latest series of decadent cupcakes, including his crème brûlée cupcake.

Even so, August wasn't taking any chances. He tiptoed through the back entrance on the balls of his feet, like his "fans" (and he was still going to hurl) could hear the tread of his shoes against the tile. Yes, that was a ridiculous thought, and he undoubtedly looked ridiculous, but he had to do what he had to do. Football drills were coming in handy once again.

Creak!

August made a quick left into the kitchen as the bathroom door started to open from the inside.

Nicholas spun around from the counter where he was mixing ingredients. "Hey, dude, what are you doing here?"

August frowned. He could say, "I'm terrified I'm going to run into someone who wants me to sign her bra," or he could deflect. He went with the better option. "What do you mean what am I doing here? I work here."

Nicholas sent him a give-me-a-break look. "Yeah, but I thought you were off being a TV star."

August rolled his eyes. "I finished that."

Nicholas wiped his hands on a towel and tossed it aside. "How did it go?"

August grimaced. "Fine. I think. Maybe." He'd tried not to think about it on the ride back to the shop. Or the business cards an assistant producer and the makeup artist had slipped into his pocket as he departed the station. Or the butt pats and the almost-pat to another part of his lower body he'd avoided.

No sounds emanated from the hallway. He cracked the door open and peered around the edge.

"Hiding from your fan club?" Nicholas asked, his snicker filling the room.

August looked over his shoulder at his best friend. "Being smart."

The hall was empty. The only sound he heard was the normal chatter from the front of the store. Maybe the customers were just their regulars. Nothing for him to hide from. Not that he was *hiding*, really.

"Sure, dude." Nicholas came to stand next to him and crossed his arms across his chest. "I can go out there and distract them."

Maybe this time that distraction would involve a striptease, which actually might not be the worst thing in the world. Nicholas could go viral and August would be in the clear.

He sighed. Yes, he could take Nicholas up on his offer, but no. One, he was a grown man and could fight his own battles (or at least walk through a crowd of women) and two, he'd made the decision to pursue this opportunity. There was no backing out now. He'd vowed to lean into the SugarBae thing, and that was that. That was how he lived his life. His word was his bond, for better or for worse.

"No, I'm good. Is Donovan in his office?"

Nicholas grinned. "No doubt. He and his computer with its sales figures are attached at the hip."

August easily returned the smile. They all had their strengths, which made them such good friends and business partners. Though they all wore whatever hat was necessary when it came to their business, they each took the lead role in a different area. Donovan had the best head for business and made sure they were reaching their financial goals. He probably knew to the cent how much profit they'd made last week. Nicholas was in charge of the kitchen. He loved coming up with new cupcake flavors and shared his kitchen reluctantly. August was a jack-of-all-trades, helping out wherever he was needed and handling any repairs and ordering that needed to be done.

"I told him I'd talk to him when I got back."

Nicholas nodded, returning to his latest creation. "Okay, man. Let me know if you need any advice on how to juggle multiple women."

August rolled his eyes again. "Thank you for being so generous. I'll remember that."

He slipped out of the room with Nicholas's laughter ringing in his ears. Thankfully, the coast was clear and he traversed the hall to Donovan's office none the worse for wear. He gave a perfunctory knock and slipped inside.

He recognized his mistake immediately.

He'd given himself no time to prepare for Sloane's presence. No time to steel himself against her impact on him. No time to wipe his expression clear before the need that clawed at him showed on his face.

Oblivious to his emotional turmoil, she grinned—no, more like smirked—at him. "August! Just the person we wanted to see."

She wanted to see him? Hope, that infernal bastard, uncurled near his heart. Wait. No, she said "we," not "I." He nodded stiffly at her, his best and usual response when he unexpectedly ran into her, then turned to the room's other occupant. "What's going on?"

Donovan jerked his chin toward the empty chair in front of his desk. The chair less than two feet away from Sloane. "Have a seat."

Since he had no real, logical reason not to do so, August sat. Sloane's light honey scent drifted toward him. That scent haunted his dreams. He faced Donovan. "What's up?"

He gestured toward his computer. "We watched your appearance on *Good Day, San Diego*."

Right. It was the twenty-first century. Streaming was a thing. "What did you think?"

Donovan's nose and eyes scrunched up. "Well, umm . . ."

"It was a disaster," Sloane supplied, as matter-of-fact as only she could be. Her plush lips tipped into a wide smile before he could decide if he was impressed or insulted by her candor. "But luckily for you, I'm here to help."

It was his turn for his mouth to gape open like a goldfish waiting to be fed. "Uh . . . what?"

She clasped her hands together, and crossed one leg over the other, angling toward him and giving him a brief flash of firm, mouthwatering thigh before she tugged her skirt down. "I've reconsidered my brother's job offer and have decided to come work for Sugar Blitz."

Donovan side-eyed her. "She needs to do a big splashy social media campaign for a job she wants, and she decided our little company was worthy of her talents."

He was supposed to laugh at the sarcastic comment, at the natural ribbing of siblings. But he couldn't. Not when his heart had climbed up into his throat and rendered him mute. This couldn't be happening. He'd reconciled to himself long ago that he and Sloane could never be a "we," and he didn't believe in torturing himself. Self-preservation was a thing he wholeheartedly believed in.

Sloane rolled her eyes at her brother before turning those beautiful eyes toward him. "As true as that may be, after that little performance this morning, you definitely need my help."

Before he could think it through, August's chest puffed up. Perhaps insulted was winning out. "What was wrong with my performance?"

She ticked the points off on her fingers. "You were stiff. You gave one-word answers, even though she asked the most leading questions ever. When you talk, and yes, we know you don't do a ton of that, you usually have a dry sense of humor. We got none of that today."

"Any other faults you want to mention?"

She wagged her finger at him. "There's that dry sense of humor I was talking about." She bobbed her head side to side like she was thinking about the question. "No, I think that's it. For now."

"Thanks." He shouldn't be grumpy. She was right, of course, but that didn't mean he had to like it.

Sloane beamed at him, clearly relishing getting on his nerves. "Any time."

August's lips twitched. That was the thing about Sloane. She could always make him smile when very few could. Even when he was determined to be in a bad mood. Her eyes gleamed at him, like she could read his mind. For a moment, the years melted away, and they were kids again.

Donovan chuckled, jolting August back to the present. "I really want to stay for the rest of this riveting conversation, but it might get bloody, and I told Jada I wouldn't get any new scars before our wedding. And my shift out front is about to start." He stood and strode to the door. "I also have faith that you both have Sugar Blitz's best interests at heart and can come to an understanding on how to proceed."

August bit down on his tongue to prevent himself from protesting and sounding like a fool. He watched helplessly as his best friend abandoned him, leaving him alone with his biggest temptation. Not that Donovan had any idea. August kept that secret to himself. It was so ingrained in him, it was like second nature. Though Donovan knew they'd had a friendship as teens, as far as he knew their relationship had cooled when Sloane went away to college. Donovan assumed Sloane liked to antagonize him just for fun now that she was living in San Diego. The full nature of their history was the only secret August kept from his best friend.

Silence made an uncomfortable companion in the room. He should break it. And he would as soon as he thought of something to say. He was the one Donovan and Nicholas counted on to see beneath the surface and get to the heart of the matter. The one who could keep steady when the world was tilting off its axis. But he was never on sure footing when it came to Sloane Dell, which is why he usually kept his distance.

"It looks like it's just you and me, kid," she said. She sounded about as thrilled about the idea as he did. He couldn't blame her. He'd hurt her, and he didn't doubt for a moment she'd gotten over it and moved on, but he knew as well as anyone, scars lingered and could start itching at a moment's notice.

He nodded again. Not for the first time, he wished he had a hint of Nicholas's suaveness or Donovan's logic. She sprang into action, leaping up from her chair, and started pacing around the room. She wore a white tank tucked into a red skirt that ended at mid-thigh, the better to showcase her terrific legs. Her braids swung back and forth as she traversed the small space. "Before we can move forward, we have to acknowledge the elephant in the room."

He blinked. "We do?"

They never had before. The Madrigal family from *Encanto* had nothing on them. Fuck not talking about Bruno. He and Sloane didn't talk about that night.

Sloane nodded. "I've made a complete about-face after a year of saying I wouldn't work for Donovan, and it's weird."

Oh. That.

A small smile played across her lips. He shouldn't notice that they were covered in a purplish-red color that highlighted their fullness, but he did. And he would beat himself up about that later.

He cleared his throat. "Was Donovan right about you doing this for another job?"

"Yes. I need to prove to my potential boss that I can lead a campaign, and if I have to ride my brother's coattails to do it, then so be it. At least it's only temporary."

August shook his head. "You know he doesn't think that way. He never has."

She sighed. "I know, but others do, or might, and I don't like it."

She never had.

"Regardless, I arrived this morning ready to work." She threw her shoulders back, while a sly smile played across her tempting lips. "When I did, I learned, to my complete astonishment, that you booked a segment on *Good Day, San Diego*."

"Which was a terrible idea, according to you."

She held up an index finger. "No, I never said that. The ultimate goal is to bring attention to Sugar Blitz, and you did that in spades."

August shifted uncomfortably in his chair. "But . . ."

"But you could have used some coaching beforehand. I'm not sure that interview was the right move out of the gate. But I'm here now, and I have ideas." She'd resumed pacing. He tried not to notice the gentle sway of her hips, the way the skirt hugged her ass. He failed. Miserably.

He swallowed hard. Would she notice if he adjusted his pants? "How so?"

Her hands whirred in front of her chest, in constant motion. "We put you front and center. Give the people what they want."

His stomach lurched. "Do we have to?"

"Yes. That's why you went on the show, right?"

He reluctantly nodded.

Sloane's head tilted to the side. "Why did you go on the show? That's so unlike you."

He could never forget that at one point in time, she'd known him as well as anybody.

"I was looking to do my part to market Sugar Blitz as we get ready to open the new location."

Her eyes narrowed. "You do plenty around here."

"I could do more." Melinda's words rang in his head. His head knew it was ridiculous. His heart was another matter. The critical thoughts were often so hard to keep at bay. If he did more, then maybe the next person wouldn't find him so unwantable. Like Melinda. Like his father.

Sloane looked like she wanted to argue. He lifted his chin and met her gaze head-on. She pursed her lips and nodded finally, then resumed pacing. "Okay, then. In that case, we need to highlight Sugar Blitz and the cupcakes, of course, but what people really crave on social media is the human connection. They want to laugh and cry and feel seen. That's why you went viral, and we need to lean into it. People want to know SugarBae."

He groaned each and every time he heard that ridiculous nickname. This time was no different.

Sloane continued, undeterred by his reaction, her hands whirling all over the place. "They know you're a football player and part owner of a cupcake shop. But that's what you do, not who you are."

Beautiful, impactful words from a beautiful, impactful woman.

She stopped when she noticed him watching her. "Sorry, I talk with my hands. It helps me think."

He knew. She was in her element. It was the sexiest thing he'd ever been fortunate to witness.

"I'm going to give them that," she continued. "And that's going to lead to them coming down here to buy cupcakes and put money in y'all's pockets. You want to be a star, right?"

No. "Yes."

But he was committed. It was time for him to come out of the shadows. Time to take control of his life and make himself worthy of . . . His eyes flickered to Sloane. Make himself worthy of someone to love.

Clearly unaware of his inner turmoil, Sloane's lips spread into a wide smile. "If that's what you want, then I'm going to make it happen."

August held back another groan. Barely. "What exactly are you thinking?"

* * *

She was thinking he was the sexiest man to ever sexy. But that's not what he was asking and it sure as hell wasn't what she should be thinking. She'd gotten over her crush years ago. Had had several real relationships since. Those relationships had ended not because she was still pining over August, but because she'd realized the relationships were nearing their expiration date. Her last boyfriend, Jim the Jughead, had made her finally realize she missed her family and San Diego, and she'd come home. When she'd needed him most, he'd fumbled the ball.

Her father, who had a gambling problem, had fallen off the wagon and started putting pressure on her, almost daily, to send him money. It brought back not-so-fond memories from childhood when his financial instability had placed a great strain on their family, and her mother, especially. She hadn't known what to tell her dad or what to do. She loved him, wanted to help him, but she knew giving him money would only make the situation worse. She'd agonized and agonized before going to Shana, who encouraged her to put her well-being first. She'd offered paying for counseling instead. Her father had turned her down, angrily declaring that she didn't love him. Jim had never seen what the big deal was or why she was so conflicted and hurt by her father's words and actions. "Just give him the money," he would say.

After that ordeal, it became clear that men were fine to have fun with, but giving them the power to hurt her? Been there, done that, not going back again.

She would never again find herself in the position of hoping a man would treat her better.

Still, none of those inarguable truths had stopped her heart from melting as she watched August on that morning show. He'd looked so uncomfortable, yet determined to do a good job, even if he had no clue what that entailed. He'd been adorable.

He looked adorable now. He'd forsaken his usual attire of T-shirt or Sugar Blitz polo for a blue button-down shirt. The top two buttons were undone and framed the strong column of his neck and his Adam's apple. Jeans hugged his firm thighs. His dark brown locs were pulled back, as usual, in a low ponytail. Did he know the style highlighted the strong line of his jaw and his amazingly sharp cheekbones?

Okay, yeah, she couldn't say any of that. She was Sloane Dell, Princess Shuri in training, hear her roar. Or something. "I'm thinking that making you a star will be fun."

He looked like he'd swallowed something both bitter and sour. When he noticed her side-eye, he straightened his face.

Sloane wasn't ready to let him off the hook. "That *is* what you want, right?"

After a moment's hesitation, he nodded once, a herky-jerky motion that inspired exactly zero confidence. Why was he insistent on doing this? She'd spoken the truth earlier. He did plenty to make Sugar Blitz a success. There was no need for him to seek out the spotlight.

But she didn't have the right to press. They were no longer friends. Maybe they'd get there again, but there would never be more. He'd made that plain years ago.

Sloane inhaled sharply. "What are you doing?" The question slipped out before her brain could catch up to her mouth. He was unbuttoning the sleeves of his shirt and rolling them up to reveal forearms peppered with dark hair and roped with veins that were begging to be licked. By her. No. That was a terrible, no-good idea. Right? No. Yes.

He looked at her like she was a few pancakes short of a silver-dollar platter at IHOP. "Getting comfortable. These long sleeves are working my nerves."

She shook her head. "Right. Sorry. Whatever. Back to the topic at hand. I don't know if you've taken a look out front, but your fan club has assembled, and they don't have any intentions of leaving until you make an appearance."

His face twisted into a half frown, half grimace. "Why? Did you post something on Instagram?"

"No, I didn't have to. *Good Day, San Diego* hyped your appearance on social media, an appearance you scheduled, might I add?"

"Social media is the devil," he grumbled.

She would not find his consternation cute.

"Hey, you're lucky they didn't camp out at the station to ambush you as you left. Here, they're likely to be distracted by cupcakes and coffee."

The half frown, half grimace made another appearance. "Right."

Sloane forced out the next sentence because she was a professional, and this was a professional situation, and she had a job to do. "And need I remind you that you announced on local TV that you're single. An announcement that will surely hit the national and international airwaves of the internet soon. I'm gonna keep it real. When you announced your singledom, a loud cheer went up in the store. Donovan and I were standing next to each other in here with the door closed, and we couldn't hear each other for a good ten seconds."

Just because her heart had seized up when he said it didn't mean anything. It wasn't like she didn't know he was single. He was her brother's best friend, after all, and she and her brother were close. If August or Nicholas had found the love of their respective lives, Donovan would've mentioned it at some point. But then she'd panicked, because what if her brother didn't? What if he decided to do something crazy like respect his friend's privacy or something? It would've been worse than when August married his ex-wife, which was one of the most painful days of her life. She'd blocked the whole day and situation out of her mind at the time. But at least she knew it was happening. This time she'd have to finally acknowledge and accept there was no hope for them to be together.

But then August had said he was single, and she could actually breathe again.

August visibly blanched.

Concern had her taking a step forward. "Are you okay?"

"Yeah, I'm fine." He rubbed his palms up and down his thighs. His massive, muscled, marvelous thighs.

They hadn't even started yet, and this was already a disaster. What had she gotten herself into? "You don't have to do this, you know."

She'd find another way to boost Sugar Blitz's social media profile.

His head tilted to the side. "I don't? Didn't you just say there were a bunch of women out there dying to meet me? How would it look for me and Sugar Blitz if I disrespected them by not making an appearance?"

Sloane swallowed. Good point. "True, but you look a little ill. It's not good when Black people look that pale."

"Nothing a good Mike's Hard Lemonade can't cure."

They shared a smile that could only come with a collective memory.

Chapter Ten

Twelve years ago . . .

Sloane tiptoed up the stairs. All the lights were off. Miracle of miracles, her mom hadn't waited up for her. It would have been very, very bad if she had. Thank God she was the youngest child. Her mom had gotten all of her overprotectiveness out of her system with her older children. Sloane was allowed to get away with murder, according to her siblings. She'd never been happier about that state of affairs than she was now.

Sloane was just sober enough to know she was tipsy. Her best friend, Stephanie, had made sure she got back home safely.

Getting up to her room was her last mission. She stealthily climbed the stairs.

Creak! Dang it! She'd forgotten about the stair that squeaked. Her siblings would be so ashamed of her. They'd taught her the secrets of their ways years ago, if only to keep her quiet about their escapades.

"Sloane, that you?" her mom called out from her bedroom.

"Yes." Sloane overenunciated to make sure no hint of slurring slipped through.

"Good night."

"Night."

She collapsed against the door when she made it to her bedroom without further incident.

Her head was a little fuzzy, but she managed to get out of her clothes and into her pajamas without too much difficulty. She snuggled under the sheets and stared at the stars she'd glued to the ceiling when she was eleven. The room only spun a little.

She wasn't a rule breaker. A go-getter, yes. A rule breaker, no. She'd gone to the party and said no to any and all drugs and most of the alcohol offered. Her friends had gotten annoyed with her when she sat in the corner instead of flirting with the boys from school. She didn't want to talk to any of the boys there. None of them were August. But, not wanting to be a total loser, she'd accepted the Mike's. She'd only had one and a half bottles.

She was still kinda wired. Kinda buzzed. Not in the mood to go to sleep. She wanted to talk to someone. Someone who wouldn't judge her for being a wee bit drunk. Which ruled out her brother and sister. They'd both have conniption fits. In their minds, she was still five.

August. She wanted to talk to August. He wouldn't judge her. She grabbed her phone and made the call. He answered on the third ring.

"Sloane. Is everything all right?" He sounded worried. "Are your parents fighting again?"

Oh, shit. It was close to midnight. She'd never called him this late before. "No, my dad's not here. I'm sorry. You were probably busy or asleep."

"Neither, actually."

"Oh." She should say something else, but his voice did something for her. Despite his claim, a hint of sleep clung to his voice, making it ever so much deeper. The sexiest voice on the planet had just gotten better.

"Are you okay?"

"Yeah, I'm at home. Went to a party."

"Sloane Dell, are you drunk?" He sounded amused, not judgmental.

"Say it a little louder, why don't you?" she hissed. "Is my brother there?"

"No, I'm in my room. He's out with some friends. And you didn't answer my question."

"It was just Mike's Hard Lemonade." She sounded sulky. She couldn't help it.

His chuckle sent a shiver down her spine. "How much?"

"One and a half bottles."

"Enough to do damage, huh? Make sure you leave a trash can by the side of the bed, in case you wake up in the middle of the night, needing to throw up."

"Thanks, Dr. Hodges." She paused. "You didn't go out with Donovan . . . or your girlfriend?" See, she wasn't in denial. She could talk about Melinda without sounding like a jealous harpy. Sloane Dell was the very picture of maturity.

"I did for a while, but I hit my limit of peopling and came home to recharge."

She made a face at the starry ceiling. "And I called, interrupting your peace."

"It's okay. I'm just chilling. What are you up to?"

"I was thinking about watching *Notting Hill*. It's my favorite."

"That's the movie with—"

"Julia Roberts and Hugh Grant. And if you badmouth it, I will—"

His laugh cut her off. "What? I was just going to say it's old."

She gasped. "It is a classic, sir!"

"Yeah, okay."

She harrumphed. "What are you up to?"

"Umm . . ."

Now, she was unbelievably intrigued. "Spill it, MOTY. Unless it's porn, which, if that is what you're up to, you can keep it to yourself."

He groaned. "It wasn't porn."

"Then what?"

"It's going to sound really nerdy."

"Okay, now I really want to know."

"I'm reading August Wilson's *How I Learned What I Learned*."

"How old is that, hmm?"

He laughed again. "You got me. You got me. I'm taking a class on August Wilson. I have to read it."

"So you don't want to read it?"

"No, I do. He was my mom's favorite playwright."

Sloane sat up in her bed. "She named you after him."

"Yeah." He sounded a little shy. Her heart melted a little more.

"That's cool. Read it to me."

"You want me to read to you?"

"I usually stick to romances, but yeah." Anything to hear his powerful voice. "You must have a soft spot for him, too, if you're reading his work on a Saturday night."

He laughed again. She'd never tire of hearing that sound from him. He always sounded half-surprised that he was capable of such a whimsical activity. "I do. I've read all his plays."

"Read it to me. Please. I need a bedtime story to fall asleep."

"Okay, okay. If you get bored, let me know."

"Never."

Sometime later, she fell asleep to the sound of his soothing, mesmerizing voice.

Chapter Eleven

We want SugarBae! We want SugarBae!"

Sloane's eyes widened as the chanting from the store increased in volume and fervor. "I'm invoking the right to change my mind. I don't think it's safe for you out there. We need to get out of here before they storm the office and rip your clothes off."

August made a face. "Agreed."

She quietly opened the door and peeked out. Luckily, the crowd was still at the front of the building. "Let's go."

They made a quick left and exited out the back a few seconds later, none the worse for wear. "Follow me." They tiptoed quietly down the alley until they reached the corner. Sloane sneaked a peek. There was a line out the front door of Sugar Blitz, but the crowd wasn't looking their way. She and August hurriedly made a left.

"To the park?" she asked, pointing ahead down the block. August nodded.

A park was great. Out in the open, away from temptation. Not that he was tempted by her, as he'd made perfectly clear. And even if she was tempted by him, there was no way in hell she would act, because of that whole humiliating history thing. Still, better to be safe than sorry.

There were only a few people milling about. A couple walking their two identical Jack Russell terriers and a mom pushing her kid on a swing.

August settled next to her on the bench. Only a foot, a mere twelve inches, separated their bodies. It was totally cool.

He rubbed his impressive thighs with his hands. It was totally cool. It was totally not an erotic action meant to entice and mesmerize her. She shifted her gaze from the mesmerizing action.

She was an adult, and she was going to have a very adult conversation with him.

Besides, if he felt even an inkling of the attraction she felt for him, he'd had ample opportunity to say so. And he hadn't. Because he didn't. In any case, she wasn't a teen anymore. She'd had her fair share of relationships, real relationships she hadn't conjured up in her head, and yeah, she was so over August. Men in general, really. She had no time for men and their shenanigans. Not after the Jim the Jughead disaster.

So it didn't matter that August could still make her hormones do a happy dance whenever he was near.

What *did* matter? The elephant in the room, aka her past actions. And now that they were committed to spending more than the bare minimum of time together, they needed to at least address said elephant. She had no desire to do so, but as she'd officially accepted the offer from her brother and watched August on *Good Day, San Diego,* she'd finally acknowledged to herself that this was the only correct course of action if they had any hopes of moving forward successfully. Damn, being an adult sucked!

Sloane squared her shoulders and took a deep breath, inhaling the salty air courtesy of the nearby ocean. She willed her heartbeat to slow.

"We need to talk."

Sloane blinked. She hadn't said that. August had.

She turned to him. "About what?"

"The past."

Shock swept through every cell in her body. Yes, she'd planned to speak to him about it, but she'd never expected him to bring it up on his own. He never had before. Then again, neither had she. But he was right. Just like old times, they were on the same page with no words being spoken. Her heart tugged in remembrance of those good times.

But that was then, and this was now. She metaphorically girded her loins, nodded, and forced her lips to move. "You're right. We do. If you don't mind, I'd like to go first."

He nodded, his focus squarely on her. Like nothing could break his concentration. She was his world. Which she would *not* find attractive. Nope, not her. Not today. Not ever.

"What happened happened, and it was unfortunate for the both of us. While we've never spoken about it, I believe we can both agree it has colored our interactions ever since." She sounded like a jaded professor giving a lecture for the hundredth time to a group of students who couldn't care less. It didn't matter. *Get through this, girl. Get through it.*

"However, we're going to be working closely together on this project, and we both want it to be successful. Therefore, I'm proposing that we agree to leave the past in the past." Her voice quickened as she began to lose steam. Bravado only lasted thirty seconds or so, apparently, especially when the cause of her bravado was staring at her like he was. She tried not to squirm under his scrutiny. He always seemed to see underneath the surface, which she'd thought was so romantic as a teen, but as an adult, she had no use for his astuteness, so she kept going.

"I'm sure you never think about it, because why would you? And I prefer to never ever think about it, and I'm sure we both know why. We need to concentrate on the present, which is that we both want the best for Sugar Blitz. That leads to only one conclusion. We can be professionals, right?"

There. She was done. A bird cooed in the distance. It was a miracle she could hear it over the pounding of her heart.

"Right. Professionals." His voice, his face gave nothing away. Which was totally fine. Totally professional.

She held out her hand. "Deal?"

He grasped her hand in his large one. She swallowed as an electric charge sizzled up her arm. His mesmerizing eyes locked on hers. "Deal."

Yep. Totally fine. Totally professional.

Chapter Twelve

August flicked the light on in the storage room of Sugar Blitz's soon-to-be newest location. Damn, what had he come in here for? His concentration had been shit since that conversation with Sloane yesterday afternoon.

He'd planned to apologize for hurting her, for never acknowledging that she hadn't been alone in her feelings back then. But she'd spoken first . . .

August rubbed the back of his neck. He got why she wanted to leave the past in the past. Why rehash a painful period in your life when you didn't have to? Acknowledging it at all made him admire her even more. So he'd decided to honor her wishes and swallow his apology.

Besides, she no longer loved him. Hell, if she ever had. They'd been teenagers. What the hell did teens know about love? After all, teens were known for living in the moment and feeling everything, no matter how minor, so intensely. And it's not like she'd stayed locked in her room and pined after him after the incident. Over the years, she'd dated Jim, James, Paul, and Tyrone, or whatever the fuck their names were. Shit, he didn't know. He hadn't kept track of her relationships because he tried his best not to be a creep, and why torture himself like that, but Donovan had mentioned boyfriends here and there over the years, and he'd been to enough Dell gatherings over the years to even meet a date or two.

But it didn't matter now. She didn't want him. He'd had his chance, and he'd blown it. He was never great verbally, especially when caught off guard, but it didn't matter. He'd hurt her. And she'd moved on, as she should have. So he needed to buck up and act like the grown-up he was. Respect their deal and play his part, even if lingering doubts had kept him up for half the night.

But he was stepping out of his comfort zone. Seizing the day.

August blinked. Shit.

What other clichés could he spew?

August's shoulders relaxed as a burst of laughter bubbled up from his chest. He focused on the box he'd come in here for, grabbed it, and headed to the front of the store.

A quick, brisk knock sounded on the door. His shoulders tensed up. None of that mattered, starting now.

He deposited the box on the floor against a wall, then strode to the entrance and unlocked the door. "Hey."

"Hi." Sloane strode confidently past him like she hadn't spent the night reciting all the defensive schemes in the Knights playbook as sleep eluded her. Not that he'd done that or anything.

She looked terrific, per usual. She wore hip-hugging jeans and a plain white T-shirt that looked anything but as it clung to her full breasts. Worse—and why was there always a worse?—she'd tied the ends of the shirt at her waist. Which meant he was being tortured with teasing glimpses of her abdomen's smooth brown skin. Yep, that was enough of that. He raised his gaze. Her braids were caught up in a high ponytail, drawing attention to the long, lickable column of her neck.

Shit. How was this supposed to work?

Yesterday, after agreeing to leave the past in the past, they'd decided to meet this morning to start on their social media campaign. And obviously that was a terrible idea. But he wasn't a quitter.

Sloane turned to inspect the space, thankfully none the wiser about his NSFW thoughts, which was a good thing because they were, in fact, at work. He was here to whip this place into shape before its grand opening.

Which meant he needed to keep his eye on the prize. August silently groaned. Good Lord. The clichés were coming fast and furious this morning.

With her back still to him, Sloane propped her hands on her back, drawing his eyes to her ass. Pure perfection.

He sighed. *FML.* It was going to be a long day. Week. Weeks? Speaking of—"How long are you planning on working on this campaign?"

His voice came out gruff, damn near unfriendly. Or so he'd been told before.

She whirled to face him, one eyebrow lifting to mock him, clearly not intimidated. "Good morning to you, too, August. Trying to get rid of me already?"

Trying to save my sanity. "No. I'd like to know how much time we have to work our magic. Are you going balls to the wall or do you plan on taking a more leisurely approach?"

She sauntered closer, her alluring hips swaying side to side. He ordered himself not to back up. He was a grown-up and could handle one woman who sent his senses racing every time he was within fifteen feet of her.

Her lips curved. "I always go balls to the wall. Our goal is to boost Sugar Blitz's profile, and we do that by capitalizing on your current popularity and making you a social media star."

Whoa. He held up a hand. "I've been thinking about that . . ."

Sloane's head cocked to the side. "And?"

He'd practiced this in the mirror this morning while he shaved. He could get through it. "I want Sugar Blitz to be a social media star, and if I have to throw myself out there a little to make that happen, then so be it, but I don't want to be front and center."

Sloane's eyes widened as her index finger lifted in an *aha* gesture. "I knew it! I knew you didn't want to do this. Why did you agree in the first place?" Her expression softened with concern. "Are you okay?"

He hadn't prepared for that. "Because."

She peered deep into his eyes, silently pleading with him for more. But he couldn't. He wasn't ready to admit that his insecurities along with his general shyness and anxiousness had woken him up in the middle of the night. Not to her or anyone. Hell, barely to himself.

When he remained silent, she nodded. Sloane went into motion, pacing back and forth, her head down, deep in thought. She stopped in front of him and lifted her head. "Okay. No one wants to force you to do something you're uncomfortable with." She bit her lip. "We won't do the campaign."

Both his hands flew up. Shit. He was not handling this right at all. "Wait. That's not what I said. I want to do a campaign."

"You do?"

This he could answer.

"Yes. Look." He spread his arms wide. "We've poured a lot of money into renovating this space with no guarantee people in this neighborhood give two shits about cupcakes. Still, we agree it's a worthy risk, so if you can help us build awareness for this location and the business in general before we open, that would be great."

Sloane went back into motion, circling the room, deep in thought, until she ended up in front of him again. "And you'll . . ."

"Be here as needed."

She nodded. "Okay. I'm in." Her lips, covered in a plum-colored gloss, lifted. "Again. We'll figure it out. Let's get started, shall we? Want to show me around?"

Yes. Right after he got his fill of staring at her luscious mouth. No. That was the wrong answer.

"August?"

He started. "Yes, sorry. I was just thinking about all the stuff I have to get done before we open."

She nodded, looking around at the piles of stuff in the room. "Makes sense."

Who said he couldn't pull a credible lie out of his ass when the occasion called for it?

Sloane ran an appraising eye over the room again. "This place is different from the original."

Sugar Blitz Two wasn't located in downtown San Diego. It had a smaller footprint. While the building that housed the original location had a modern feel to it, this building hadn't seen much refurbishing since the '80s, if then.

He'd fallen in love with the space the moment the real estate agent drove up to the place. Its potential was obvious. The big open windows that let in sunlight and unencumbered views to any passersby who might be tempted to give in to impulse and stop in for a cupcake. Brick archways, wainscoting on the walls. All architectural details his mother had loved.

He shrugged. "I know, but different is good."

Enthusiasm shone in her eyes. "Agreed. Each location should have its own personality. Even though y'all are about to be a franchise, that doesn't mean you can't expand your brand, so to speak. The buildings can be different, as long as the cupcakes remain the same."

August's lips quirked. "Nicholas would throw a fit if quality suffers."

"My brother too. Are y'all planning on hiring other bakers?"

"Yes, all of that is in the works. They must meet Nicholas's very stringent qualifications first. We've narrowed the pool down to three."

Sloane nodded. "What do you plan on working on in here? As far as my untrained eye can see, a lot of the major work has been done, but not everything."

"Hanging up sconces, painting, a little electric work." He pointed to a stack of boxes leaning against a wall. "Putting together the tables and chairs we ordered."

"Light work, huh?" She threw a soft smile his way. His heartbeat stuttered for a second. Apparently, teenage crushes weren't so easily dismissed.

Her brow creased in confusion. "Why are you doing all this yourself, instead of . . . ?"

His lips quirked. "Instead of hiring someone else to do it?"

"Yeah."

"Because I like it. I spent a lot of time with my grandfather growing up. He did carpentry and handiwork. He would take me with him on his projects sometimes."

Her eyes softened with understanding. One day he'd stop noticing how her emotions always showed in her expressive eyes.

"I love that you two had something you could bond over," she said.

August agreed. Pops wasn't a man to show affection with words. He showed he cared with his actions, taking August under his wing. "Yeah, he was the best. Let me show you around."

He led the way down the hall, showing her the three small offices he and his partners had all agreed were necessary. They could each have their own space to retreat to the next time they unintentionally went viral. After that, short stops at the supply closet and bathrooms followed. The last stop was the most important. He pushed the door open and flicked the light on. Her soft gasp sent a frisson of pleasure sweeping through him. He might not be as business savvy as Donovan or a culinary genius like Nicholas, but he cared about and took as much pride in their endeavors as they did.

The kitchen was top notch. Like they had at the first location, they'd spared no expense in the room where the magic happened. High-tech, expensive equipment. Quartz countertops. A large stainless steel industrial refrigerator. All-new racks and baking equipment. Donovan had gotten them the best deal he could on the equipment, but they'd still spent a pretty penny on it all.

Which meant they needed to make this location a success, and he needed to play his part to make it happen. Whatever it took.

"Okay, yes, this is amazing," Sloane said. "Y'all did the damn thing in here." She took her phone out of her ginormous purse and snapped a few photos. Then, she damn near blinded him with the flash of the camera.

Blinking, he held up his hands and edged his way to the left, hopefully out of the frame. "What are you doing?"

She lowered the phone and shot him a look. "Well, I *was* taking photos of the co-owner, who I noticed was obviously proud of his hard work. But now that look of pride has been replaced with a scowl, which I don't think is the right message to send to Sugar Blitz's social media followers."

Oh. August pushed his lips upward.

Her head cocked to the side, her nose scrunching up. "Is that supposed to be a smile? It's giving Beast when Lumiere, Mrs. Potts, and Cogsworth decided he needed to woo Belle and told him to stop scowling."

Oh, great. Now she was comparing him to a cartoon character. Is that how she saw him? As grumpy and stubborn? Set in his ways? Brooding? And wasn't it true? Shit. He didn't have time for introspections that were going nowhere.

His faux smile faded. "I wasn't prepared."

"Oh, I know," she shot back.

His lips tugged upward, a little more naturally this time. Sloane with the dagger always.

"Candids are better than posed photos, though we'll want some of those as well," she continued.

"We do?"

"You're the one doing the renovations, so yeah. By default, you have to be in the photos. You're the one everyone wants to see. You're SugarBae."

He groaned. "Not you too."

Her eyes twinkled. "What? SugarBae."

"Don't call me that."

"Why not? It's so accurate."

Now she was laughing at him again. Somehow, he could still hear the snickers even though she covered her mouth with her hand. She dropped her hand and rolled her lips inward when she noticed his expression. She held up a hand. "Sorry. I'm going to stop laughing." A giggle escaped. "I promise. Seriously though, what's the issue with me taking some photos of you doing your thing? You're the one who said you'd be here to participate as needed. And need I remind you, you *did* go on *Good Morning, San Diego*."

"And as you so eloquently expressed, it was a complete disaster."

Sloane moved to stand directly in front of him. Close enough to touch. Close enough to reach out to the tie at her waist and tug her toward him for a kiss. *Another kiss.* Okay, yeah, no, he wasn't going to think about the past. *Focus, August.*

"I'm sorry," she said. "I shouldn't have said that. It wasn't a complete disaster."

"Just three-fourths of a disaster?"

"Well . . . yeah." They shared another smile. Her plum-colored lips drew his attention yet again. Would her lips taste like the fruit?

Sloane sighed. "I shouldn't have laughed at you. I apologize. You're new to this and this isn't exactly in your wheelhouse. But that's why I'm here. I'm here to help, and I'm happy to be here."

Her hand fell away, and she took a step backward. He took a step forward, drawn to her like a moth addicted to fire. She didn't step away.

"Are you? Happy to be here?" He peered into her eyes. There, the truth lay. Always.

"Yes. Yes, I want the job with SDT, but I'm happy to help you reach your goals. You know I love Sugar Blitz. The only reason I haven't taken my brother up on his offer is I—"

"—don't want to ride his coattails," he finished for her. "I remember."

His eyes greedily tracked the movement of her lips as they parted slightly as she exhaled. "Yes. You always listened and remembered."

Yes, he had. And she'd done the same for him. As much as they'd avoided each other over the years, how easily they slipped into their old routine.

She stepped away. "But that was a long time ago."

In other words, back up.

"Right. Let's get to work." Work never let him down. Seeing the fruit of his labor bloom. Much better than dealing with messy emotions. He turned on his heel and headed for the front of the store. That didn't stop him from cataloging her every movement as she hurried to catch up with him.

His salvation lay in the boxes stacked against the wall. After grabbing a box cutter off an already-assembled table, he pulled one of the boxes toward him and sliced through the cardboard. He did his damnedest to ignore the click of the phone. This is what he'd signed up for. What he lobbied for. Just because he hadn't actually thought it through meant nothing. Maybe he wouldn't have gone on *Good Day, San Diego* if he'd known that would lead directly to working with Sloane. Or hell, maybe he would have done the show even sooner.

When it came to Sloane Dell, he never knew which way was up.

Her chuckle interrupted his twisting thoughts. His gaze shot to her. She was grinning at her phone. At the photos she'd taken of him? He was frowning. He could feel himself frowning. He couldn't help it.

"What's so funny?"

"You look so fierce even though this is the most routine task ever. Your fans are going to eat it up with a spoon."

He grunted. She laughed harder. The movement caused her shirt to ride up, torturing him with more, extended glimpses of her smooth skin. Would it be as soft as it looked? Taste as good as it looked?

He shook his head, like that mundane action stood a chance in hell of ridding his brain of those incendiary thoughts. "Come here."

Her laughter halted. "Why?"

"If you're going to be here, you're going to help."

She shook her head. "That's not what I signed up for."

"If you're here, you work. Those are the rules."

"Says who?"

He grinned. He couldn't help himself. "Your brother."

His smile widened when she groaned. That was the "contract" Donovan had made them all agree to when they were in the process of opening the first location. She and Shana, her sister, had shown up one day to suss out the scene. Donovan, in work mode, had given them tasks and his mantra for being in the store prior to the grand opening.

He watched as her brain tried to come up with a rebuttal. Her chin lifted as she settled on a response. "I'm here to take pictures."

She might as well have added "so there."

"You've taken a million of me opening boxes already." When she opened her mouth, he added, "You can get back to it when we move on to the next task."

She grumbled under her breath. Something about "know-it-all reading my mind."

"Thank you." His grin spread. "The rules still apply."

Her scowl deepened. "Fine, okay."

"That's the Sugar Blitz team spirit we like to see."

They shared a smile that sent curls of warmth cascading through his body. Dangerous territory, but one he did nothing to stay away from. He'd done that for the past twelve years, and the ache had never fully dissipated. What was a little more pain now that she was here to follow him for the next few weeks?

She held the box while he pulled the tabletop and legs out. He opened his toolbox and took out the needed equipment to assemble the table.

"Now you're bringing out the power tools? TikTok is going to get the vapors."

August shot her a look.

She grinned harder. "And that expression is only going to stoke the flames. Folks love a grumbly hero."

Now it was his turn to mutter to himself. Why had he thought this was a good idea? This was the last time he let his father and ex-wife influence anything he did.

"Yes, keep that up. It's perfect." She'd grabbed her phone and started snapping again.

He growled louder. She laughed.

August rolled his eyes. "Time to make yourself useful. Can you hold the leg while I screw it on?"

Could he handle the task by himself? Yes. Was he a glutton for punishment? Absolutely.

But it was nice to have someone else there to share in the joy and pain and annoyance when the holes didn't line up perfectly as he muttered to himself about shitty craftsmanship.

By design, he lived a fairly solitary life. Had come to rely on and prefer that state of affairs. Relying on others, expecting more from them, was fool's gold. Very few broke through that wall. His ex-wife who he'd known since childhood, Donovan, and Nicholas. And once upon a time, Sloane.

He and Donovan had become fast friends as freshmen, teammates and roommates in college, trying to prove themselves to coaches who were more comfortable with upperclassmen who already knew what was expected of them.

He'd damn near collapsed in relief when he and Donovan had been drafted to the same team. Then, the next year, Nicholas had been drafted by the Knights, and basically glued himself to August's side. As a running back, Nicholas had said he wanted to become simpatico with August, the fullback who led the way for him on the football field.

He'd forgotten what sharing that kind of camaraderie felt like with a woman he cared about. He could admit that. He cared about Sloane. He always had. He was just having a hard time remembering why they could only enter and stay in the friend zone.

They put together five tables before taking a break. He retrieved a couple bottles of water from the refrigerator and handed her one. He tried not to notice the long, smooth column of her throat as she swallowed. He failed. He barely stifled a groan when she licked away a drop of liquid that had caught on her bottom lip. He was definitely being punished for some long-forgotten sin.

She wiped some sweat off her brow. "Why aren't Donovan and Nicholas here to help with this manual labor?"

"They have enough things to do to keep them busy at SB1, not to mention the hiring and dotting of *i*'s and crossing of *t*'s with various contracts with this location. We agreed I'd take lead on these renovations. I enjoy it. Them, not so much. They help out as needed."

Her tempting lips lifted. "And you get to be alone." She tipped her bottle toward him. "Well, until I showed up."

He wasn't the only one who could claim to know the other well. He shrugged.

He could never forget that. They'd revealed so many secrets and innermost thoughts during those conversations he'd told himself were innocent. A shadow crossed her face like she too remembered. Were they fond memories or did she regret revealing so much of herself back then? They hadn't been this close alone for this long in years by mutual, tacit agreement.

He had to defuse the situation somehow. "Well, you always were a spoiled brat."

Her mouth dropped open in surprise, like he expected. Her infectious laugh followed like he hoped. Then she pushed him. That he hadn't been expecting. Her palm landed on his bare arm right under where the sleeve ended. He felt like he'd been electrocuted.

She snatched her hand away. "Sorry."

Before he knew it, he was reaching for her as she stepped away. He clasped her hand and halted her retreat.

"You have nothing to apologize for."

She didn't answer. She stared down at where their hands were clasped. He did the same. He should let her go. Pretend this moment meant nothing. Instead, he turned her hand over and traced a line in her palm as a corresponding heat traveled through his body. "Sloane."

Finally, she looked up. Her eyes devastated him. Guileless. Rich, honey brown. Memories swamped him. Whatever he'd been about to say deserted him in a rush.

Somehow, they were standing closer together, only a whisper separating their bodies. He raised her hand to his chest, where his heart was racing. He needed her to feel how she affected him. How she always had.

"August," she whispered, longing and need coursing through the two syllables.

Her lips were so close. So tempting. So necessary for him to taste. His eyes drifted shut as he lowered his head.

"What's going on here?" a voice boomed from behind them.

Chapter Thirteen

The intrusion snapped Sloane back to reality.

She stepped away from August. Away from temptation.

She gave not one damn if that decision made her a coward.

She'd been so close to drowning in August's beautiful eyes and for-getting everything she'd told herself over the years. She was over him. Over. Him. Not that she'd ever had the chance to be *under* him—and wasn't that a pity, she thought, as he stared at her with hot, glittering eyes. He was a man of few words, but in this instance, his thoughts were easy to read on his face. He was thinking about what could have been if they hadn't been interrupted. So was she.

Or maybe she was just horny, and any good-looking guy would have gotten the same reaction from her.

Yeah, right, her wicked inner bitch who had no time for foolish-ness whispered. She shook her head and brought the people who'd walked into the building, courtesy of a front door that was apparently unlocked, into focus. Three people. Two women, one man. All of them with identical, suspicious, and—dare she say it—unwelcoming expressions on their faces.

They all looked old enough to be Sloane's parents' ages or older. The Black man and woman held hands. Her skin was a smooth sienna, proving once again that black don't crack, with the man a few shades lighter. Her gray hair was styled into a stylish bob. She peered at August and Sloane through silver wire frames. Her tapping foot indicated she wanted answers, and she wanted them now. She'd been the one to speak. The man was a few inches taller than her with a paunch highlighted by his polo shirt tucked into his khakis and his belt pulled tight. His hair, cropped close, was a stately salt and pepper.

The other interloper looked to be Latina, with her honey-gold skin and dark wavy hair. She didn't look any more welcoming than the other two.

"Excuse me, can I help you?" August said. His voice came out strong. Sure. Not like he was still thinking about the kiss that never was. Impressive, really. And a little insulting, but now was not the time to obsess about that.

The threesome didn't look intimidated by the tall, buff pro athlete questioning them. They continued to sweep their gazes around the space. Like they had every right to be there. Ahh, to be old and unbothered. Sloane aspired to reach that state of mind someday.

"The real question is 'Who are you?'" the Black lady finally said.

"I'm August Hodges, and I own this building. Co-own."

That earned him a simultaneous sniff from the trio. Sloane was intrigued. Who were these people? "I'm Sloane Dell."

This time the simultaneous sound from all three members of the Old Folks Triumvirate came in the form of a disbelieving "tuh."

The guy stared at them hard, his bushy eyebrows doing all the talking. They were saying "yeah right." He harrumphed. "We saw the way you were looking at each other. Making googly eyes."

Guess he was tired of his eyebrows having all the fun. Sloane's insides burned with embarrassment.

The Black lady slapped him on the arm. "Ben, really."

He looked nonplussed. "The younger generations always think they invented sex."

She nodded. "True."

Strangers who were the same age as her parents talking about sex was only slightly less embarrassing than her parents talking about sex. Sloane cleared her throat. "How can we help you?"

"I'm Ben Franklin, and you can wipe those smirks off your faces. It's a fine upstanding name. This is my wife, Cynthia. And this is our next-door neighbor, Rosa. We came to have a look around. Heard some banging and wanted to see what the folks who bought this place were up to." The man started whistling, folding his hands behind his back, obviously trying to look unsuspicious, but accomplishing the exact opposite.

Sloane exchanged glances with August for the first time since the almost *whatever*. *What is going on?*

"Turning this place into a cupcake shop?" Rosa asked, as she swept her gaze all around the room.

August nodded. Sloane followed his lead. Keep it short and simple. Share no incriminating details. Though not spoken, this was a low-key interrogation.

"There's a bakery a couple of blocks down," Cynthia said.

Sloane nodded again. She'd passed the French bakery on her way here. But she knew her brother. He and his partners had undoubtedly done their due diligence before deciding to open the new Sugar Blitz location here and concluded there was room enough for both businesses.

"Whatcha got planned?" A seemingly simple question accompanied by more casual meandering that was anything but. "Painting the walls?"

Sloane exchanged another glance with August.

"Yes," he said.

"Hmm," all three said in unison.

"When do you plan on opening?" Cynthia asked.

"Two weeks."

"This the furniture and artwork you plan on using?" Ben followed up.

Sloane nodded again. She wasn't sure where the Three Musketeers were going with this interrogation, but the less ammunition they gave them, the better.

"Never seen you around before, but here you are making a lot of changes, I see."

"Well, we won't hold you up any longer," the ringleader, Cynthia, said. She turned on her heel in a sharp move any drill sergeant would admire and led her two cadets out the door.

A tense, prolonged silence followed. Sloane searched for something to do with her hands. She finally settled on resting them on her hips.

"That was weird, right?" August said, his eyes narrowed in suspicion.

Sloane briefly met his gaze. "So weird."

She had a feeling they were talking about more than the visit from the Three Musketeers.

Chapter Fourteen

Twelve years ago . . .

There's my baby," Sloane's mother, Sandra, cried out when Donovan walked through their home's door for the first time since they'd dropped him off at college a few months ago. He walked straight into their mom's open arms.

Sloane barely spared her brother a glance. The man behind him was much more interesting. Enthralling, really. She'd seen photos, of course, but she would have recognized August anywhere. It was the way he carried himself. With self-assuredness, but in no way conceited. A little shyness that could easily be misconstrued as aloofness. But she knew better, thanks to their phone calls. And he'd come home with her brother for Thanksgiving.

Her breath caught. He was better looking than she'd thought, and she'd thought a lot while scrolling through photos on Facebook. Thank God for Google Images. He wasn't considered a star player like her brother, because he was a fullback, so his photos were a little harder to find, but she was nothing if not a determined teen girl. Where there was a will, there was most definitely a way. The photos that existed? She'd seen them all. Multiple times.

He hadn't seen her yet, so she took the opportunity to ogle in peace. No need to pretend—to herself anyway—that that wasn't what she was doing. His locs brushed his shoulders. She'd thought they were black, but they were actually a rich dark lustrous chocolate. They were getting longer. His hair framed his face. Drew attention to his high cheekbones and sharp slant of a nose and the sumptuous curve of his full lips. Sloane bit her lip to stop a sure-to-be-embarrassing sigh from escaping. At least her sister, Shana, was still upstairs. She'd always been able to read Sloane like her favorite book.

"You must be August," Sandra said.

"Yes, ma'am," August answered in a voice that was even more potent in person than over the phone.

"'Ma'am.' The boy has manners. I like that." Sandra wrapped her arms around him like he was her own child.

Sloane smiled. No surprise there. Her mom was a hugger and had never met a stranger. After a slight hesitation, he returned the gesture.

Do not be jealous of your mother.

"Hey, Sloane." Her brother had reached her side. She reluctantly tore her eyes away from his teammate and turned to Donovan. He looked more and more like their father every time she saw him. And she'd keep that thought to herself. Donovan didn't like being reminded of that fact.

Not that she blamed him. Their relationship with their father was tempestuous at best. Their father tried, even succeeded sometimes, but when he didn't? Before the divorce, their mother had suffered, though she'd tried to hide it, and that hurt had only manifested her children's.

She smiled up at him. "Hey, Donny."

He blanched and looked over his shoulder, no doubt to make sure August hadn't heard. He hated that nickname. "Hey, cut that shit out. I told Mama not to call me that around my friends."

She knew. "But you didn't tell me." A loophole she'd planned on exposing as soon as she overheard him making the request to their mom during their last phone call. How else was she going to earn her annoying younger sister badge, especially now that he was away at college most of the time?

His eyes narrowed, but he drew her into a hug anyway. Just like she knew he would. They were close, and he couldn't stay mad at her for long.

"Good to see you too, Sloaney-Baloney," he said just a touch too loudly. Or maybe it just sounded that way to her sensitive, mortified ears. She broke his hold and glared up at him.

Donovan smirked. Close didn't mean he wouldn't seek revenge at the earliest opportunity, clearly.

"Sloaney-Baloney?"

That came from behind her. From August. Oh, God. He'd heard.

She whirled and forced out a sound that could only be called a laugh based on the loosest definition of the word. A strangled, mangled cry for help was more like it. What else was she supposed to do? Acknowledge that Donovan had embarrassed her because she had the world's biggest crush on her brother's best friend, and admit it in front of her unsuspecting brother and mother, not to mention the aforementioned best friend? Yeah, no. None of that was about to happen.

"Yeah, it's a childish nickname my brother knows I hate with the fire of a thousand suns." She sounded halfway normal, which was more than she could have asked for. She would just ignore how her heart had started beating at quadruple its normal rate now that they were standing less than five feet away from each other. Probably closer to three feet. Close enough for him to transmit the world's most potent pheromones, that was for damn sure. She was officially a horny teenage girl, and she'd never been happier.

The side of August's mouth kicked up, like he was unused to smiling.

"Feel free to call her that whenever she annoys you." From behind her, Donovan slapped his hands on her shoulders and squeezed.

She rolled her eyes. "Thanks."

"Donovan," their mother warned.

"Let me make the formal introductions, since I don't believe helping her with her homework a few times counts. Sloane, August. August, Sloaney-Baloney. Sloane," he corrected at their mother's warning murmur. "Friend-roommate-teammate, meet little sister."

Sloane's shoulders stiffened under her brother's hands. She hoped he didn't notice. August hadn't told her brother they actually talked at least once a week?

August still watched her, his expression unreadable. She didn't know what to do. Her palms were sweaty, her tongue was stuck to the roof of her mouth. Crushes were awful, heart-palpitating, why-do-I-do-this-to-myself things.

Finally, August held out his hand because he, apparently, had the sense to realize one of them needed to act in what was becoming an increasingly insanely awkward situation.

She forced her hand away from her side. Went absolutely still as their palms met for the first time and a glorious zap of electricity crackled up her arm and then through her body. She concentrated on the connection. On how his large hand swallowed hers, but his grip was gentle. Kind, even. Lifted her eyes to his.

His voice, that she'd only heard through the phone, rumbled in that way she'd come to anticipate. "Nice to officially meet you, Sloane."

And she swooned. Not literally, of course, because she had enough self-preservation not to commit that cardinal sin. But in every other sense of the word, she was a goner.

Crush Level: Infinity.

Chapter Fifteen

Sloane half-heartedly snapped a few photos of the interior of the new Sugar Blitz location. Sooo exciting. But at least she could lie to herself that she was getting some work done. And taking the pictures allowed her to not think about what had almost happened yesterday during the nanosecond it took her to press the button on her phone.

Was August avoiding her? Probably, but no more than she was avoiding him. Isn't that what you did when you almost kissed someone you vowed to never want to kiss again?

Some might say she was hiding out and avoiding a conversation. Those people would be correct, but she didn't care. She could do the mature thing and discuss what had almost happened with him, but maturity was highly overrated. Limiting her embarrassment was her only real course of action.

And it's not like he was making much of an effort to speak to her about it. He was in the kitchen counting bags of sugar or something. She hadn't really caught what he mumbled as they crossed paths that morning. Yesterday, after the Three Musketeers departed, they'd decided to call it a day rather than talk about what had almost happened.

Was he actually attracted to her or had he gotten caught up in the moment? Even if he *was* attracted to her, so what? She refused to go down that road again.

Her decision to stay away from him meant she was currently failing at her job to document his every move, but she'd look for her courage a little later.

Sloane snapped a couple more shots, then quickly scrolled through the camera roll until she came to yesterday's final photo. August wielding a hammer, giving her epic side-eye. Damn, he was ridiculously handsome.

Wait. What was that?

Sloane cocked her head to the side. A hum of noise like a . . . chant. She moved closer to the shop entrance, where the murmuring was coming from.

Were they saying . . . ?

Oh, God, they were. She rushed to the front window. A crowd of about ten marched back and forth outside the store, all holding picket signs and chanting "No, no, we won't go. We don't want yo' sto."

Oh, shit.

Worse, they were attracting the attention of passersby—both those on foot and those in cars. More than one vehicle slowed as it went by.

Oh, shit! "August! August!" She hurried back toward the kitchen. As she turned the corner, she slammed directly into a brick wall. A warm, delicious-smelling brick wall named August. Her nose planted directly into the soft cotton of his T-shirt. It smelled like detergent, sugar, and August. She inhaled. Sue her. She was only human. Hopefully, it was inaudible and didn't make her sound like the sex-deprived fiend she clearly was. At least she didn't reach up and lick his exposed collarbone. She had a little bit of self-respect left. Just a smidge, but she held on to it like a talisman with all her might.

That is until she met his eyes. He stepped back, but his hands remained at her waist. Never had she been so jealous of denim. If he tried even a little, he could reach under her waistband and touch her skin.

"Hey, hey, are you okay?" His dark eyes probed hers and then slid to inspect every inch of her body. He didn't mean it that way, obviously, but it felt like a caress nonetheless. Her nipples pebbled under his scrutiny. Yes, she was officially a sex-deprived fiend. Thank God for a decent bra and shirt.

He briskly ran his hands up and down her arms. Totally harmless. "What's wrong?"

His concern, his fierceness, his determination to fix whatever had befallen her wormed its way past her defensive walls and aimed straight for her heart. At that moment, she couldn't have looked away from his penetrating gaze if her life depended on it.

"Sloane." His voice rose. "Sloane. What's wrong?"

She blinked. Right. She had gone looking for him, yelling his name, causing him to believe there was a problem. Which there was.

She pointed behind her. "There are protesters outside."

He blinked. "What?"

"You heard me."

He rushed to the front windows. Sloane lengthened her stride to catch up with him. It was the first time she'd ever seen him in a hurry. He always moved at a measured pace, always considering his surroundings, including the people in his space. Even on the football field, he seemed to move at his own pace, often anticipating his opponent's next step before he made it.

He yanked open the door and stepped outside. "What's going on out here?"

Cynthia stepped out of the picket line. "Oh, look, it's the two lovebirds. We're exercising our First Amendment right to protest," she said with a flourish as the other picketers cheered her on.

Sloane twisted her lips into a facsimile of a smile as a non-protesting pedestrian gave her a clear "girl, what's going on here?" look. Sloane gave her best "nothing to see here, folks" smile.

"Why are you protesting?" August asked.

Cynthia's chest puffed up. "We don't like what you're doing to our community."

Her husband, Ben, stepped out of the picket line to join her. "You're destroying it! And you don't even care as you two kids make googly eyes at each other."

Sloane barely stifled a groan.

"How are we destroying the community?" That came from August, who had apparently decided to ignore the inflammatory ending of the sentence. Good plan. She would follow his lead.

Cynthia stepped closer to August and glared up at him. "This used to be a business run by hardworking folks, who were part of this neighborhood. You come here with your money thinking you can just change things. You ran them out!"

August held up his hands. "This building sat empty for eighteen months before we purchased it."

The old man harrumphed. "You still bought it and are intent on destroying what made it great. We don't care that you're football players. You're trying to change this neighborhood, and we're not going to let you. You're trying to drive us out and turn this whole block into your little playground that only the rich can afford."

Sloane's attempt to stifle a groan was less successful this time, but she managed it. She couldn't stop a full-body shudder, however. They were accusing the Sugar Blitz owners of gentrification. She knew her brother. She knew the neighborhood they'd grown up in and the harm gentrification had done to it—driving out long-term residents who couldn't afford to stay as rents skyrocketed in the quest for "progress." He would never want to be part of such an endeavor. He would be horrified, actually. And so would his friends and business partners.

"No, we're not." August kept his cool, laying out the bare facts as he saw them, like always. Another reason to admire him. If she was in the business of admiring him, which she so was not.

Waving her sign in the air, Rosa joined her friends. "You're not from around here. You don't care!"

"Yeah, you don't care. And we're not going to let you do it." Cynthia tapped a clipboard she was holding.

August sighed. "Everything we've done for this location is above-board. We have the right permits. We purchased the building legally. We're following all local ordinances."

Cynthia's face made it clear she was unmoved by these facts. "You didn't ask anybody if we wanted you here."

Sloane stepped next to him. She couldn't keep quiet any longer. "That may be true, but it's also true that they didn't have to do that. You don't have a legal reason to be here."

The older lady sniffed and tapped her clipboard again. "Maybe not, but there's more than one way to skin a rabbit. We're gathering signatures from everybody in the neighborhood who doesn't want you here. They're all pledging not to step foot in your store and to tell everyone they know not to either. Once we work our magic, we'll see how long your business lasts."

Sloane's stomach dropped to the pavement. This was a disaster for several reasons—for Sugar Blitz and for her own professional aspirations. The shop hadn't even opened yet and trouble was brewing.

Ben adjusted his glasses and lifted his chin. "My wife is spot-on. We're going to be out here every day until you go away."

The other picketers nodded in unison.

Sloane met August's gaze. The look on his face was clear to read. Mainly because it echoed the thought running through her head.

What. The. Fuck?

Chapter Sixteen

"They're really boycotting us." Donovan sank back in his desk chair, shaking his head, his logical side clearly unable to accept such a predicament. "We've been a part of this community for close to a decade."

"They don't care," August said. He understood his best friend's confusion, but he'd had a few hours to adjust to the idea that opening a second location wasn't going to be smooth sailing like they'd planned.

They'd gathered at the original Sugar Blitz store to discuss the tenuous situation. Something needed to be done, and soon, before the Three Musketeers garnered any more attention and turned the situation into a real shitshow. He'd hoped that they only planned to picket for one day. He'd swiftly realized the error of his ways when he showed up to work that morning.

Hence, this meeting.

"Yeah, they said something about not caring about football. It's a violent sport that offers nothing positive to society and drains taxpayers' money by forcing hardworking citizens to pay for billion-aires' fancy stadiums," Sloane added.

Donovan shot his sister a look. "Thanks, Sloane."

She shrugged. "I'm just repeating what they said as I walked by this morning. I did speak in your defense."

"And?"

"They didn't . . . care," she answered, her nose wrinkling. It was cute. Everything she did was cute. He needed help. Like now. There was never going to be a Sloane and him. The sooner he accepted that the better.

"That's because they haven't met me yet," Nicholas said.

August didn't bother rolling his eyes. Nicholas was always going to be Nicholas. He expected nothing less. Beside him, Sloane snorted.

"What a brilliant suggestion," Donovan said, the words dripping with sarcasm.

August froze. Because he always seemed to have his eyes on her, he saw the exact instant that the same realization dawned on Sloane.

She snapped her fingers. "You know what? That *is* a brilliant suggestion!"

"What is?" Donovan asked. "Letting him work that questionable Nicholas Connors charm on some elderly folks who can see bullshit coming a mile away?"

"Hey, I will have you know my bullshit is worth a million bucks *and* it smells nice," Nicholas said, pressing a hand to his chest in affront.

This time, August joined Donovan in a groan, while Sloane rolled her eyes.

"No, you fool," Sloane said. "We need to hold a town hall. Get ahead of the story and narrative. They caught us flat-footed. We can't allow it to happen again. We need to show them that y'all are on the residents' side."

August nodded, completely on board with the idea and pleased that they were on the same page, but also determined not to make more of it than that.

She turned to him. "You'll have to be there, August. You're the one they know. And sorry, you might have to speak."

Wait. What? That was *not* part of his plan.

"All three of you will charm them naturally," she continued.

Donovan smiled. "It's perfect."

"Yes, that will be perfect," Nicholas said. "We gotchu, August."

August wasn't so sure.

* * *

August sat quietly in a squeaky folding chair on a mini-stage they'd set up in Sugar Blitz Two along with rows of folding chairs for their expected audience. Good thing he wasn't known for talking. His throat had dried up as nerves sank their claws into him. At first, he'd been somewhat okay. Only a few people had trickled into the shop, and he'd thought that maybe the threat of a boycott was overblown. Foolish, foolish thought.

As the clock on the far wall ticked closer to seven, the trickle turned into a stream, then a damn downpour. Now the room was standing room only. Which would be great if they were open for business, but nope, they were here to convince these fine folks of San Diego that they weren't here to ruin their neighborhood. Apparently, Sloane's social media efforts were paying off. She'd posted the meeting on all their social media channels, sent out an email blast to their customers and local media outlets, handed out flyers to the protesters, and hung more flyers in the storefront windows of other businesses on the street.

He couldn't blame the residents for showing up. Gentrification rarely, if ever, benefited the residents who made their home there before the "updating."

Yes, they'd sunk a lot of money into this enterprise, but it was more than that. He'd seen the good their first location had done, bringing together neighbors and fostering a sense of community. He had no doubt they could do the same thing here.

Donovan stood at the corner of the stage reviewing his notes, while Nicholas worked the crowd. Cynthia Franklin might not care about football, but she didn't speak for everyone. Plenty of people in the crowd were happy to take selfies with San Diego's star running back. Hopefully, they would be open-minded about the new location.

Jada, Donovan's fiancée, approached him. "Hey, August. You ready?"

She owned an event-planning business and had handled all the nitty-gritty details of setting up the town hall. She'd been moving throughout the room, directing traffic and marking things off on the very official clipboard she carried. She was in her element. That made one of them.

August sighed. "I guess."

She offered up a sympathetic smile. "I have faith in you. We all do. Just be yourself." The walkie-talkie clipped to her waist buzzed. "Sorry. Duty calls."

August nodded. "No worries."

She hurried away and he went back to concentrating on trying not to sweat through his clothes. He was unsuccessful.

"Hey, aren't you August?"

He looked up. A pretty woman, in her mid-to-late twenties, stood before him. He nodded. "Yes."

She slowly looked him up and down, missing absolutely nothing in her perusal, like he was a prize cow at an auction. "I'm so happy I came tonight. Your photos don't do you justice. At all. You are way finer in person."

His eyes skidded to Sloane, who was only a few feet away. Undoubtedly, she'd heard. She didn't react, however. Her head remained buried in her clipboard, though he knew she'd worked closely with Jada and planned for everything, including any potential deviations from the plan. Why would she react? They were nothing.

The woman cleared her throat, bringing his attention back to her. "Umm, thanks."

The woman's smile spread wider. She sidled closer, licking her lips. "What do you think about getting together after this meeting?"

Sloane stepped up to the mic. "Thank you everyone for coming tonight. Let's get started."

Grateful for the lifeline, August shrugged. The woman backed away slowly with a flirty wiggle of her fingers. "We'll talk after the meeting."

August pushed his lips upward, hoping it looked like a smile rather than the grimace he had a bad feeling it resembled.

"I'm Sloane Dell," the social media guru continued. She wore a lightweight red sweater and black slacks that skimmed her curves, which only served to make him want to burrow underneath to discover her hidden treasures.

"We don't care. We want to hear from him," someone in the crowd yelled out, pointing at August.

"Yeah, SugarBae, show us what you got!" another audience member called out.

Fuck. That was not what this meeting was supposed to be about.

It was naïve of him, and he tried his damnedest to never be naïve. Life had taught him how foolish that was, but he'd hoped the SugarBae thing would die a swift death. Apparently not. Heat swamped his face and tied his tongue into knots. He wasn't supposed to let them see him sweat, according to Sloane, but this was already a disaster. His supposed best friends, Donovan and Nicholas, were too busy chuckling to offer him any sympathy.

"You'll be hearing from all three owners of Sugar Blitz, don't worry, but we called this meeting specifically to discuss the opposition to our newest location." Sloane, the consummate pro, took control of the situation. It was incredibly sexy. Which was incredibly unimportant.

Thankfully, the crowd subsided.

"I hope you'll indulge us and let the owners talk about their background and what they envision for the store, then we'll open the mic for any comments or questions. Sound okay?" she asked in a charming voice. The audience responded with nods and even a few smiles. Yeah, she was good at this. "First, we'll start with Donovan Dell."

Donovan rose and gave a short speech about the first shop's economic impact on the neighborhood, and how it had become a gathering spot for locals looking for cupcakes and community.

August looked out into the crowd. A few people seemed to be taking Donovan at his word, but more than a few looked skeptical. They'd decided to go with Nicholas next after Donovan's facts, to hit the crowd with some fun. People, especially heterosexual women, were extremely susceptible to his charm.

Nicholas took his place at the mic and offered up the smile that had several audience members gasping and covering their hearts. "Thank y'all for coming. I want to tell y'all a story about why we chose this location. I've been volunteering with the Boys and Girls Club and I drive through the neighborhood often. I love the vibe here. Neighbors and friends looking out for each other. When I saw that the building was up for sale, I knew this was the spot for our next location."

A true story. A few more people seemed interested and willing to listen. The crowd looked to him next, but it wasn't his turn yet, thank God.

"Before August speaks, we'll open the floor for questions," Sloane said.

Cynthia's hand shot up in the air. "You talked all that good talk," she said without waiting to be called on. "But you still ain't from around here."

"No, we're not, but we've all come to view San Diego as our home and want to see it thrive just as much as all of you," Donovan said.

Cynthia sniffed. "That's all good, but you're still making too many changes. Making stuff too fancy."

"There used to be a restaurant in this space," Rosa called out.

August nodded, along with Donovan and Nicholas.

"We heard you drove them out of business, so they'd be forced to sell."

"Yeah, that's what I heard too," someone August recognized as a picketer said.

Several gasps lit up the store. Chants rang out. "No, no. We won't go. We don't want yo' sto'." Soon, others joined in the chant.

August winced. Damn, he hadn't realized the place had such excellent acoustics. He exchanged looks with Nicholas. It didn't take much to read the "fuck" Nicholas muttered.

"Hey, hey." Donovan returned to the mic and held up his hands to get the angry crowd's attention.

Someone pointed at August. "We want to hear from him, since he always has something to say."

Always? Dear Lord, his outburst from the other day was the gift that kept on giving. He, who only liked to talk when required, now had a reputation as a jabbermouth. If it wasn't the most ridiculous thing, it would be funny. He glared at Donovan and Nicholas, whose shoulders were shaking. What was his life?

Sloane gestured for him to stand. "August, would you like to join me?"

He reluctantly lumbered to his feet. A cheer rose from the back of the room. "SugarBae, SugarBae!" chants rose up. Were these excited chants better than the get-out chants? Before he could decide, Sloane spoke. "August, would you like to address the concern that you drove the last owners out of business, forcing them to sell?"

He fought the urge to scratch the back of his neck. "It's not true."

Sloane stared at him expectantly.

What? What else needed to be said?

Someone in the audience cleared their throat. Someone else shifted in their seat. Fuck. They expected him to say more. After all, he was the wordsmith who'd read those boys for filth. Shit. This was just like the morning-show interview from hell.

Sloane's eyes softened, as though she sensed his plight. "That's right. You know why I know it's not true? Because this building used to be a Mexican spot." She spoke to the audience. "And I have it on good authority that Mexican is your favorite, and you'd never be party to shutting down such an establishment."

Her comment prompted a few chuckles from the audience. His lips twitched. She'd always kidded him about his affinity for Taco Bell, despite being born and raised in San Jose and having tons of MexiCali options at his disposal.

"This is true." He spoke into the mic when she gestured for him to move closer.

"So why don't you tell everyone here the true story?" She spoke directly to him, keeping his focus on her, not giving him the opportunity to freak out because everyone was staring at him. August's anxiety immediately calmed. Though they were in a room full of people, it felt like it was just the two of them, just like it had been all those years ago when they talked on the phone.

August gazed into her beautiful, understanding eyes. "When we talked to the real estate agent, she told us the previous restaurant owners had fallen behind on the rent, so they had to close the restaurant."

"You didn't force them out of business." Her voice was steady. Sure. She believed in him.

He shook his head. "No, we would never do that. They were already closed by the time we expressed interest."

"Barbara and Raul would have told us if they were struggling," someone in the audience yelled.

Sloane nodded at him. She believed he could handle this, which meant everything. He turned back to the crowd. "Maybe not. I understand pride. We all do, I think. People rarely like to admit when they're struggling."

Cynthia shot up from her seat. "That's all well and good, but we heard you were buying other buildings around here. Is that true?"

August exchanged looks with Nicholas and Donovan. "Uh . . . yes."

"See, they are trying to drive us out of here!"

Benjamin and Rosa hopped up. In unison with Cynthia, they chanted, "No, no. We won't go. We don't want yo' sto'!"

* * *

The chants jarred Sloane back to reality. And out of the little cocoon that only included her and August she'd inadvertently wrapped herself in.

She swallowed hard as she surveyed the crowd and fought the urge to cover her ears. While some looked on curiously, others joined the chanting.

This was worse than she'd thought. This is what she got for accepting a job before she knew the full parameters of the assignment. She'd obviously known the guys had bought the building for the new location. She hadn't known they'd bought the whole block. That changed things.

Hell, *were* they trying some gentrification crap? Ergh. She was going to kill all three of them.

"We won't do that," August said in that tone that showed quiet confidence and offered little to no room to argue. When he brought out that authoritative voice, people listened. This time was no different.

Sloane took a deep breath. Now wasn't the time to get answers to her questions. Not with an attentive audience hanging on his every word.

She spoke into the microphone. "You've heard it right from the horse's mouth. Sugar Blitz wants to be part of the community, not change it. Thank you all so much for coming. The town hall is now adjourned, but please feel free to stick around and talk to all three owners individually. They'd love to hear from you."

Despite the protestors' claims that no one wanted a Sugar Blitz location in their neighborhood, audience members still took the opportunity to get up close and personal with the football-playing owners. While her brother and Nicholas garnered their fair share of requests for selfies and autographs, the attention they commanded was nothing compared to that of August. He seemed to be taking it in stride. Somewhat. He didn't look completely comfortable, but he was hanging in there. And just because his line was comprised mostly of women batting their eyelashes at him meant nothing. A particularly bold woman invaded his personal space and gave him a bold up-and-down look before whispering in his ear. Sloane's hand clenched at her side. Okay, mostly nothing. She turned on her heel and headed toward her brother and Jada.

"You and August did good," Donovan said.

"Yeah, your chemistry was great," Jada said. "I'm so proud of you," she added to someone who'd walked up behind Sloane.

Sloane didn't need to turn around to know that "someone" was August. She could always sense him. Sense when he was within a ten-mile radius of her.

Sloane shrugged away the compliment and its importance. "Must be us spending the past few days together. Gave us enough time to get our routine down. Anyway, we need to talk about their gentrification claims and you owning several buildings on the block. That's something I needed to know *before* we called a town hall."

She shot pointed looks at August and Donovan.

August had the decency to look slightly guilty, at least. Her brother, on the other hand, puffed up his chest and held up a hand. "Now, Sloane."

Jada groaned. "Wrong answer, honey."

"Correct." Sloane tipped her chin in acknowledgment at her sister-in-law-to-be, then turned to glare at Donovan. "Don't 'Now, Sloane' me, big brother."

"Excuse me?" The woman from earlier, the one who'd stared at August like he was an ice-cream sundae and she had the world's biggest sweet tooth, stepped into their circle. "You dating him?" She jerked her chin toward August.

"We're not done discussing this, guys." Sloane sent another pointed look to each of the Sugar Blitz owners before turning her attention to the newcomer. The urge to lie was strong. Really, really strong. Overwhelming, really. But that made no sense. Because they weren't dating and weren't going to date. So she pasted on a smile and said, "Oh, no, we're not."

"Good."

The woman turned her back to Sloane and planted herself directly in front of August.

"That was such a great speech tonight." She trailed her nails down his bare, muscular arm. "You're so worthy of the SugarBae title."

All of a sudden, memories of watching WWE with her older siblings when they were kids washed over Sloane. Jumping off the top rope and tomahawk-chopping this lady seemed like a good idea, for some reason.

"Paige, honey, what are you doing over here?" a woman asked, joining their little circle.

"Oh, Mama, I'm just talking to SugarBae."

Oh, good Lord. Sloane barely stifled a groan. The day just kept getting better. Mama was Cynthia.

Chapter Seventeen

Knock, knock!

Oh, thank God. Sloane rushed to her apartment door and threw it open. "Finally. You're here!"

Her best friend Felicia lifted a brow. "Well, when your BFF sends an SOS, I believe I'm contractually obligated to come running."

Since Sloane had indeed sent that message the moment she returned home from the town hall, she could only be grateful. "And that's why I love you." She waved Felicia inside. "Come in, come in."

"And because I am the best friend ever, I brought reinforcements." Felicia held out a small, flat box.

Sloane gasped. How had she missed that and the familiar, heavenly smells emanating from inside? "Have I told you that I love you?"

"Not today."

Sloane eagerly took the box and yanked it open. Ooey, gooey cheesiness food porn greeted her. She looked up. "Cheese fries for the win!" But these weren't just any cheese fries. They were loaded with bacon, chives, and jalapenos. Also known as heaven on earth. "Thank you!"

She beelined to the kitchen for a fork and knife and met up with Felicia in the living room. She settled on the couch. "Do you want some?"

Felicia looked at her like she smelled a trap. "Do I want to come in between you and your favorite food? No, I value my fingers too much."

"Hey, I'm not that bad. Okay, yes I am," she continued when Felicia side-eyed her. "But I mean it. You are more than welcome to *a* fry."

"Such a generous offer, but I'm good."

"Okay." Sloane barely got the word out before she stuffed the first—okay two—delicious fries into her mouth. When her stomach had been sated a few minutes later, she leaned back against the sofa cushions and patted her abdomen. "Now, that was the good stuff. Thank you again."

Felicia angled her body toward her on the couch. "You're welcome. Now tell me what's up. I miss you."

"I miss seeing your face every day too, but I had to leave." She made a face, remembering why she'd quit.

"Girl, I get it. So spill. Tell me why I got the emergency 'help' text? I'm assuming this has something to do with your new job."

Sloane had already spilled the details about her interview with San Diego Today, her old foe Preston, and how she'd come to work for Sugar Blitz.

"Is this about working for your brother?" Felicia added. "I know you never wanted to do that."

Sloane wrinkled her nose. "I still don't, but I do want his business to succeed. Besides, it's temporary. A means to an end."

Felicia's head tilted to the side. "Okay. So, maybe the text was about working with your forever crush? I mean, I am your best friend. I've listened to and remember *all* your ramblings over the years."

Sloane held up a finger. "Hold up. First of all, he's not my forever crush." He couldn't be. She couldn't be that ridiculous. Could she? No. Absolutely not. "That was back in high school, and it's fine. I'm working to get him out of his shell and capitalize on his social media fame, so their new location is a success. Even though he kinda doesn't want to do that anymore, so I'm trying to respect his wishes, but still have a successful campaign. It's fine." Sloane popped two more fries into her mouth. See. Totally fine.

Felicia crossed her arms and lifted her eyebrows.

Sloane swallowed. "What? It is!"

"Ma'am. I know you. I remember how you talked about how he barely speaks to you, and you get back at him by teasing him whenever you can. I also have social media, and have seen SugarBae become all the rage."

Sloane lifted her chin. "Yeah, well, a man who recognizes the importance of women is rare."

"And it didn't affect you at all?"

Sloane shrugged as nonchalantly as possible. "I mean it was nice to hear, but whatever. Anyway, we had a town hall tonight because some residents aren't happy about Sugar Blitz coming into their neighborhood. They've been protesting." She stuffed another fry in her mouth and swallowed. "Anyway, you should've seen some of the women. And their mothers! Offering their daughters up to him like he was Prince Charming."

"Does that make you Cinderella?" Felicia snatched a fry off Sloane's plate and popped it into her mouth.

"You're my bestie and you bought these, so I won't cut off your fingers—this time."

Felicia swallowed. "I know. Love you too."

Sloane narrowed her eyes. "Hmm, mmm."

"Now, answer my question."

Sloane threw her hands up. "What? About being Cinderella? No, I'm not! For one, I'm not looking for love right now. Men are nothing but trouble. You and I have talked about that on multiple occasions. Two, he's not my Prince Charming."

"Then why are you stuffing fries in your mouth faster than you can chew?"

Sloane swallowed. "Because they're amazing. Anyway, you should have seen August. He was acting weird, and I don't get it."

Felicia settled her arm on the top of a cushion and rested her cheek on her fist. "Weird how?"

"He smiled at them!"

"He smiled at them," Felicia repeated slowly.

"Yes!" Why didn't her friend understand the urgency of the situation?

"That's a problem because . . ."

"Because he doesn't smile." And when he did, the action lit up the whole room. He saved them for rare occasions, and just because she felt like a million bucks when she got one out of him meant nothing.

Felicia shrugged. "Maybe you're rubbing off on him. You did task yourself with bringing him out of his shell."

"That didn't mean he should be smiling at people who want nothing more than to lick him like a lollipop!"

"Riiiiight," Felicia said.

"You won't believe this. The one who was doing the heaviest flirting is the daughter of the protesting group's ringleader. He can't be interested in her, right?"

"Right."

"And that's all there is to it. Let's move on." Sloane chewed and swallowed another fry.

"Sure. Sounds like you have other issues besides August smiling at people?" Felicia continued, moving on like the good friend she was. "Something about protestors."

Sloane dropped her head back and groaned. "I thought this would be a fun, easy assignment with the whole SugarBae thing. They already have a strong brand that just needed some social media help. I figured I could work with August on his concerns and hesitations. But then the protesters showed up. We hoped the town hall would allay their fears, but I'm not so sure. The residents are worried about gentrification, which isn't helped by the fact that August, my brother, and Nicholas, their other partner, basically bought the whole block. I know their intentions are good, but . . ."

"The road to hell is paved with good intentions."

"Exactly." Sloane blew out a breath. "I'm just trying to keep it all together. We're going to talk about this whole buy-the-block thing tomorrow and what exactly that means, because I am not about driving residents out of their neighborhood."

"Except you don't own the buildings, and you need to make them look good if you want this job."

Sloane shook her head. "Thanks for the reminder."

Her phone chimed with a text. Sloane grabbed the device from the coffee table and groaned. "Why me?"

Felicia scooted closer. "What now?"

Sloane showed her the screen.

Her bestie made the Chrissy Teigen "yikes" face. "Sucks to be you, my friend."

Chapter Eighteen

August flipped the light switch. Bright fluorescent light flooded the room, bathing the gleaming kitchen appliances, floors, and counters in what some considered a harsh light. He sighed in satisfaction. He and his partners had worked hard to have this amazing place.

Behind him, his companion groaned.

"Why? Why are we here?" Sloane griped. "Who did I piss off in my former life?"

He turned to face his helper. "Is that a whine I hear?"

She grumbled something under her breath. Something like "I'll show you a whine."

August crossed his arms over his chest and lifted his eyebrows. "You're the one who said you wanted to be present to chronicle my every move to build awareness for Sugar Blitz."

Last night, after he'd gotten home from the town hall, Nicholas had texted him to ask if August could cover his morning shift, because Nicholas had a meeting with his agent he couldn't get out of. Something about a snag with an endorsement deal. The meeting

would require him to leave in the middle of prep. August had played
sous-chef enough times to know what was expected. Show up at
5 A.M. to make the day's cupcakes. He'd immediately texted Sloane
to join him in the morning fun.

She growled. "You know I'm not a morning person."

"Lucky for you, it's the middle of the night."

She growled louder.

August struggled to hold back his laughter. "You can always
go home." A snicker slipped out. Okay, maybe he wasn't trying
that hard.

"And have you calling me a quitter? Ain't no way." Sloane rubbed
her eyes. It was adorable. Her braids were pulled back into a high
ponytail. Her pout only highlighted how full and tempting her bare
lips were. Which was not the point.

"I'm going to get started." August tapped on the tablet screen he
carried. Nicholas had sent him a detailed plan about which cupcakes to bake, where the recipes were located, where the ingredients
were located, and even a little note about how the oven could be a
smidge tricky in the morning. All things August already knew, but
Nicholas guarded his kitchen like a helicopter parent, so August
didn't mind much.

August kept scrolling. Even if the plan was ten—no, make that
eleven—pages long.

"Ooh, yes. Give me more wrinkled brow. Your fans are gonna
love the intensity."

August looked up and glared. Sloane had her damned camera
trained on him, snapping away. She lowered the device. "You might
want to work on that scowl. You don't want to scare your fans away."

It was his turn to growl. Sloane's smile widened. He stepped
closer until only a foot separated them. Her gaze skittered away for
a second before returning to his. Her throat worked up and down

twice, and yes, the long, sleek line was mesmerizing, conjuring up fantasies about tracing the skin with his lips, but that's not why he'd come over here.

He bared his teeth. "Be sure not to take any blurry photos. I mean since you're so sleepy and all."

She gasped, any lingering traces of sleep on her face replaced by hot-blooded ire. She stepped closer. "How dare you? I am a professional!"

He smirked. "Who was whining three minutes ago. Try to keep up."

"And you try to keep that scowl off your face as you bake. Leave the hard stuff to me, *SugarBae*."

Undoubtedly that word had never been uttered with such derision. August smiled to himself. Starting with their first conversation all those years ago, Sloane had never been interested in taking shit from him. And just like then, he found her attitude ridiculously appealing.

His attraction to her, which had reignited when she moved to San Diego, only continued to grow by leaps and bounds. And there was absolutely nothing he could do about it. She'd made it clear she didn't want to go there, and he couldn't blame her. He wasn't worthy of her. Not after what he'd done. He doubted he ever would be.

He went back to work and tried to ignore that through all the sugar and buttercream, he could still smell her honey scent. Sense her presence. He also couldn't ignore that she was snapping away. He was not a cover model. He leaned out of the shot. When she didn't say anything, he tried it again.

She lowered her phone. "Would you stop?"

"Stop what?" he asked innocently.

"You know what. Stop being petty and stand still so I can take clear, non-blurry photos. This whole thing was your idea, remember?"

Yes, he remembered. A moment of weakness. He dodged one more time. It was so worth it when she let out a tiny scream of frustration. He wasn't perfect. Sue him.

"August."

"Okay, okay." He stopped acting like a child and went back to measuring ingredients. Her honey scent still filled his senses, but a man couldn't have everything, could he?

"You like baking, huh?" she asked a few minutes later.

He looked up. "Yeah, I find it relaxing."

"Me, too. Whatcha making?"

"Peanut butter chocolate. It's one of our top sellers."

"Oh, okay. Hmm."

He looked up. "Did you say something?"

She waved her hand. "Oh, no."

He returned to his task.

"Hmm."

Okay, he wasn't imagining it. "What does that mean?"

"What does what mean?"

"You're hmming."

Sloane rocked back on her heels. "Oh, nothing."

Eau de bullshit was wafting through the air. "Yeah, right. Spill it, Sloane."

"It's just . . . you know, you have an interesting technique."

His eyebrows lifted. "By interesting you mean wrong."

"Oh, no, I would *never* say that."

"You would just think it. Do you even know what you're talking about?" Never let it be said that he couldn't jump into Pettyville.

Sloane sniffed. "You're not the only one who knows how to

bake. Just because I don't make time for it doesn't mean I don't know how to do it. Baking is a strong Donovan tradition, as you well know."

"Hmm."

Her eyes narrowed. "You also know good and well I've helped out here before."

"Once."

"At least three times, you annoying hermit."

"You've resorted to name-calling, I see." He was having way too much fun. He wagged his finger. "Tsk, tsk. How unbecoming."

"I can bake you under the table any day of the week."

"Put up or shut up."

A competitive gleam entered her eyes. "You're on. Give me the tablet."

He loved seeing that fire in her eyes. He also loved living, so he handed over the tablet. "Why don't we make this interesting and see who can bake the best batch?"

The idea clearly intrigued her. "Who's going to judge?"

"Donovan and Ella are scheduled to work the morning shift. They can do it."

"They love me best, so advantage me. What do I get when I win?" She snapped her fingers. "Ooh, I got it. If I win, you do a photo shoot and you do as I say during this campaign. No dodging photos, no whining. I lead. You follow."

"And if I win, I get right of first refusal on all posts and photos before you post."

"You're on." The light of battle in her eyes matched the resolution of her tone.

August was only a tiny bit scared. Only a tiny bit turned on. "You have to follow the recipes exactly. We have a reputation to uphold."

Sloane nodded. "I don't want Nicholas's ire to rain down on me if I screw up, so I'll follow the recipes. But I'll still win because I'll add the Sloane *razzle dazzle*."

He snorted, amused as always by her. "I'm going to pretend you didn't say that. I'll also continue to do what I'm doing and ignore your little hmms as I bake."

"I'm going to set up the camera to get footage."

Of course. He respected the hustle even if he didn't like it very much.

She whipped around. "And you can't work while I do it."

He held up his hands in supplication, then waited patiently while she exited the kitchen and returned a couple of minutes later with two tripods procured from somewhere, set them up, and checked the lighting. She set up his phone and hers at different angles to get as much of the kitchen as she could.

Finally, when she was ready, he laid out the rules.

"You bake six varieties and I take the other half. We choose by random order. We follow the recipes exactly, making sure to put Sugar Blitz quality and consistency first."

Sloane snapped a salute. "Yes, sir. I will do all that and add my *razzle dazzle*."

"Still pretending you didn't say that, as I remind you that if you happen to burn a batch, oh well. I'm winning." He lifted up his wrist to inspect his watch. "We have two hours."

"Got it." Sloane made a beeline for the refrigerator.

He followed at a more sedate pace. "What are you doing?"

"Making sure I get the best eggs."

"Are you serious?"

"Yes." Her voice came from inside the door of the massive refrigerator.

He stepped behind her to find her, indeed, inspecting all the eggs, which were all roughly the same size and quality, like they were individual frames in the Zapruder film. August cleared his throat.

"Hold your horses. I'm almost done."

Two could play this game. He made his way to the cupboards and grabbed a bag of flour. The only bag.

"What are you doing?" she said.

"Getting my supplies together." He stepped aside and let her take his place.

"Where's the flour?"

"I've got it. You can have it when I've made all my cupcakes."

Her eyes widened. "What? That's not fair."

He shrugged. "All's fair in love and cupcakes."

She wasn't the only one obsessed with winning. You couldn't play professional football and not be competitive as hell. He usually left that side of him on the football field, but this situation was unique. And he was having so much fun with her. Like when they were kids. He'd missed this. Missed *them*.

Sloane's mouth fell open. "You're diabolical. Where's the rest of the flour?"

He shrugged. After shooting him a glare that would have incinerated a lesser opponent, she sprinted out of the kitchen to the supply closet where there was, indeed, more flour, but the door was locked. August kept one eye on the door while he measured out flour.

Sloane came careening back into the room. "The door was locked!"

"You don't say." He nonchalantly cracked an egg he'd selflessly liberated from her stash.

"I'm still going to win."

"Yes, I know. With your *razzle dazzle*."

Sloane squeezed her eyelids shut. Her chest rose and fell as she took a deep breath. When her eyes reopened, the panic had receded. Determination and grit had replaced it.

A chill slithered down his spine. Oh, shit.

She marched over to him and held out her hand. "Give me the flour."

Like the mature adult he was, he held the bag over his head. "Give me some of your eggs."

She gasped. "Absolutely not. There are more eggs in the fridge."

"But not the best eggs, according to you. No eggs, no flour."

Her jaw worked side to side as she considered her next move. "Fine." Her shoulders slumped and her chin burrowed into her chest. "You win."

Now he felt like the worst piece of shit. "Hey, Sloane, I was just kid—"

He never saw it coming.

"Ouch!" She'd kicked his shin! He dropped the bag on the countertop as pain radiated up his leg.

Sloane grabbed the flour and ran to her station, cackling. "Gotcha, sucker. Victory is mine!"

August shook his head. "You are ridiculous."

"As are you, sir. As are you."

He screwed his face into an exaggerated grimace. "You wounded me."

She flicked her hand at the wrist, dismissing his pain. "You'll be fine."

He placed a hand over his chest. "Your sympathy soothes my soul."

"You're welcome."

They shared a smile. Again, it was like no time had passed. Her smile was like a punch to the stomach. Breathing was no longer possible. She truly was beautiful, never more so than when happiness bloomed across her face.

* * *

Sloane took a step backward. She had to. A stoic August was a sight to behold. A smiling August was breathtaking. Whipping eggs suddenly became the most important task in the world. Anything to avoid the wonder of his gaze. "I'm still going to win, ya know."

He snorted. "Whatever, dude."

They worked in silence for a bit. She kept tabs on him, of course. There was a competition to be won, after all. When he looked like he was ready for the oven, she grabbed her pan and sprinted across the room.

"What are you doing?" he asked from behind her.

"Getting the good oven."

"Both ovens are exactly the same."

"Nicholas likes the top one, so that means it's the best."

He opened the other, *lesser* oven and slid his pan inside. "Have I mentioned that you're ridiculous?"

"Not in the past ten minutes, no."

They returned to their stations and got to work, preparing their next batches. Sloane carefully scrolled through her tablet to make sure she was following Nicholas's directions exactly.

"How's it going?" August called out.

"With baking? Fabulous. I'm going to make cupcakes that will have you weeping with joy because they're so good."

His lips quirked. "Good to hear. And life, in general?"

Sloane cracked another egg open. "Other than trying not to freak out about being unemployed, it's going swell."

He stepped around the counter toward her. "Hey, you're going to get that job. And even if you don't, you'll get another."

At least he didn't mention getting a loan from her brother. That was never, ever going to happen.

She shrugged. "I hope so. Nothing's guaranteed, no matter how much I wish it were." She'd had that lesson drummed into her over and over through the years. "This is a good distraction, though."

And she wasn't just talking about baking cupcakes. He'd always been willing to listen. To care about what was going on with her. How had she forgotten that? It felt good, nice to let down her guard and be vulnerable with someone. No, not with someone. With August.

She looked up to find his eyes pinned on her. Like he could read the words she'd left unspoken. Like he shared her thoughts. Wanted what she wanted. She swallowed hard as the air backed up in her lungs.

"Happy to help." One of his brilliant, rare smiles slowly made an appearance.

Her eyes caught on his beautifully molded lips. What if she bridged the gap? Tasted those tempting lips?

Ping! The oven timer. Sloane jumped, jarred back to the present. They were in a kitchen. Baking. She coughed and stepped back from temptation. They couldn't. She couldn't. "Let's get back to work. These cupcakes aren't going to bake themselves."

She held her breath, waiting for him to respond as his gaze, dark and penetrating, remained focused on her. Then, he slowly nodded and went back to baking.

Sloane slowly exhaled and studied him out of the corner of her eye as she crossed the room to the oven. Her hormones were still rioting, begging her to finish what she hadn't started. Was there anything sexier than a man knowing his way around a kitchen? Well, a man cleaning up after himself in the kitchen, maybe.

She shook her head. She didn't have time for this. Wouldn't have time for this. She opened the oven and pulled out the strawberry shortcake cupcakes. They smelled wonderful. Looked even better.

Suddenly, she became aware that she wasn't alone. August stood behind her, which shouldn't have been a big deal, but she could feel the heat radiating off him, seeping into her body. Making her want to snuggle into his chest. Making her want . . . everything. No. She squeezed her eyes shut for a second, then set the pan down and took off her oven gloves.

"They look good." He still stood too close. Or maybe that was her overactive imagination. She turned. He was close, his attention focused squarely on her.

"Thanks," she whispered.

"You have flour on your nose." He wiped away the offending ingredient. The act shouldn't have sent a streak of heat skittering through her system, but it did.

She lifted her hand to . . . what? Ward him off? Instead, her fingers curled over his chest. His heart beat fast and sure under her palm, scalding her with his heat. She gasped. "August."

Suddenly his mouth was on hers. Or maybe hers was on his. It didn't matter. His lips were exquisite, soft and full. Deliberate as they demanded entry. She had no issue acquiescing. Giving him anything he wanted. She opened her mouth on a moan. A shiver raced down her spine as their tongues met and slid sensuously against each other. Wanting more, Sloane explored his mouth. August took the kiss deeper, and she was happy to drown.

More, more, more.

She pressed her chest against his, dug her nails into his shoulders. Groaned when he slipped a leg between hers and pressed against her. He was so hard. He nipped her bottom lip with his teeth and kissed away the sting. Then, the kiss got wilder. Hotter. He lifted her on the counter. Ever grateful, she took the opportunity to wrap her legs around his waist and crowd closer.

As quickly as it started, it was over.

He stood a foot away and stared at her with wide, unblinking eyes. "I'm sorry. That shouldn't have happened."

"What?" Chest heaving, lips tingling, lust rampaging through her system, Sloane stared at him. Then, she heard it. Other voices outside the door.

"I'm sorry," he said again.

"Are we interrupting something?"

The question had come from her brother.

Sloane hopped off the counter, which brought her much too close to August. She took two hasty steps to the left. "What?"

Donovan and Ella were standing at the room's entrance. Ella's grin was almost as wide as the doorway. Donovan looked both shocked and confused.

"Are we disturbing something?" he repeated.

Sloane looked around. They hadn't wrecked the kitchen, but there was stuff everywhere, not to mention the phone cameras she'd set up at different points to capture it all. She had flour all over her. She wiped her hands on her apron, which did nothing but add another layer of flour to the covering. Clearing her throat, she stepped away from temptation and tried to take control of the situation, even though her mind was still swirling and her hormones were still raging.

What had they done? Why did she do that? She couldn't get involved with the guy who broke her heart. She couldn't let a man be that important to her again.

Focus. She needed to focus. "August and I are having a contest to see who can bake the best cupcake, and you two are going to be the judges. And it's a blind taste test, so you can't pick your best friend/employer." She sounded only a little bit shaky. She'd take that as a win.

Donovan eyed them both while Sloane held her breath. Had he seen them? *Heard* them? "Hmm," he finally said. "Okay, then."

Sloane slowly exhaled.

"Donovan might have to be impartial, but there's nothing in the rules that say I can't pick who I love the best," Ella said. "So of course I'm going to pick you, Sloane."

"Blind taste test it is then." August clapped his hands, sounding completely unbothered by what had just gone down.

Sloane snorted because that was the expected reaction.

"That won't be necessary," Donovan said. "We can be impartial, right, Ella?"

"Yeah, I guess," Ella said.

On autopilot, Sloane went and retrieved her cupcakes and handed them to Ella and Donovan. "I made these. Pretend this is *GBBO* and give your honest assessments."

She crossed her fingers behind her back as the judges both took generous bites of her strawberry shortcake. They both emitted moans of approval. She barely restrained from smirking at August. She really wanted to win. Did it matter, in the grand scheme of things? No, but wins had been hard to come by lately. And if kissing her was such a mistake, then she needed to best him in something. Prove to him the kiss meant nothing to her, as well. Even though it absolutely did.

"The texture is almost perfect," Donovan said. "A smidge too soft, but that's coming from an expert. The average layperson would never notice."

She resisted chucking something at her brother's head.

"I love the extra whipped cream. Our customers will love that," Ella said.

Next, they tried August's chocolate raspberry swirl. Again, the judges moaned in appreciation at the first bite.

Which was a good thing. They did plan to sell the desserts, after all. Were the moans a little louder, a little more appreciative than for hers, or was she losing her mind? Either option was viable at this point.

"The raspberry and chocolate mix perfectly," Ella said.

Donovan nodded. "But I'm wondering if this was cooked a tad too long."

Sloane rolled her eyes. Her brother was being difficult on purpose. His grin confirmed it. She bared her teeth at him. He laughed and stepped back to confer with Ella.

"We have a winner," Ella declared solemnly a few seconds later.

Sloane squeezed her eyes shut and rocked back and forth on her heels. Her heart was pounding.

"The winner is . . ." Donovan paused dramatically like he was, indeed, the host of *GBBO*. She'd kill him later when she had the time.

"The strawberry shortcake!"

Her eyes popped open. She jumped up and down and squealed. "I win, sucker! Take that!"

August lifted an eyebrow. Right. Decorum. She cleared her throat. "Good competition. Your cupcakes were undoubtedly amazing."

His eyebrows climbed higher. "Really?"

"Oh, yeah, I'm sure they were, but mine were better, and you have to do everything I say."

The corner of his mouth lifted. "Your wish is my command."

If only.

"Sloane. Sloane," Donovan said.

She jumped. "Sorry. August and I'll talk about our social media plans later. But now that I have you here, dear brother, I have something else I want to talk to you about. Nicholas isn't here, so two out of three will have to do."

Donovan and August exchanged an uneasy glance. She wasn't deterred. "You three own three buildings on the same block as Sugar Blitz Two and none of you bothered to mention it."

Donovan and August exchanged another glance. However, Sloane wasn't interested in best friend telepathy at the moment. She waved her hand. "Spill it, gentlemen."

With a sigh, Donovan leaned against the counter. "We weren't trying to hide it from you. It just never came up, and I don't see the problem anyway. We're not planning on doing anything evil."

"You don't see the problem?" Sloane turned on her heel and marched to the end of the room and turned back. "Let me break it down for you. I know y'all, so I don't doubt that you have the best intentions, but residents don't know that. They don't know you. What they do know is what's happening all across this country, namely outsiders coming in, raising rents, and driving out longtime residents all in the name of so-called progress."

"We would never do that," August said quietly.

She found his quiet resolution way too attractive, but she would think about why she insisted on torturing herself later. She nodded emphatically. "And I won't let you. Donovan, we're from Oakland. We've seen firsthand how gentrification can harm communities, especially our people."

Donovan blew out a breath. "I know, Sloane."

She threw up her hands. "Then what's the plan?"

August stepped in front of her. Close enough to touch. But he didn't. Longing swept through her for that phantom touch. He looked deep into her eyes. "Sloane. We have some ideas, but we haven't decided on anything. We do know we aren't going to drive people out."

Again, his innate sense of calm and purpose effortlessly lured her into a trap he wasn't even trying to set. By force of will, Sloane stepped back and went to retrieve her phone. She unlocked it and started typing.

"What are you doing?" August asked from behind her.

She turned to him. "Putting in a reminder to set up a meeting when all three of you are available to discuss these ideas and come up with some better ones."

His lips spread in obvious appreciation. "I would expect nothing less."

Chapter Nineteen

Twelve years ago . . .

Sloane paused outside her mom's bedroom. Her mom was on the phone. Her voice was muffled, but Sloane made out "Where were you?" Sloane's dad had promised to stop by, since Donovan and Shana were in town for Thanksgiving. The sun had set without an appearance. With a sigh, Sloane continued on her way. Her destination was never more important.

A few minutes later, the door behind her creaked open. She slid her pilfered goods to the side away from the moonlight, then collapsed in relief when she saw it was August. "Hey."

"Hey," he said. "You look guilty. What's up?"

She held up the silver tin. "I'm eating a whole pie by myself."

The side of his mouth tilted up. "Didn't your mom tell you to save some for guests?"

"Yes, but I needed it. Y'all don't."

He nodded. She waved him over and held her breath as he settled next to her on the first step of the back porch. This was the first time they were alone together in person. She would not freak out. Hopefully. "What are you doing out here?"

"Didn't feel like sleeping."

She nodded in understanding. A restlessness she couldn't shake thrummed through her veins. "Can I ask you something?"

August clasped his hands together between his bent knees and sighed. "Let me guess. You want to know why I'm here celebrating Thanksgiving with the Dells instead of with my own father?"

"Yeah."

"My dad is off being the great Dale Hodges, celebrated chef. Thanksgiving isn't a time for family. It's a time to build his reputation." He shrugged, like he didn't care, but even the shadows created by the moonlight couldn't hide the sadness that filled his eyes.

"I'm sorry. Does he come to see you play?"

"No. Football isn't really his speed."

And that hurt him. Which hurt her. "I'm sorry he's not the parent you deserve."

August shrugged. "It is what it is. Coach gave us a few days off and your brother insisted I come home with him."

Sloane's stomach cramped, but she couldn't leave the most obvious question unasked. "And your girlfriend?"

"She's with her mom. It's not my place to talk about it, but it's a volatile situation. I wouldn't have been welcome."

"Well, you're welcome here." So very, very welcome. Crushes were the worst.

"Thanks."

She had one more pressing question. "Why didn't you tell Donovan we talk about stuff other than calculus?"

"I didn't know if you wanted me to," he said, his soulful gaze never wavering. "Privacy is important."

She stared at him with wide eyes. "Wow. Thank you."

His shoulder lifted. Clearly he was uncomfortable with

compliments. Sloane bit her lip. She'd had no idea how attractive humility was until that very moment.

"Enough about me," he said. "What brought you out here?"

Sloane leaned back against the post and stared up at the night sky. "I don't know. Trying to figure out my future. Do I stay close to home or go across the country for college? When will my mom stop putting on a fake front and admit she's not getting the financial help she's supposed to get from my dad?" She shrugged. "My siblings are lucky. They don't live here anymore. It's just me. She tries to hide it from me, but she worries about the bills that never stop coming."

"That's a lot."

She shrugged again. Like it was that easy to reconcile her feelings. "It is what it is."

"Such wise words."

"Shut up, MOTY." Laughing, she reached out to push him. Her hand landed on his chest, right on top of his heart. His T-shirt offered little resistance to the warmth underneath. A fierce heat traveled up her arm. The urge to curl her fingers around the fabric and bring him closer surged inside her. Her breath caught. They were so close on the small porch, knees almost touching. Her movement had brought her closer. Their mouths were only inches apart. His lips had parted. Her breath caught. That look in his eyes . . . like he could feel it too.

He laughed, though it sounded forced. "Only if I can have some pie."

She dropped her hand. "Right! Yes. Sorry, I should have offered you some. It's really good. My mom did her thing." She stuffed some in her mouth to stop her rambling and thrust the pan at him. He cut off a slice with the knife and popped the dessert into his mouth. She was no longer hungry for pie. She stared, rapturously, as he chewed, and the pie slid down his throat. His Adam's apple bobbed up and down. She wanted to lick it so very, very bad.

August swallowed. "This pie is fantastic."

And he had a girlfriend. Time to act like she had some sense. "I know, right! Everyone is always debating pecan pie or sweet potato pie for Thanksgiving. They can have it. Give me my lemon meringue and I'm a happy camper. My mom always makes me one for holidays and my birthday."

"Your mom is the best."

"She is. My dad, on the other hand." She sighed. "He tries, but addiction is hard to break."

"I get it about not-great dads." He looked at her like no one ever had. Like he really saw her.

"Is that how you and Donovan bonded?"

His mouth curved upward. "Something like that. As for college, do what's best for you."

She nodded. "Thanks for the reminder." She took a bite of pie. "This pie makes everything better. Eat it with me so I can lie convincingly to my mother when she asks about it tomorrow."

"You're going to throw me under the bus, you mean."

"It sounds so harsh when you put it that way."

He side-eyed her. "Does it?"

Sloane laughed again. He always made her laugh. And he was so, so handsome. She looked her fill, but she didn't touch. "Just eat it!"

"Your wish is my command."

Chapter Twenty

August unlocked the back door of Sugar Blitz Two and held the door open for Sloane. Because he was a glutton for punishment, he deliberately took in a lungful of her scent as she passed by. Though they'd cleaned up after their little contest, he could still smell the sugar and frosting on her. It mixed deliciously with the honey scent from her lotion. He'd watched like a lovesick fool as she'd smoothed it on her arms during the drive over.

He followed her down the hall.

"Now that I've won our contest because I'm the better baker, we need to discuss what's next with our social media campaign."

With a sigh, August sat in one of the chairs he'd put together yesterday.

Sloane continued, clearly undeterred by his lackluster response. "I have some ideas on how to capitalize on your popularity to make sure this location is a success." She nodded decisively. He instantly went on guard. While he appreciated her assertiveness and go-get-it-ness, he was wary when that focus was turned his way.

A dangerous smile curved her lips. "We should make a TikTok."

He jumped up. "Or we should not."

She waved away his objection. "I'm sure there's a dance going around we could learn."

His blood ran colder than the ice in Antarctica. "I'm sure there's a chance I will never do it."

She made a sound of sympathy and patted him on the arm. "I know there's a stigma in our community about not having rhythm, but we're not a monolith. If you don't have rhythm, it's okay. It's a little embarrassing, but I can keep a secret."

"I have rhythm," he growled.

Her face blanked. She licked her lips, her eyes sweeping up and down his body. Where had her mind gone? Was she thinking about their kiss and other ways he could demonstrate rhythm? Ways they could find rhythm together?

He dragged in a breath and slowly exhaled. "Sloane."

She jumped, then cleared her throat. Her gaze focused on him again. "I'm just kidding, dude. You're so easy."

"Oh. Okay." He needed a distraction from this conversation. Oh, look. He needed to finish hanging a sconce. He moved toward a wall and picked up the lamp.

Sloane followed him. "What I'm not kidding about is doing an Instagram Live."

Grimacing, he whirled to face her. She was close, as close as earlier when they'd . . . Wait. No. He wasn't supposed to be thinking about that. They were talking about him doing something that sounded wholly unpleasant. So he would think about that instead. "Why would I do an Instagram Live? I'm not entirely sure what that is, but it sounds horrible."

His scowl deepened when a laugh slipped past her lips. She did a piss-poor job of disguising it by coughing. She held up a hand. "Sorry. No more laughing. An Instagram Live is a live video chat on

Instagram. You broadcast live from your account and your followers can watch you doing whatever you're doing as you do it." She side-eyed him. "And you know that already. You're just stalling."

True, but he saw no reason to admit it. Instead, he cleared his throat and gave the nail that was already securely screwed into the wall another whack with his hammer for good measure. "I ask again, why would *I* do an Instagram Live?"

"At the risk of reigniting the same argument we've been having for the past few days and repeating myself, might I remind you that you agreed on recording your involvement in the renovation. You also said you'd do what I recommended after I won the baking contest."

"The contest was rigged." Was he being an ass? Yes. Did he care? No.

She moved between him and the wall, bringing that delectable body of hers way too close for his peace of mind. As always, she smelled like all his hopes and dreams come true. And he'd told her kissing her was a mistake. Why had he done that? Another mistake in a long line of mistakes when it came to Sloane Dell. If he had the time and a little privacy, he'd bang his head against the wall.

She narrowed her eyes as her lips parted. "I'm going to assume what you actually meant to say when you stated that blatant mis-truth was 'You're right, Sloane. Please continue.' And I'm also going to ignore that scowl. Even though you and your partners haven't decided what to do with the other buildings yet, the residents are still fired up and they're not going to be satisfied with a simple 'wait and see' answer. We need to respond to the protestors and their petition in some way now."

She was so fucking sexy when she was demonstrating her smarts. He took a half step back, just to give him some space to breathe. To try to think clearly.

She held up a hand. "Yes, the town hall was great, but a lot of the people there were distracted, and the ones who were really worked up are outside protesting as we speak." Her voice, the look on her face, became earnest. "Yes, it's only four people, but people are walking by and taking notice. Tomorrow, it could be five, then ten again. We need to do more to get ahead of the story and control the narrative."

August stifled a groan. Sloane being right meant suffering for him. "By hosting a news conference on Instagram?"

Her eyes widened in unabashed glee. "Ooh, we could do that."

His stomach dropped to the wooden floor.

Smiling, she patted him on the arm. "Kidding again. That's a terrible idea."

If he didn't want to kiss her again, he'd kill her. "My ego and I thank you."

She waved her hand. "You're fine."

"I am? Why, thanks."

She squinted. "Are you engaging in word play, trying to get me to say you're fine? 'Cause I'm not going to do it."

Time for some payback. Shake her up a little like she did to him on the regular. "I wasn't, but it's nice to see where your mind immediately went to. Do you think I'm fine?"

She balled her hands into fists, closed her eyes for a second, and drew in a deep breath before leveling him with a no-more-bullshit glare. "You thought you successfully distracted me. You thought. Back to our discussion. The IG Live won't be a press conference. It'll be a chance for you to highlight what you're doing in the store and what's to come. I'll throw a few softball questions at you, people will be happy to see SugarBae *and* be absolutely appalled that anyone's against you spreading joy and happiness with cupcakes in this neighborhood. Win-win."

She beamed, clearly pleased with her little speech. That made one of them.

"Except for the part where I talk as little as possible, and I don't like cameras in my face."

"Yes, this is true, but that's why I'm there. To keep the conversation going and give you something, or in my case, *someone* other than the phone camera to focus on."

She was right in one regard. Focusing on Sloane had never been an issue. She was beautiful, her hands waving, eyes shining bright with her idea. She lived for this. And he lived for . . .

"Fine. But I'm only doing it for five minutes."

Her nose wrinkled. "Let's play it by ear. I'm in charge, remember."

Saying no to Sloane Dell had never been his strong suit, but he was going to gird his loins and keep the Live as close to five minutes as possible. Sweat had already started to preemptively bead on his forehead and palms, and they weren't even doing anything. He set the hammer on the floor before he dropped it on his foot.

He just needed to play it cool. Fake the funk for a few minutes, that's all.

Sloane reached for his hand and squeezed before letting go quickly. Gazed at him with concerned eyes. "We don't have to do this if you don't want to."

He sighed. So much for his Oscar-winning turn as Cool August. He balled his hand into a fist, missing the brief connection. Missing their longer, more heated connection from earlier.

"I thought it would be a quick, fun way to connect with fans and show them how Sugar Blitz will be an asset to the community without you actually having to speak publicly. But making you miserable isn't part of the plan."

Get it together, man. "You're right. I'm nervous. There's no point in lying about that, but I'll be okay." He'd gotten himself into this mess. It was his responsibility to get out of it. Somehow.

She still looked unconvinced, so he continued, "Hey, if things go left, we can always end the Live abruptly, undoubtedly leading to wild speculation on social media about what happened and increasing overall interest in the shop."

Her eyes widened, and she excitedly lifted on her toes. "Ooh, maybe we should try that." Her grin and the heels of her sneakers fell when she noticed the look on his face. "Or maybe not."

* * *

Sloane peeked at August out of the corner of her eye as she pretended to fiddle with the camera settings. The panic in his eyes had subsided, but she still wasn't sure this was the best course of action. Social media was her thing, not his. She could come up with another idea to circumvent the protestors' message. It wasn't like the detractors had gotten very far with their petition. Maybe she should chill. Even if that went against her nature. It wasn't like her to just wait for the other shoe to drop. She took action. Made shit happen.

"I'm fine, Sloane. You can stop worrying about me," he said from where he'd resumed using a leveler to find the studs in the wall. How did he do that—know what she was thinking and what was going on around him without her saying a word? It was his superpower.

"I know. I just—" Her words flittered away to nothing as her mind blanked when his massive palms landed on her unsuspecting shoulders.

He squeezed. "I'm fine."

She nodded and stared at his shirt because talking was beyond her at the moment. It shouldn't matter. He wasn't even touching her. He was touching the cotton of her shirt. There was no skin-to-skin contact. Didn't matter. She felt like she'd been scalded. Thank God, he didn't seem to notice.

"Really," he added when she didn't respond.

He stilled as though he finally recognized the instance for the momentous occasion it was. He dropped his hands to his sides. All she could hear was the loud beat of her heart in her ears. They were standing close, so close she could count his individual eyelashes. She'd always been jealous of his thick eyelashes. She could count the whiskers that lined his ridiculous cheekbones and jawline. And his mouth? It was right there, his full lips moving as he continued to reassure her he wasn't going to pass out live on Instagram.

Earlier, when he'd been so emphatic about having rhythm, her mind had swan-dived into the gutter like she was an Olympic gold medalist diver. Reasons for why they couldn't, shouldn't happen had flown out of her mind. And she was doing it again. Ways to convince him that the kiss was a great idea crowded her brain. But no, she couldn't. He'd rejected her twice now. There wouldn't be a third time. Giving a man a chance to hurt her again—like August had done, like Jim had done, like her father had done—was nowhere in her life plan.

She stared into his mesmerizing eyes that radiated nothing but honesty and kindness.

But what if . . . what if this time was different? What if he'd been surprised by the kiss and didn't really think it was a mistake?

What if he was the person she could trust? What if he was the person she could be vulnerable with? What if he was the person who could be a genuine partner to her?

What if, what if, what if. Scary, scary questions that she wasn't ready to seek answers to.

Sloane drew in a stuttering breath and stepped away. "Okay. You need to change."

His eyebrows shot up. "Excuse me?"

She waved at his red-and-black T-shirt. "It's cool that you're repping the Knights today, but during the Live, you need to rep Sugar Blitz. It's easy promo."

His face cleared. "Oh. Okay. I'll be back." He turned with unnatural grace for someone of his size and headed to the back of the store.

Sloane sucked in a lungful of August-less air. She ignored how empty the room seemed without his presence. She went back to fiddling with the settings on the camera while her brain continued to whirl. It took her a while to realize it had been more than a few minutes since August had disappeared. What was going on? He'd been the one reassuring her he was up for this. Was he okay? What if he wasn't?

She hurried to his office and knocked on the door. When no answer was forthcoming, she opened the door. And immediately forgot how to think or breathe.

He wasn't wearing a shirt. *Alert, alert!* August Hodges was *not* wearing a shirt.

Her greedy eyes inhaled the wall of delicious flesh that defined his magnificent back. Muscles rippled in perfect synchronized motion as he lifted his arm. Scrumptious, delicious brown skin her lips and tongue longed to taste. Dampness instantly settled between her legs.

She must have made a whimper full of intense hunger, or maybe he just sensed he was no longer alone—and she was going to go with the second, less embarrassing option—because he turned. Holy fuck! The front was better than the back. He was a professional athlete who took his fitness seriously (even though he owned a cupcake shop franchise), so she shouldn't be shocked by how fucking good he looked. But it was one thing to be intellectually aware of something and another to be confronted with it up close and personal. A quick perusal registered an eight-pack. A trail of hair bisected his abs and led to . . . She jerked her eyes upward.

His eyebrows lifted. "Sloane?"

His tone was amused. No doubt her tongue was hanging out her mouth like a dog eagerly tracking the bowl of water its parent carried.

Dignity. She needed to find it, and soon. She lifted a hand as he reached for the teal Sugar Blitz polo on his desk. Let a mocking, flirty smile spread across her lips. "Please stop on my behalf."

He shot her a look. "I do so appreciate being treated like a piece of meat."

The finest, rarest cut of beef. Filet mignon. Dignity, Sloane. "What's taking you so long? Everything okay in here?"

"Yeah, sorry. Nicholas called to tell me I left the pans in the wrong spot this morning. I told him to go to hell."

His torso remained uncovered, making it extremely difficult to concentrate on his words. *Dignity, Sloane.* She replayed the last few seconds through her head and forced out a laugh like she was supposed to.

Finally, he lifted the shirt above his head and slipped his head through. Sloane silently cried "nooo" as his wonderful brown, toned skin was covered up inch by merciless inch.

"How do I look?" he asked.

Like someone she wanted to jump and have her wicked way with. But no, that was the incorrect answer and not the one he was expecting or wanted. Right. She needed to get it together. She took a more objective, less lusty inspection of him. The teal popped against his brown skin. His jeans were perfectly worn in. He was handsome as ever. His locs were pulled back in his customary ponytail, which served to highlight his sharp cheekbones. He looked comfortable and casual. Approachable. Attractive as fuck. Very August.

"Great. The camera's gonna love you."

She should know.

Chapter Twenty-One

Twelve years ago . . .

Sloane stepped farther out onto the porch. Away from the chaos that reigned in the frat house behind her. She took in a deep lungful of smog-infested LA air instead. At this point, it was better than the *lovely* combo of weed, body odor, and puke smells inside.

She was having the quintessential college experience. Or something. Attending a frat party with a bunch of cool college kids. Or at least that's what she'd assumed would happen when her brother told her about the party.

But the reality was not living up to the hype. Watching people fawn over her brother and his teammates because they played football was quite an experience.

She'd made the campus visit, ostensibly to see if she wanted to be a UCLA Bruin. The real reason was to see August. Duh. It had been a few months since Thanksgiving. She'd wanted to see his ridiculously handsome face again and leapt at the convenient excuse.

Not that she'd had much chance to see or talk to him so far. She'd spent the day touring the campus and participating in prospective student activities. Afterward, she'd met up with Donovan, who told her about the party.

And still she'd had little to no August face time. When he wasn't surrounded by other students wanting a second of his time, his girlfriend, Melinda, was there. His perfect girlfriend who was way cooler than Sloane would ever be. And the worst thing was she couldn't even hate her. Melinda had been nothing but gracious to Sloane, even opening her closet to Sloane so she didn't look like a total dork at the party. Okay, she hated her just a smidge. If only because she had the right to hug and kiss August whenever she wanted.

That display of affection had been the last straw that sent Sloane skedaddling out of the party.

Sloane blew out a breath and took a seat on the top step. Damn, this sucked sooo hard. Why had she come to LA? She could have made her decision about college without ever stepping foot on this campus or subjecting herself to the horror of watching the guy she liked love on someone else.

She nodded at some kids who stumbled up the stairs and into the house. Looked like they'd started the partying earlier. Yeah, this was the *best*.

A couple of minutes later, the door opened behind her.

"Sloane? What are you doing out here?" August asked.

She twisted around so fast she almost tumbled off her perch, and wouldn't *that* have been fabulous? "What are *you* doing out here?"

She jumped up and moved closer to him, drawn to him like a magnet.

August jerked his chin toward the house. "Waiting for Melinda. I'm partied out. Some people from her animal rights group came and they're having an impromptu protest planning session."

Yeah, Melinda was way cooler than Sloane. "Animal rights isn't your thing?"

The corner of his mouth kicked up. It was adorable. He was adorable. "I support when I can, but it's her passion." He pointed at the phone in her hand. "I interrupted you. Scrolling Facebook or Twitter?"

Sloane shook her head. "Good guess, but no. I'm reading a book."

"What kind?"

The best kind. Not that everyone shared her opinion. She gave him her best death glare. "I'll tell you, but if you make fun of me, I'll kneecap you and all your fawning fans will keel over in agony."

He covered his heart with his hand. "Promise."

"It's a romance. Brenda Jackson, the queen." She glared again.

He pointed at his face. "This is me, opening my mouth, but not to say anything mean."

She nodded regally. "You may continue."

"Do you read a lot of romance?"

She nodded. "It's my fave. People working hard for their happily-ever-after and being rewarded for their efforts. It gives me hope that it can actually happen. My parents weren't the greatest example."

"Cool."

Sloane stared at him. "That's all you have to say?"

"Yeah."

They stared at each other, then burst into laughter. By silent mutual accord, they settled against the windowpane and stared out into the street.

"We always seem to find ourselves on porches," she said.

"It's good to see your face, Sloane." He bumped shoulders with her. How she didn't melt into a puddle of goo, she would never know.

"Yours, too." She twisted to study his profile. It was sheer perfection.

"Have you made a choice about college yet?"

"Not yet." Though the choice was becoming clearer by the second.

Chapter Twenty-Two

*T*he camera counted down. Three, two, one.

Sloane pasted on her hostess-with-the-mostest smile. "Hey, everyone, I'm Sloane Dell, the social media manager for Sugar Blitz, and I'm here with August Hodges. Some of you might know him as SugarBae."

Beside her, August groaned. She laughed. "And don't we just love that modesty. We've been reading the messages y'all have been sending in—some of them very NSFW—and August wanted to thank you by doing this Live."

"Hey, everybody." He waved. He looked halfway comfortable. She'd take it.

"We don't want to take up too much of your time, but we did want to let you know a second location of Sugar Blitz is opening soon in the Emerald Hills neighborhood. August is here doing some renovations to make sure the place sparkles and shines before we open to the public. We know y'all have been asking to hear from SugarBae, so here he is. Put your questions in the chat, and August will answer them."

She and August began walking through the store, like they'd rehearsed. "August, this place has come a long way in the last week. Take us through what you've done." She panned the camera as he spoke.

"I painted the walls, hung up some photos. Did a whole lot of cleaning. Tried not to freak out when a spiderweb came out of nowhere and attacked me. Went through an inspection with the city. And put together a whole bunch of tables and chairs. Real glamorous stuff."

Sloane laughed. She checked the screen. Their viewer count was steadily climbing. The hearts were flowing. "Ahh, the glamorous life of a small business owner. Not to be a downer, but there's been some concern about the role you and your partners plan to play in Emerald Hills—that you're only concerned about profits and don't care about the people here. I hate to bring up the G-word, but . . ."

"You have to. Gentrification. It's happening everywhere. My partners and I want to be a part of the community. We want to give, not take or change. Be good neighbors."

"But you're rich. Rich people tend to forget about us regular folk."

He chuckled. "Yeah, we're rich. But we weren't always. My father is a successful chef, but it took him a long time and a lot of work to get there. We know what it's like to struggle. To work hard. To be proud of where you come from. We have no intention of driving people out. We're here because we want to be part of the community, not above it."

Sloane couldn't take her eyes off him. His sincerity was so apparent and unbelievably attractive. "That's amazing." *You're amazing.* Nope. Not the time. "Now let's get to the good stuff. And I know you hate this question, but it's the number-one question in the comments. Does SugarBae have a significant other?"

"You are correct. I do hate that question. And the answer is no, I don't."

She knew that already. Duh. But still, a little puff of relief escaped past her lips. *Not going to happen, Sloane.* She focused on the screen and read another question.

"'How did you get so awesome? A lot of men, even well-meaning ones, rarely understand the contributions women make to society.' That comes from Sydney4Ever."

"Thank you, Sydney4Ever, for saying I'm awesome, even though I'm not sure I agree." He shrugged. "I live in this world. I observe what's going on. It's easy to do when you care about the truth. The truth isn't always easy or pleasant, but it's always necessary if you want to make the world a better, more equitable place."

That was probably the most she'd ever heard him speak at once. But it was obvious that it came straight from the heart. That's why he'd gone viral. Even when he wasn't trying, he connected with people because they sensed his innate goodness.

"Great answer, August. Since you are such a truth teller, how do you feel about giving some advice? We've gotten a lot of DMs, some of them definitely not safe for work, but others are more innocent in nature."

The corner of his mouth kicked up. "Let's do it."

Sloane read from a notebook she carried. "I'll keep the account private to keep the peace, but one of your followers wrote 'My boyfriend wants me to move in with him because we live far away from each other, but the reason we do is because my job is on the other side of town, and I love my job. Should I choose him or my job?'"

Sloane was insanely curious to see how he would answer. They'd agreed he wouldn't know the questions beforehand, to maintain authenticity.

His head tilted to the side as he considered the question. "My first instinct is to say drop that loser and stick with the job. But, not knowing more than what you just said, I'd say have a talk with him. Maybe compromise is the answer. It's good that he wants to spend more time with you, but will it be quality time if you're stuck in traffic for two hours every day. Maybe, when your lease is up, you can find a place that's midway between both jobs."

Sloane checked the phone. More hearts filled the screen. The comments were flying by so fast she couldn't keep up.

"More great advice," Sloane said. She turned the phone, so that both she and August appeared on screen. "That's all we have time for today, folks. Thanks for joining us. Stay tuned for more Lives, with more renovation tips and love advice from August Hodges, SugarBae himself. Until next time."

Sloane ended the session to the sound of August growling in her ear, which was half parts funny and sexy as hell.

She turned to him with wide eyes and an innocent tone. "What?"

"Why do you keep pushing that SugarBae bullshit?"

"Well, let's see. That's what the internet knows you as, and we're trying to get and keep the internet's attention, which isn't easy to do. Also, because it's funny and brilliant and I'm ridiculously jealous of whoever came up with it." A snicker slipped out before she could stop it.

His glare intensified, which only made her laugh harder.

"Sloane." His serious tone tipped her off that they were no longer joking.

She swallowed. "What's up?"

"About earlier? When we kissed . . ."

Sloane blinked. Oh, wow. He was really going there. She swallowed hard. "Yeah?"

"I said it was a mistake. I just meant—"

Sloane lifted her chin. "You just meant that's not why we're here.

We're here to work. There's too much water under the bridge for us to go there. I get it."

His lips pressed tightly against each other for a beat. "Right."

Did he not agree? Her traitorous heart fluttered in unwise hope.

"Hello, there," someone called out.

The voice, familiar and completely unwelcome, came from the front door. Once again, they would need to do something about leaving the door unlocked. Paige, the flirt from the town hall and Cynthia's daughter, stood there, holding a dish, dressed like she'd stepped off a Fashion Week runway. Sloane hated to admit it, but she'd kill for the red dress that slipped oh-so-artfully off Paige's right shoulder. But so what? Sloane's attire of jeans and a T-shirt was completely appropriate for the situation and location. So there. Take that, ye olde insecurities.

It took Sloane a moment to realize Paige wasn't alone. Two more women stood beside her.

"Oh, hey, Paige," Sloane said oh so casually. "What's up?"

Paige sauntered over, her red stilettos click-clacking on the wooden floor, all red lips and stunning white teeth. "We wanted to properly welcome August to the neighborhood. We saw the Live, so we knew you were here."

Great, this was all Sloane's fault. Her big bright idea for people to get to know August had backfired spectacularly. Wait. No. She didn't care if August had fans.

"We came right over." Paige trailed a fingertip down August's bare forearm.

Sloane didn't growl. Barely even glared. Didn't yell at Paige to take her hands off her man, who, okay—objectively speaking— was not her man, but that was beside the point. She congratulated herself on her restraint.

"I told my parents I was coming to get intel, so they wouldn't object," Paige added.

Intel on what? The shape of August's body? How much body fat he carried? Sloane very much doubted Paige cared about the store's impact on the neighborhood.

August's lips tipped upward. "Thanks. But you didn't have to come all the way down here."

"Of course we did." One of the other women, this one wearing a purple romper, which Sloane begrudgingly admitted was really cute, came over. Clearly not in the mood to be outdone by Paige, she stepped entirely too close to August and cooed. Like, actually fucking cooed like a baby. "I'm Desiree, by the way."

"Nice to meet you, Desiree," August said. Sloane wanted to yell at him to ignore his manners, but that would make her look super jealous, which she totally was, but there was a huge difference between feeling an emotion and broadcasting it to the whole world. She'd learned that lesson long ago. Made it much harder to deny said emotions and put you in a vulnerable state, which she never wanted to be in again.

"And I'm Terri," the last member of the triumvirate added. "We brought gifts. A man like you, who owns a cupcake shop, must love sweets."

"But we know we couldn't compare to your cupcakes," Paige said breathlessly. "Sugar Blitz cupcakes are the best on the West Coast."

Laying it on a bit thick there, aren't we? Sloane turned away before they could see her rolling her eyes.

"So we brought pie. We actually made them for the church bake sale, but we'll make more later. We thought you could tell us which pie you like best," Paige continued. Each woman held out a towel-covered tin.

"Oh, I can't do that," August said.

"Oh, but you must," Sloane said.

It was his turn to glare at her. But she was having fun now. Ridiculous situations called for ridiculous responses. "This will make for great social media content."

The three women wasted no time in procuring a table to lay out their goods. A knife and fork were whipped out from somewhere. Sloane hid behind her camera, recording it all.

"This is my famous apple pie," Paige said. *Famous to who?* The snarky thought had barely crystallized in Sloane's brain when Terri snorted. Seemed they were on the same wavelength about one thing at least.

August, still looking like he wished a sinkhole would open beneath his feet, took a bite. "It's good."

Paige beamed.

Desiree was next, with a pecan pie. "I serve this every Thanksgiving, and my family always raves about it. Everyone always asks for seconds."

August dutifully took a bite. And chewed. And chewed. "It's good," he said after finally swallowing the pie and taking a gulp of water.

Desiree's face fell like an undercooked soufflé. "Maybe I used a little too much corn syrup this time. I just wanted it to be extra special."

August shook his head. "Don't worry. It was great."

August truly was a good man, and her feelings for him were her problem to deal with.

"Okay, me next," Terri said. "My blueberry surprise is next. Step aside. The queen baker is here and I do not play in the kitchen."

She leaned down to place her pie directly in front of August. A good move, Sloane had to admit. The woman had cleavage for days. Her V-neck top did a great job of highlighting her assets.

August's version of a smile made a reappearance. "Great, thanks." He chewed slowly, nodding his head in appreciation.

Sloane distracted herself by taking photos. Better than pretending she was wrestler Bianca Belair and taking all these women out.

Paige stepped forward. "So which pie wins?" Desiree and Terri quickly joined her, jockeying for position in front of August.

"Ladies, you can't expect me to choose. That wouldn't make me much of a gentleman." He actually sounded sincere.

He could be charming when he wanted to be. And kind. Sloane would not find it attractive. Except she did. She totally did. The women all sighed in appreciation. Sloane barely refrained from joining them.

Terri turned her way. "Did you get my good side in the pictures?"

Was she for real? "I did my best," Sloane answered.

"Sloane, put down the camera and have some pie," August said. He pointed at the deadly pecan pie.

"Oh, I couldn't." She held up her phone. "I'm here to record the action, not to be part of it."

His shark teeth made an appearance. "Sure you can. Our guests were so nice to stop by. I'm sure they don't mind sharing."

"Nope," Paige said.

"Whatever you say, August," Terri cooed.

"'Course not," Desiree said with a bright smile.

Sycophants were gonna sycophant. And she could and *would* kill August later. Sloane accepted a fork from Paige and took the teeniest tiniest piece of the pecan pie. That was still too much. It was positively awful. It tasted like mud and pecans baked in paste dyed brown. "Mmm."

August stood. "Thank y'all for coming, but as you know we still have a ton of work to do before the shop happens."

"I know my mother has her doubts, but I can tell you have the best heart. Say the word and we'll come back at any time," Paige said. There went her damn finger again, tracing August's bare forearm. Sloane bit her lip hard to hold back a growl.

"Any time," Terri chimed in immediately.

Sloane stuffed a bite of Paige's apple pie into her mouth to stop herself from snorting. *Ooh.* Okay, this was good stuff. Not as good as her mom's lemon meringue pie, but delicious all the same. Credit to August for not showing favoritism. Sloane studied the plate. One more bite couldn't hurt. Maybe Paige wasn't all bad.

"All the other SugarBaebies are going to be so jealous we got to see you," Desiree said.

Sloane choked on the pie. SugarBaebies? What the hell was a *SugarBaeby*?

"I'm sorry. All the who?"

"The SugarBaebies. That's what August's fans call ourselves."

Oh, good Lord. She rolled her eyes. She couldn't help herself. How had she missed that trend on Instagram? If it wasn't in fact, horrible, the appalled look on August's face would've been hilarious.

"He's the best, and he deserves the best." Paige's finger went to work again on August's arm. Clearly, she meant herself. "I'd love to get to know you better."

"So would I," Terri said.

"Me too," Desiree added.

"The SugarBaebies just want you to be happy and find a good woman," Paige said. After they took a group picture with August (and Paige got one more grope in for good measure), the women left.

"Don't say it," August said after the SugarBaebies departed.

"Say what?" Sloane said. Although she knew exactly what he was talking about. Not that he had to worry. She wouldn't have made that suggestion in a million years. She could only be pushed so far. She knew her limits.

"That if I go out with Paige, then her parents might back off with their boycott if they think their daughter is happy."

She hated that he could read her mind. "I'm not going to lie. The thought did cross my mind, but I wasn't going to say it."

"Why not?"

"Why not what?" Although, again, she knew what he was asking.

"Why weren't you going to say it?" Clearly he had an infinite amount of patience and wasn't about to let her get away with BS.

She stood and began gathering the extra pie and plates the Sugar-Baebies had left behind. Anything to avoid looking him in the eye. "Because it's not any of my business who you go out with."

"Even if it would help you out by generating a lot of social media buzz."

She shrugged. "Even then. I'm not a pimp. You can date whoever you want. That's it."

He stared at her for a long moment with unreadable eyes. "Right."

Chapter Twenty-Three

Sloane settled into the chair behind August's desk at Sugar Blitz Two. He'd loaned her the office for her upcoming meeting since his was the only one that had a desk and would offer a half-way decent backdrop. He hadn't done too much decorating, but elements of his personality were clear to see. A few tools on the bookshelf. One of the hair ties he used for his locs. A framed photo of a woman holding the hand of a toddler August. His mother, presumably. A few empty boxes cluttered the space, but it was far from a disaster zone.

She imagined she could smell his scent lingering in the office. Her computer dinged. No time for fanciful notions. Time to get this job.

Emily from SDT appeared on the screen. "Sloane, I'm glad you could meet with me today. I don't have a lot of time and I'm sure you're busy, which makes Zoom calls the best. Neither of us has to fight traffic for a fifteen-minute meeting."

Sloane's smile came easily. "Absolutely."

"As you know, I wanted to talk to you about your progress with your social media campaign."

Sloane nodded and kept her eyes on the screen. She'd memorized her notes. "We're making good progress. Our follower count is up thirty percent on Instagram and forty percent on TikTok since my original meeting with you. Sales at the open location have risen by fifteen percent in the same time period. I'm really pleased."

"That's great." Emily pursed her lips. "But sales aren't what I wanted to talk to you about."

Sloane pinned the smile to her face, relieved the camera was focused on her face and not her bobbing foot. Nerves were skateboarding up and down the inner walls of her stomach. "They're not?"

"No. I saw a story in the *Union-Tribune* about some neighborhood residents not being pleased about the new location. They aren't happy you're moving in and are making a ruckus."

Shit. The nerves did a twisty 720 in her belly. Shaun White would be proud. Sloane injected an upbeat tone into her voice. She even added a slight chuckle. "I'm not sure 'ruckus' is the right word."

Emily lowered her glasses to peer down her nose at Sloane, an impressive maneuver given the medium. "Whatever word you choose to use doesn't change the fact that they're not happy."

Sloane spoke as calmly as she could. "It's just a few people. It's all under control."

"Are you sure?" Emily asked.

Sloane clenched her hands into tight balls in her lap. "Yes. This is a minor speed bump."

"I was talking with Preston and he's lined up a celebrity endorser to tweet and make a few TikToks about the exercise bike he's marketing that he assures me will go viral."

Yeah, because the ass-kisser liked talking out of his ass. "That sounds great."

See, she could be professional when the situation called for it.

Emily chuckled like she didn't fully believe Sloane's words of praise. "It is, but you don't want to get too far behind the eight ball. I like you, Sloane, but you've got to show me something. I've checked out the social media accounts. You're quick-witted. I really love what you've done with the whole SugarBae thing, but you could be doing more."

Sloane nodded. "I'm doing my best to show that August, aka SugarBae, and by extension, Sugar Blitz, are more than a viral speech."

"I understand, but the fact is you were handed a golden opportunity when SugarBae went viral. People really responded to it and him. They're really interested in him and his personal life. Give the people what they want. I've noticed the follower uptick has slowed a bit the past few days. Yes, I keep my own stats. Is there a way he can get the protestors on his side? They're fairly quiet now, but that doesn't mean they will stay that way."

The nerves in her stomach completed five straight 360 flips. "I . . . ummm . . ."

Emily sighed. "You want this job? You've got to earn it."

Right. No biggie.

* * *

"Sloane?" August entered his office, but no erstwhile social media manager was waiting. Her abandoned laptop and notebook on the table were the only indications she'd been inside. Where was she?

His phone chimed with a text. He dug the device out of his pocket and read the message from Sloane.

I needed some air. I'll be back this afternoon.

August blew out a breath. Damn. Had her meeting not gone well? He hoped not. He knew how badly she wanted that job. So bad she'd agreed to work with the man she typically avoided. But maybe she was fine, and he was overreacting. He'd ask when she returned.

As he turned to exit, his eyes fell on the open notebook. He jerked back in pure shock as he registered the words on the page. What the hell? He circled around the desk and collapsed into the chair. With shaky fingers, he picked up the red journal.

* * *

When the front door opened thirty minutes later, August set aside the chair he'd been attempting—and failing—to put together due to his inability to concentrate and quickly rose from the floor. "Hey. You okay?"

Sloane came to a stop a few feet away from him. "Yeah. Why do you ask?"

"Your text said you needed some air."

Her left shoulder lifted. "We've been cooped up in here. I wanted to take a walk. Stretch my legs."

"That's it?"

"Yep." Her poor attempt at an upbeat tone did nothing to hide the turmoil swirling in her eyes. Damn, he hated seeing her this way.

"Okay. Well, I'm glad you're back. I wanted to talk."

"Why? You never talk."

A grin tugged at his lips. Being around Sloane was good and

bad for his self-esteem. He . . . appreciated a plainspoken woman. "Today is different."

She crossed her arms. "What's going on?"

"I changed my mind about going out with a SugarBaeby."

Her eyes blinked rapidly, her mouth falling open, but she recovered quickly enough. Because she was Sloane and could never be kept down for long. Another thing he . . . appreciated about her.

"Wow," she said. "That's . . . not what I expected you to say. That's great."

Yeah, great. He was going to help her get that job if it was the last thing he did. This was the least he could do for her. Even if it was the last thing he wanted to do. But they were never going to be a "we." Hell, could he blame her? The past still swirled between them. She hadn't disagreed with him about their kiss being a mistake. He'd blown another chance and it was time he accepted that. Besides, if he wanted to be bold like he said he did, there was no time like the present. Even if the thought of it made him want to throw up.

Now, her face turned suspicious. "Why?"

She did know him, more than he'd realized. More than anyone other than Donovan and Nicholas. He decided to play dumb.

"Why what?"

She hit him with a don't-play-that-shit-with-me look. "Why the change of heart?"

Telling her he felt bad for her and wanted to help her out would go over about as well as telling her she wasn't a good social media manager. He'd lose a limb or two in the process. He rather liked having limbs.

The truth was he'd seen her "Pros and Cons of Getting August to Date a SugarBaeby" list in her notebook.

Pro: Nail the SDT job down.

Con: Coerce August into doing something he doesn't want to do.

Pro: Pay rent and student loans.

Con: ???

Pro: Great social media content!

Con:

She'd actually written something there, but had scribbled it out, so he hadn't been able to read it. He'd tried to think of what it could've been, but ultimately it didn't matter.

He couldn't let her lose an opportunity because he was uncomfortable doing something people did every day—date. He'd be damned if he was the reason she didn't get the job of her dreams. He wanted the best for her. He cared about her. Always had. Always would.

"I realized you were right."

"How?" Suspicious eyes let him know she was still smelling bullshit.

"I need to step out of my comfort zone if we want this social media campaign to be a success. It will make great content, and maybe I'll meet someone special."

"By going on a date with a SugarBaeby."

"Yes." He still refused and always would refuse to use that term. "It makes sense. They're active on social media. They live in the neighborhood. Paige thought it was a great idea."

"You—you already set up a date?" Astonishment covered her face and filled her voice. He would hazard to say she'd never been more shocked in her life.

"I have." He'd done it before he lost his nerve. "I wanted to broach the idea with her first since there would be the expectation that the date be chronicled on social media. That's still the plan, right?"

Now she looked like she'd swallowed a whole lemon. "Yep, that's still the plan." She went silent for a beat. "Paige doesn't have an issue with the social media part?"

"No. We agreed we'd go on a date, see if there's a connection. Even if there isn't, her follower count will get a boost."

Her face smoothed into a bland expression. "Great. Seems like you two have everything figured out. It'll be a little weird spying on your date, but I'll be there with bells on. In the background, of course."

"Silent bells?" He smiled. "No coaching me? I was looking forward to you giving me instructions through Bluetooth like you're my personal Cyrano."

Finally, a spark of humor lit her eyes. "You'll survive."

Chapter Twenty-Four

Twelve years ago . . .

Sloane paced back and forth in her bedroom. This was it. She'd practiced her speech over and over again the past two weeks, ever since she got word that her brother was coming home for a day during spring break, and he was bringing August with him.

She stopped in front of the dresser mirror and inspected herself. Not that she was an expert, but her makeup looked great. Thank God for YouTube tutorials. For her outfit, she'd gone for casually sexy. She had no clue if she could pull it off, but she had to try. The jean skirt barely covered her ass, and it showed off her long legs to perfection. Her top dipped a little more in the front than the shirts she usually wore, but it offered a tasteful amount of cleavage. She tugged the collar down. Maybe tasteful wasn't what she should be going for.

She checked her phone. It was after 1 A.M. Everyone was asleep, or at least in their bedrooms. Still, she tiptoed down the stairs, avoiding the step that squeaked, made a detour through the kitchen, grabbed the lemon meringue pie her mom had made, and escaped out the back door to the porch.

When she was settled, she held her phone between shaking hands. Was she going to do this? Yes. She had no choice. Not if she didn't want to live her life with regrets. She sent the text.

She knew he'd be up. He said he often had trouble sleeping. Two minutes later, she was rewarded with the creaking of the door behind her.

"Sloane, what's—"

She stood to greet him. His mouth dropped open. "Wow. You look nice."

"Thanks." She shyly held out the pie. "Want some pie?"

"Yeah, yeah."

They settled on the porch and ate. Well, he ate and she watched him. Her stomach would not be happy with her if she tried to put anything in it. Finally, he set aside his plate. "What's up? You couldn't sleep?"

She shook her head. Time for her speech. "I have a lot of decisions to make. I've been accepted to UCLA and Northwestern. Both are dream schools. I can either stay here close to my family or go halfway across the country."

He studied her with dark eyes. "Which way are you leaning?"

"It depends."

"On what?"

Say it! Say it!

After a moment of hesitation, she answered.

"This."

She bridged the gap between them and pressed her lips against his for the first time in reality. In her dreams, she'd done it a thousand times. Reality blew fantasy out of the water. His lips were soft and plush. When his mouth parted on a gasp, she instinctively licked the seam between his lips. Anything to be closer to him. He tasted delicious. Warm and sweet. Her lips slid once, twice against his.

Then, she felt it. A light pressure as he returned the kiss, his mouth capturing hers. The kiss was perfect. The moment was perfect.

Then, she felt nothing. Her eyes flew open.

August had stumbled to his feet and put the width of the porch between them. His eyes were wild, his chest heaving. "Sloane! What the fuck was that?"

She rose to her feet and closed the distance between them. "August, I want to be with you. For real. I love you, and I think you love me too."

He shook his head. "No, you've got it all wrong."

She couldn't give up. This was too important. "Do I? We talk all the time. We share our dreams with each other. Our deepest thoughts."

He waved his hands, like that would negate what she said. "I have a girlfriend. I'm going to marry her."

Sloane stumbled back. "You're going to . . . *marry* her?"

His eyes squeezed shut for a second. "Yes. We've known each other since we were twelve. We promised we would always be there for each other and get married."

No, she couldn't accept that. Wouldn't. It made no sense.

"But you love me. Whatever you have with her can't compare to what we have."

"Sloane, we talk on the phone. That's it."

Wow. Pain lanced straight through her, but she wouldn't let it fell her. She couldn't. "All the time. We talk all the time. Way more than whatever you told my brother, and don't give me that BS about respecting my privacy. You didn't tell him because what we have is special, and you don't want to share it with the world."

He shook his head. "Sloane, no."

She spoke through tears now. She couldn't stop them. All her dashed dreams poured out of her in wrenching gasps. "I can love you better than she can. I already do, and you know it."

"Sloane, you're just a kid. I'm marrying Melinda. I promised her. Whatever you think we have is all in your head." He went back into the house.

Leaving her broken and alone.

Chapter Twenty-Five

Felicia and Sloane's older sister, Shana, both stared at Sloane like she'd lost her ever-loving mind.

"Let me see if I got this straight," Felicia finally said from her perch in Sloane's living room armchair. "You're helping the guy you've been in love with for a decade date other women. How and in what world does that make sense? Cuz in this world, the one *we* live in, I'm not getting it."

Lying to her best friend and sister should be illegal, but she'd been lying to herself for so long she didn't know how to stop. "I don't know. I mean, it does make sense. I mean, I need to get over him. I mean, I was over him. I *am* over him. And hey, I haven't been in love with him for over a decade." That would make her pathetic. Ridiculous. Her, fixated on a man? No way, no how. Her happiness depended on herself, not a man. "It was a teenage crush. I'm no longer a teenager, so I should be over him, right? Right?"

Felicia's face scrunched up in polite disagreement. "Maybe."

Ugh. "We kissed. He said it was a mistake. I agreed, because it was."

Shana, who was sitting next to her, twisted to give her a big-sister look. "Are you sure? After all, I was the one who was there to dry your tears when he broke your heart." Very true. Once August and Donovan left, she'd run straight into her sister's room and confessed all. She'd be forever grateful her sister had been home for spring break that week, too.

And yet . . . "That was a long time ago, so yes, I'm sure."

"We can beat him up if you want."

Sloane glared at her sister. "Why are you here again?"

"Officially, to have a girls' night without my darling husband and children. Unofficially, to live vicariously through my sister and her love life."

"I don't have a love life," Sloane said through gritted teeth.

"Well, you should."

Felicia held up her hands. "Sorry, Sloane, but I agree with Shana. Maybe you do need to go on a date. If August can date, so can you."

Sloane rolled her eyes. "It's not a competition."

"No, but you've wasted too much time thinking about this dude. If you're not going to pursue him, find someone else. Time to get back on the horse and ride him over and over again, honey."

Felicia and Shana shared a high five across the living room table.

"You're terrible. Both of you." Sloane tapped her nails on the arm of her sofa. "But it was his idea. He set up the date himself, so obviously he wants to do it. If he wants to step out of his comfort zone, it's my duty to help him."

Shana wrapped an arm around her shoulders. "Even if it kills you?"

Yes. She shook her head to rid it of that unwanted reaction. "It's not. He's a client. Getting involved with a client is ethically murky, at best."

Felicia side-eyed her. "It's a temporary assignment."

I know. "And I'm not going to embarrass myself over him again.

Once was more than enough. That was enough embarrassment for two lifetimes."

Felicia opened her mouth like she was going to argue and offer up more salient points. Sloane couldn't let her. No more wishing and daydreaming. She wasn't seventeen anymore.

"And also, it's one date. One. I'll barely be there. I'll be all the way across the room."

"Reading body language. Trying to interpret their facial expressions. Seeing if they're leaning into each other. Laughing at jokes. Touching."

Hell on earth, in other words. Sloane fell back on the couch and grabbed a cushion. She yelled into its microfiber material, then smacked her face with it a few times for good measure.

"Feel better?" Felicia asked.

That would be a negative. *Whack!* One more time just to see.

"No." She groaned. What the hell had she gotten herself into? "He's going to be with another woman. Just like last time."

Shana's brows creased with worry. "All kidding aside, you've got to stop blaming yourself for what happened."

"Do I? I went full Meredith Grey: 'Pick me, choose me, love me.' Do you know the levels of embarrassment I still feel all these years later?"

"First of all, Shonda Rhimes will answer for her crimes one day. More importantly, you were a kid, not a grown-ass adult like Meredith, so your foolishness was way more understandable."

Was it?

Chapter Twenty-Six

*W*hat the ever-loving fuck was she doing here?

Oh, yeah.

She, Sloane Renee Dell, was here to document August's date with a woman who wasn't her.

How had she gotten here? Could she leave? Just walk out and continue walking toward the sun until she got too close to it and melted like the Wicked Witch of the West?

Sloane blew out a breath. Okay, she was being melodramatic. That imagery made no sense.

But hell, wasn't she a mashup of Icarus and the Wicked Witch? She'd thought she could handle hanging out with August for eight-plus hours of the day and old feelings wouldn't come rushing back to the surface. Wasn't she evil for using him to advance her own agenda, even if he was fully aware of said agenda and had agreed to it? Even halfway participated in it?

Was continuing to participate in it.

Oh, God. Sloane sat up straighter on her stool. None of that mattered at the moment.

She'd taken a seat at the bar because it gave her a good view of the front door. And didn't it just.

August and Paige were right outside the restaurant. She could see them through the door's oh-so-helpful wide-paned window. He looked better than anything she'd seen on the menu. Dark-wash jeans skimmed his powerful thighs. A lightweight red short-sleeve sweater complemented his rich brown skin and molded to his wide shoulders and muscular arms. Paige was wearing a cute dress, but whatever.

Sloane's gaze drew inexorably back to August. Not only was he ridiculously handsome, he was also courteous, holding the door open for Paige and slowing his stride to match hers as they went up to the maître d'. He hadn't spotted her yet. Good. Maybe she could fix her face before he did. Wipe the drool off her chin.

The host led them to a table toward the back of the restaurant. Sloane settled her tab at the bar and followed at a discreet distance. She'd already informed the restaurant's manager she was there to chronicle the date and not to be weirded out if she or the staff saw Sloane taking photos. Still, she didn't want to be too close—for her own peace of mind and for the sake of the date. It was supposed to be real. August was going to make an honest effort. So she'd give the potentially soon-to-be happy couple their space and pretend her heart wasn't splintering into tiny little pieces inside her chest.

And at the end of this adventure/fiasco—she couldn't decide which was more accurate—thanks to all the successful promo, she'd get a job out of it and August and Sugar Blitz would have a successful launch of their newest location. Everyone wins. Throw some confetti. Hold a parade through downtown San Diego.

But first she had to get through this date. A stabbing pain hit her square in the chest. Sloane slammed a hand to her ribs like she could stop the ache from spreading through her entire body. Oh, my God, he was on a *date*. Four-letter words were truly the worst. But there was no time to freak out. She'd save that for later. She had a job to do.

Earlier, she'd scoped out a table in the opposite corner hidden behind a potted plant where she could watch through the leaves and take pics. She made her way to her hiding spot and got into position.

Sloane took a deep breath and focused on her subjects. August and Paige had settled at their table and were currently inspecting menus while they chatted. Nothing strange or noteworthy about that. She snapped a quick pic and captioned it "First-date vibes" in her notes before returning her attention to the potential soulmates.

Playing armchair psychologist wasn't her thing, but she couldn't help but notice their body language. Paige was doing most of the talking, which was the least surprising development ever, given August's penchant to never speak.

He doesn't have much trouble talking to you.

Although he wasn't speaking, August listened attentively. Like he cared.

They weren't encroaching on each other's space, but they did lean toward each other. They looked good together, even if it killed her to admit it. And it damned near did.

Sloane finally gave her full attention to Paige. Dark brown curls framed her face. As befitting a social media maven, her makeup was flawless, including her fabulous smoky eye application that made her dark eyes look huge and luminous. Her dress, a cute casual red sundress, showed off toned arms and was cut low enough to tease at cleavage and make her date long to see more. A perfect first-date outfit. Damn it.

After the waiter came and took their orders, Sloane took a few more photos. Her finger, working on its own accord, lingered on the zoom as she zeroed in on August's mouth and took a photo. She was a pervert. But his mouth was perfect. She'd only felt it twice against hers, but she still remembered how it felt in crystal-clear detail. How could a perfect mouth only get more perfect over the years? Both lips were perfectly plump, neither too thin or too big. They rounded enticingly as he formed words.

Sloane set the phone down. "Move," she muttered to the couple who'd stopped to talk to August instead of continuing on to their own table. One of them was blocking her view. Her displeasure stemmed from the fact that she couldn't do her job. It had nothing to do with her wanting every chance she could get to stare at August. Nope. Not at all.

Finally, the couple left. As soon as they did, the waiter returned with Paige's and August's orders. So did Sloane's server. She accepted the food with a "thanks" and turned in time to see August and Paige take their first bites. Oh, happy day.

His tongue peeked out as he raised a forkful of pasta to those perfect lips. Sloane's grip on her phone faltered as a rush of heat swamped her.

This is what her life had become. She was jealous of fettuccini and fork tines.

Get a grip, Sloane.

Paige's hands were windmilling, and her lips were moving at a rapid pace. Whatever story she was telling had her worked up. August was giving her his full attention.

Sloane couldn't make out any words, which was for the best. Whatever Paige was saying was enthralling. Second date coming right up. Yippee.

Sloane shook her shoulders, like that's all it would take to rid her of the dark thoughts.

Eye on the prize. August having a good date was for the best for Sugar Blitz and for Sloane's own goals, which did not include licking and savoring every inch of August's body, starting with those lips, like he was a butter-pecan triple-scoop ice-cream cone.

She took a quick snap, capturing the exact moment both Paige and August were laughing, because wasn't she *awesome* at her job, and added it to Sugar Blitz's Instagram story along with a few heart-eyes emojis. *Gag.* Being a social media maven officially sucked. Why had she ever thought this was her calling?

She checked the stats on the story. Every addition brought more clicks. Yippee. Time to pop some champagne. But not while she was on the job. She turned away from the *August and Paige Show* and half-heartedly stuffed a piece of bread in her mouth and chewed by rote as she dispiritedly contemplated her life choices.

So what if it made her feel like she was on a date with August and his soulmate because she'd inadvertently ordered the same pasta dish as August? That didn't make her pathetic. Okay, yes it did. But he had good taste. The seafood pasta was the best she'd tasted in a long time.

An odd noise cut through the low-level hum of chatter and dings of cutlery in the restaurant. It sounded almost like a . . . ? Sloane twisted around, her mouth promptly falling to the floor. Her ears hadn't been deceiving her. What had sounded like a sob was *absolutely* a sob.

And it was coming from Paige. Her hands covered her face, but she was definitely crying. Tears seeped between her fingers. Her shoulders vibrated with her every breath.

What in the world . . . ?

Chapter Twenty-Seven

August tentatively reached out to pat Paige's shoulder and offer up some inane words of comfort, but before he made contact, she dropped her forearms to the table and whacked her head against the table. *Thwack, thwack.*

Shit.

How had things gone south so quickly? The date hadn't been going bad, really. True, there was no chemistry, no heart-stopping moment when he spotted her. No waiting with bated breath for her to notice him or pay him the slightest bit of attention. But it was fine. Until it wasn't. One minute they were having a decent, if not great time, the next she was crying her heart out.

Wincing, he awkwardly patted her shoulder. "Hey, hey, it's not that bad."

"Yes, it is," she said in a wobbly voice through her tears. And to her, it was.

She'd noticed the waiter's nameplate, and that's all it took. Mike. Such an innocent, ubiquitous name. Emphasis on ubiquitous. Mike happened to be the name of her ex, who'd broken up with her three months ago after four years together, instead of proposing like she'd been expecting.

Despite her flirty behavior in their previous encounters, this was her first date since the breakup. She was totally over her ex. At least that was the story she'd peddled. He'd suspected that wasn't the case when Mike's name came up while they waited for their food.

"Mike never would have taken me here. He's allergic to oregano, so that means no Italian restaurants. Do you know he had the nerve to call me this morning when he saw on Instagram that I was going out with you? I knew I should've blocked him."

He'd hummed in commiseration and steered the conversation elsewhere. All to no avail, ultimately.

Another loud cry spilled from her lips. They were starting to attract attention. When they'd first entered the room, most of the other patrons had whispered and taken photos they'd undoubtedly say was in a surreptitious manner before getting bored and returning to their meals. That was no longer the case. Folks were now being bold and brazen with their phones.

He leaned down to whisper to the top of her head. "Hey, do you want to get out of here?"

She raised her face, mascara streaking down both cheeks, her lower lip trembling. "Why are men so horrible?"

He did the only thing he could do. He took one for the team. "I don't know. I'm sorry."

She sobbed harder. Wrong answer, apparently.

He needed to turn this situation around. Now. He leaned down and whispered in her ear.

Her head shot up. "What? How could you?" she screeched.

Fuuuccck.

Her expression stiffened as she noticed the other diners watching them. "Oh, my God, I have to get out of here. I need to be alone." She leaped from her seat.

Mike, the waiter, chose that inopportune time to make his reappearance. "Everything okay, guys?"

"I hate you!" she yelled in poor Mike's face before pushing past him and sprinting out of the room quicker than half the running backs in the NFL.

Shit. August rushed after her, but by the time he got outside, her car was already streaking out of the parking lot. Fucking hell. He blew out a breath. This was why he didn't date. *Wasn't it?*

He turned at the sound of a clearing throat behind him.

Sloane stood at the door with a raised eyebrow and her hands on her hips.

He'd almost forgotten she was there witnessing his worst first date ever, which was a miracle in and of itself. From the moment he'd stepped foot in the restaurant, he'd sensed her presence and spotted her at the bar, though she was sitting in the corner. It was like she wore a beacon only he had the right frequency for.

She'd done her best to remain as unobtrusive as possible, but he still knew where she was at every moment during the date from hell.

And he'd just embarrassed himself and upset another woman in her presence. Fucking hell. Yeah, he was batting a thousand tonight.

She came a step closer. "Is Paige okay?"

He squeezed his forehead between his thumb and index finger. "I hope so. She said she needed to be alone."

Sloane nodded, sympathy swimming in her brown eyes.

And now he had to go back inside and face the stares and accusatory glares and muttered denunciations as he returned to pay the bill and apologize to poor Mike.

He took another deep breath and squared his shoulders. No time like the present to face the firing squad and get it over with.

Sloane stopped him with a hand on his arm. "No need."

It took him a second to process her words. Because she was touching him. Of her own accord. It didn't matter that it was the most innocuous, meant-absolutely-nothing touch. Sloane was touching him. He hadn't recognized how much he'd been craving that contact until now. Like a man stuck in a desert for a decade who finally spotted a waterfall. Was it a mirage? He focused on the spot where her long, slim fingers pressed against the bare skin of his forearm. He'd never been so thankful for San Diego weather, where wearing long sleeves made sense so little of the time.

She was looking at him expectantly. Right. She'd spoken and was waiting for a response and was finding it very strange—no, make that *amusing* based on the grin playing at the corners of her perfect lips—he hadn't provided one yet. He replayed her last words.

"Why no need?"

"Because I apologized for the scene and paid for y'all's dinner already. Can't have them thinking Black folks dine and dash, can we?" she continued at his questioning look.

His lips quirked. "Nope. Can't have that."

"And I left a good tip. That poor waiter is probably traumatized."

August groaned. "FML."

Sloane laughed. "No, he's good. Said he has a story to tell for the rest of his life."

August rubbed his eyes. "Wow."

"That's what he said!"

August lowered his hand and glared. "You're not helping."

"Yes, I am. I paid for your dinner so you don't have to face the crowd in there, who are all waiting for act two. They're hoping we're in intermission. I need you to pay me back ASAPtually. You're the rich one, not me."

Sighing, August nodded. "You're right. I owe you. How much was it?" He reached into his back pocket for his wallet.

She squinted at him, wrinkling her nose. "It's been a long night. Why don't you buy me a drink as a down payment? Not in there," she added when she saw him looking past her at the wooden double doors of the restaurant. She jerked her chin to the right. "I've been wanting to try out that bar."

No guy to meet for an actual date there? That wasn't . . . displeasing to hear. Still, she wasn't asking him on a date. She wanted to unwind. And after the last half hour from Hades, so did he. "Let's do it."

She offered up a genuine smile and he was surprised he remained upright. Her smile was killer, and it punched him right in the gut like he'd gone a round with the champ. The smile curved her plump lips, highlighting her magnificent cheekbones, and turned her eyes, already beautiful, into sparkling orbs. And he had to act chill. Like this was no big deal. Because it wasn't. They were friends, or at least moving in that direction, and that's all it was. Hell, she'd cheerfully sent him off on a date with another woman, after all.

They walked in companionable silence to the bar, the Secret Cove, a few doors down from the restaurant. August quickly looked around as they stepped inside. She'd wanted to come here? How had she heard of the place? It wasn't a swanky place where people came to see and be seen, a place people would be constantly talking about on social media. It was clean and warm, yes, but swanky, no. Well-worn wooden floorboards creaked under their feet as they made their way inside.

"Hey, welcome," a woman called from behind the bar. "Take a seat wherever you want."

August looked down at Sloane. Fought the urge to lay a hand

at the small of her back. This was not a date. "Do you have a preference?"

She looked around. "Let's sit at a booth. It offers a little more privacy."

He nodded his agreement and followed her to the back of the room.

"What happened?" Sloane asked after sliding into the booth. "I'm gonna assume something set her off. I mean, I'm gonna hope you have at least a little bit of game and that you don't have a habit of sending women running and crying into the night."

He shot her a look as he sat opposite her. "Thanks for your faith."

After their server, a redhead named Charli, stopped by to take their orders, August quickly explained about Mike.

Sloane nodded in sympathy. "Yeah, sometimes that's all it takes to have the memories of a past relationship come crashing down on you, and before you know it, you're blubbering in a restaurant." She scrunched up her nose. "Been there, done that."

"Jim, right?"

She looked surprised he knew. "Yeah."

Like he could ever forget anything he knew about her.

"What happened, if you don't mind me asking?" What had that fool done to lose her? He'd wondered more than once over the years.

Sloane waved her hand. "Nah, it's cool. I did witness your date from hell. Basically, as you know, my dad deals with a gambling addiction. He was going through a rough time when I was in Chicago, and I had no idea how to handle it. It was a really rough time for me, my dad, and my whole family. Jim was less than supportive, to put it mildly. I knew I needed to be around my family, so I returned to San Diego." She quieted.

August covered her hand on the table. "He hurt you."

Her gaze fell to the connection, but she didn't pull away. Her eyes, full of the sadness of the past, lifted to him. "He did."

"I'm sorry." He squeezed her hand. He wished he could offer more. Do more. Whatever she needed to feel better.

Her lips lifted in a small smile. "Thank you for the apology he never gave. You're a good guy, MOTY."

His heart soared. Maybe, just maybe, there was hope for them. "Anytime."

"I know."

Charli returned with their waters, beer, and a bowl of peanuts. August bit back a growl of disappointment when Sloane slipped her hand away to take a sip of her drink.

Sloane set the glass down and steepled her fingers together. "Enough about me and my less-than-illustrious dating history. Back to you. What was the final straw tonight? One second, Paige was there, albeit crying hysterically, and the next, she was out of there like a rocket."

August winced. He could lie and save all the face in the world. But he made it a practice to never lie. People deserved the truth, even if it made him look like the biggest ass. "I might have told her to drop that zero and get herself a hero."

Sloane froze for a millisecond, then water came spewing out of her mouth. Thankfully for him, the liquid only sprayed so far before gravity took its toll. August lifted his gaze from the table, now dotted with little droplets of water, to Sloane. Her shoulders were shaking and tears were already seeping out of her eyes. Great. He'd made two women cry tonight.

"Why . . . why?" she said, in between fits of laughter. She wiped her eyes and tried again. "Why—why would you . . ." More uncontrolled giggles. It wasn't that damned funny. She held up a hand. "Okay, I'm going to stop, promise. Why would you say that?"

She ended on a snort of laughter, but August decided to ignore that little slip.

He shifted his shoulders, seeking some relief from the tightness in his muscles. Saying dumb shit made you tense up, apparently. "I was trying to lighten the mood. I was hoping to get a laugh out of her."

Sloane took another sip of water and actually managed to swallow it all this time. "Yeah, well, that didn't work. But at least you tried." She pressed her lips together, unsuccessfully, because another cackle escaped.

August took a sip of his beer. "Great. Now you're laughing."

Sloane's lips quivered again. "Isn't that what you wanted?"

"I wanted laughter *with* me, not at me."

"Yeah, well, I want fifty gold bars to miraculously show up at my front door, but that ain't gonna happen either. Where did you even come up with that expression?"

August shifted on the hard bench again. Wood was not the most forgiving of surfaces. Just his luck, he'd end up with a splinter in his ass. "When I was little, I used to come home from school and Pops would always be watching talk shows. He moved in with me and my father after my mother passed away. Maury was his number-one guy, but he made room for Ricki Lake, Montel, and Jerry Springer. He watched them, and if I wanted to be in the same room as him, I had to watch too."

Her expression softened. "That's sweet."

He shrugged. "We ended my after-school break by watching Oprah. Had to end on some class, he would always say."

She nodded. "Yes, yes, of course."

"I will have you know there were many pearls of wisdom doled out on *Ricki Lake*."

Sloane's eyes twinkled in the light. "Like the best way to duck a paternity test?"

"No, you smartass. The best way to handle it when people boo as soon as you walk onstage."

"Oh, do tell."

"You egg them on, of course."

Sloane's laughter slowly turned into a groan. "I can't believe I got us in this mess. I'm sure this story is already spreading across social media like wildfire."

Damn it. "Is it going to hurt your chances to get that job?"

She blew out a breath. "Maybe. I don't know. I hope not. I'll do my best, but controlling social media isn't actually possible, despite what us social media managers tell ourselves."

Her phone chimed. She picked it up, looked at the screen, groaned again, and flipped the phone screen down on the table.

"What's up? More bad news?"

"I . . ." She shook her head. "My best friend Felicia wants to set me up on a date."

"And do you want to date?" He was proud of himself. He got the question out without sounding like he was choking. He sounded almost normal. She had no idea his insides were twisting themselves into knots it would take a lifetime to untangle.

Sloane traced the rings, left by a thousand beer bottles, in the wooden table. "Before I quit my job, I might have said something casual. Now, I feel like I shouldn't even do that. I should be concentrating on getting a new job and reestablishing some consistency in my career."

He sensed there was more, so he forced himself to say, "But . . ."

She lifted her gaze and bestowed a soft smile on him. "But, sometimes when I'm alone with my thoughts, I think it would be nice to have someone I can share life's burdens with." She chuckled. "Someone I know will listen and understand when I complain about my boss stealing my ideas, which led immediately to me not getting the promotion I deserved, and quitting."

He understood. While there was no denying he had a good life, he sometimes had those same thoughts about wanting a partner to share life's inevitable ups and downs with.

His phone dinged, drawing his attention. "Paige said she got home okay."

"That's good. It's a no-go on another date with Paige, I'm assuming," she said.

"Yeah, pretty sure that's a safe assumption." August took a sip of his beer.

Silence fell, the only sounds coming courtesy of the '80s yacht-rock song playing in the background and the chatter of the other patrons and the clink of glasses. They drank and munched on the peanuts. They'd never hung out together, just the two of them, outside of work. Over the years, he'd always been welcome at her family's gatherings. But even then, she'd make herself scarce, or Donovan would be there to act as a buffer.

Sloane lifted her beer bottle. "Cheers to better days ahead."

He clinked bottles with her and tried his damnedest not to be jealous of the glass that was fucking lucky to touch her lips. The hint of tongue that peeked out as she sipped enthralled him.

"What?" she asked, because no doubt he looked like a lovesick fool staring at her with heart eyes.

"I've never seen you drink before," he said. Points to him for improvising on the spot.

She laughed. "I'm not a kid anymore."

"Even when you were, you weren't the type to do much underage drinking."

"Yeah, after my one indiscretion in high school, I was good."

He laughed, recalling how she'd called him that night. "Good times. You getting drunk off Mike's."

She threw a peanut at him and made a face when he snatched it out of the air. "Don't laugh at me, Mr. Good Reflexes. I was in high school!"

He cracked the shell open and popped the nut into his mouth. "Mmm, delicious. Thanks."

"You're welcome." She rolled her eyes, then lifted her chin at his beer. "Is that your drink of choice?"

"When I'm in the mood for a beer. I like whiskey, but hard stuff isn't exactly good for the body."

"Your body is in great shape." She groaned. "And no, that wasn't some kind of terrible come-on."

His lips twisted. "You sure? It sounded very come-on-y to me."

"I meant that you're a pro athlete, and I admire the work you put in to make sure the tool of your craft is in top-notch condition." A prissy note entered her voice. It was the hottest shit ever.

"So you do think I'm fine. I knew it!" What was he doing? He was flirting, duh. The better question was why was he flirting? She'd just talked about wanting to date other men. There'd been no mention of him. Hell, she'd happily sent him on a date with another woman. They'd agreed their kiss was a mistake.

"I think one date and the fawning people are doing over Sugar-Bae is going to your head." Her smile indicated she knew he was joking and was giving him shit for fun too. Like the old times.

He considered her. "How did you get into social media?"

"You mean as a career?"

He nodded.

She considered the question for a moment. "I was on it, like most people our age. I've always liked it. You can be creative and share your life and see what makes others tick. Find likeminded individuals for whatever your interests are. You might think you're alone, but I bet pretty much anything I own that you're not. It became a place of community for me. Professionally, I can indulge my nerdy and creative sides. Looking at the metrics and seeing what works and what doesn't. What's the best time to post? What app works best for what content? What content will people respond to? I love trying to bring people together over a shared interest."

"That's why you wanted me to date."

She stilled. "Right. People are invested in you, and they want the best for you. You spoke to them, and they care what happens to you. They want you to find someone worthy of you."

"And you?"

Sloane picked up a peanut and popped it in her mouth, all without looking at him. "And me what?"

"Do you want me to find someone worthy of me?"

She took a long pull of her beer before replying. "Of course. Why wouldn't I?"

Because I rejected you all those years ago.

But he couldn't address the elephant in the room. Didn't want to hear that she'd moved on long ago and never dreamed about what could have been. "This isn't what you signed up for."

She shrugged. "I signed up to make you and Sugar Blitz social media stars to ensure the success of your second location. There was no one right way to get there. Yeah, we've taken an unexpected detour, but that doesn't mean I didn't know there would be bumps in the road. And I also deserve a ton of credit for using two clichés about driving in one sentence."

August's lips twitched. He tipped his bottle toward her. "Consider credit delivered."

"Thanks. In any case, now that you have this date under your belt, you now know what *not* to say on future dates."

"Right. More dates."

August blew out a breath. How had he gotten himself into this mess? The only woman he wanted to go out with was sitting across the table, determined to send him on dates with other women.

What the fuck was he doing?

Chapter Twenty-Eight

*S*loane leaned across the table. "What did you say?"

Loud cheers from the bar drowned out August's response. They looked toward the bar, where four men had crowded another guy and chanted, "Shots, shots, shots." They whooped it up when their buddy downed four shots in a row.

Laughing, Sloane caught August's eye. "Bachelor party," they said in unison.

"Maybe we should go," she said, raising her voice to be heard over the ruckus. August tossed a few bills on the table and they skedaddled.

Outside the bar, Sloane happily inhaled the fresh air and went to slip on her jacket.

"Here, let me."

She hesitated a second before handing the denim jacket to August and turning her back to him. He stepped closer, his body heat warming her. Sloane sucked in a breath. Was it her imagination or did he linger over his task as she slipped her arms into the sleeves and he swept his hands across her shoulders to make sure the jacket settled properly? Odds were she was being fanciful, but her heart trembled anyway.

She turned. He didn't move away. He smelled wonderful. And she was ridiculous. *The kiss was a mistake, remember?* And yet she still wanted him. But that was her little secret, thank God.

Time to get moving. "My car's down there."

"I'll walk you to your car."

Ever the gentleman. Sloane headed down the sidewalk with August at her side. Like this was a date. Except it wasn't. Sloane stifled a sigh. They reached her car, but she didn't make a move to get inside. Instead, she basked in the comfortable silence between them. Basked in simply being with him.

August rubbed the back of his neck. "If I didn't say so earlier, thanks for coming tonight and enduring my weirdest date in a minute, and then staying to cheer me up when it went all the way left."

Sloane grinned. "I don't know if it went all the way left. I mean she didn't toss a drink in your face. No fights broke out."

He blanched. "You're right. It could've been way worse." His eyes crinkled at the corners, a detail she had no business noticing. She'd blame it on the one beer she'd had. The fact that alcohol dulled your senses, not made you more aware, was way beside the point.

"But still, I had a good time tonight, thanks to you," he continued, mercifully oblivious to the ramblings of her mind. "You're good people, Sloane Dell."

She was just going to ignore the warmth spreading like melted wax through her entire body. She was also going to ignore the way he looked at her. Like he really saw her and appreciated her for her, not just his best friend's little sister or the teen girl who'd thrown herself at him.

"You're welcome." Her voice came out a little softer than she intended, but he still heard her. He nodded, his eyes going all serious.

"I learned something tonight."

His voice, his face mesmerized her. She couldn't look away. "What?"

"Dating isn't so bad if it's done with the right person. It's actually kind of the best."

Breath lodged in her throat. Her vision went hazy for a moment as shock swept through her veins. She should say something. Do something other than stare up at him with eyes that undoubtedly reflected all of the surprise coursing through her and the feelings for him that had never completely gone away no matter how hard she'd willed them to. The hope that curled around her heart.

But how could she when he was staring at her with hot, covetous eyes? When her feelings were being telegraphed back at her? Or was that more wishful thinking on her part? Was she letting the teenaged girl she'd been guide her thoughts now? Was she getting lost in the past? Worse, was he just feeling the moment, recognizing that their time in the bar was extremely date-like?

It had been his idea to go on the date with Paige, after all. But no, there was no denying the interest in his eyes. The intent.

She should move away. Put an end to this. Tell him they couldn't. Tell him she should go home. Instead, her lips parted as he tilted her chin upward with a gentle forefinger. Always, always so careful with her, his gentleness belying his natural strength. Her eyes fluttered closed. A soft sigh escaped as his lips touched hers for the first time in what felt like forever, though in reality it had only been a few days. So, yeah, forever.

The embrace felt like coming home, like his mouth had been made specifically for hers. August didn't hurry. He sampled. He sipped like he was relearning the shape of her mouth. His lips slid across hers once, twice. It was almost chaste. Almost. There was a fire, a hunger behind the exploration that came through in his thoroughness, in his complete and utter devotion to his task. He was a man not to be denied. Not that she had any intention of denying him. Or herself.

A strong arm curled around her waist and unhesitatingly drew her against his hard, unyielding body.

Sloane gasped. Despite the cool spring night, his body, his oh-so-firm body, was a furnace. She couldn't wait to throw herself in the fire.

The gasp seemed to be the signal he was waiting for. Seemed to unleash something in him. His hand slid from her chin to her nape and held her in place as he kissed her like a man desperate for oxygen only she could provide. Thorough, yet hungry in his exploration of her mouth.

A dual moan escaped into the air as their tongues reacquainted themselves.

Sloane eagerly rose on her toes and dug her nails into his shoulders. He wasn't the only one with questions. With answers. She wanted him just as much. When he drew away briefly for breath, she greedily swept her tongue across the bottom lip that haunted her in her dreams. It was she that demanded entry into his mouth this time. Moaned when he acquiesced.

Sloane crowded closer. She wanted to climb him like a tree. Wanted to feel his hardness between her legs, giving her pleasure. She moaned in approval when he slipped a leg in between hers and rubbed against the spot desperate for attention. She was greedy, unashamed, uninhibited riding his thigh. Their tongues tangled together, sliding against each other in the same slow, determined rhythm as their lower body parts.

She wasn't a teen anymore. She was an adult, fully aware of her desires. She wanted him now, tonight, and tomorrow.

A burst of laughter, then music filtered through her senses. Coming closer.

She froze, then wrenched away. She ignored the way it felt like leaving the bliss of spring and plunging directly into the harsh depths of winter.

They were in a parking lot of a busy strip mall of bars and restaurants.

What was she doing? She'd told herself not to do this. Not to give in to the feelings she still harbored for him. She was shaking. Shaking with desire. With confusion. With longing to return to his arms.

Sloane squeezed her eyes shut like that small action would actually help in restoring her balance and sense of right and wrong. When she opened her eyes, August watched her with his all-seeing eyes. He didn't make a move toward her, as though sensing she needed the space, even as everything inside her tried to rebel at the notion. But she was in charge. Not her hormones. Not her feelings. She couldn't let him, let anyone, hurt her. Not again. Not ever.

"I can't. We can't. I don't . . ." She was babbling. Incoherent. Thoughts in a scramble as lust still swirled in her veins.

Where was her purse? There on the pavement where it had slid off her shoulder as she went to kiss him. Her hands were shaking, and it took two swipes before she grabbed the clutch. Another three swipes before she grasped the door handle and pressed the button to unlock the door.

"Sloane," August said from behind her.

She shook her head. She didn't want to hear again that this was a mistake. She wouldn't survive that rejection for the third time.

She wrenched the door open, got in her car, and sped off.

She didn't look back. She couldn't. Not if she wanted to keep moving forward.

Chapter Twenty-Nine

August scrolled through the photos of his date with Paige on the Sugar Blitz IG account. The images had garnered thousands of likes and hundreds of comments. Sloane hadn't wasted any time controlling the narrative of his date from hell. But she hadn't lied. She'd been honest that the date hadn't been a success but hadn't painted him or Paige in a bad light.

"All fish in the sea ain't for you" she'd captioned a photo of him eating a bite of the scallop from his pasta dish.

"When you realize you're in need of a cupcake" was the caption of Paige hurrying out of the restaurant. Sloane had sent that one last night while they sat at the bar. She was a genius. She'd edited the photo on her phone, come up with the caption, and posted it within minutes, all without losing the thread of their conversation.

August sighed. He wasn't resentful of her professionalism. Her business mind was one of the many things he liked about her. But was that all he was to her—a job, an assignment?

Was he the only one who'd struggled to fall asleep last night? The only one to lie there and replay their entire kiss—which, by the way, was such a tame word for what happened—over and over? The only one to replay the way the light shimmered in her brown eyes in the bar? The way her mouth quirked up at the corner when she was amused about something? The breathy, almost desperate sounds she made as they kissed? The only one to wonder if she made those same sounds when someone was kissing other, more intimate parts of her body?

The only one to slip his hand under his covers to find the release his body so sorely needed while fantasizing it was her hand, her mouth providing the relief?

"Shit." That line of thinking was not helping.

She'd texted that she was working from home that morning and she'd be in that afternoon to chronicle more of his adventures. Disappointment and relief had warred within him as he read the message. He wanted to see her. He always did. But he had no clue what he would say or do. He'd hoped she wanted more, and just when it seemed he was getting his wish, she ran off like the hounds of hell were chasing her.

And he'd let her.

August sighed again.

And here he was at Sugar Blitz Two. Alone. And not doing a damned thing other than obsessing about what was and what could have been.

Sloane, apparently, wasn't suffering from the same fate. He raised his phone to eye level. She'd even called up Paige and gotten a statement from her. "August is really nice, but I wasn't ready to date yet. Hopefully, he's still free when I am. Until then, I'll continue to lust after him like every other person attracted to men. He's the real deal."

Paige had posted the statement on her Twitter account. Sloane had wasted no time retweeting it and screenshotting the post to post on Instagram.

At least he could breathe a little easier on that front. The neighborhood committee wouldn't have his head about breaking the heart of one of their own. He hadn't put Sugar Blitz in a worse publicity spot.

It was official. Sloane was a certified badass. She was a certified badass he wanted more than a Super Bowl win. And the feeling had been reciprocated last night, for a few minutes at least. Fuck.

Footsteps sounded from down the hall. August sucked in a breath. Had Sloane decided to come in early after all?

When Donovan rounded the corner, August's shoulders slumped in disappointment. No. Definitely not Sloane. His eyebrows lifted in surprise when Nicholas emerged from behind Donovan. He tilted his head in inquiry. *What are y'all doing here?* he asked silently.

"To check out our investment, of course," Donovan answered. They rarely needed words to communicate. Over the years, Donovan had become a genius at reading August's expressions.

"That's the official answer," Nicholas added as he turned in a circle to take in the room's updates. He nodded approvingly. Nicholas strongly believed in aesthetics. Other than wanting to make sure the food tasted good, making sure everything looked good was his top priority.

August leveled a death glare at him. He already knew where this was going.

Nicholas, the arrogant bastard, grinned in response. "The unofficial reason is we came to get the dirt on your date."

On a scale from one to ten, August's level of surprise came in at a strong negative three. He went back to opening boxes. "There is no dirt."

"That's not what the streets are saying. And by the streets, I mean Instagram," Nicholas, the gossip hound, said.

August stopped his motion with the box cutter to glare at Nicholas again. "There is no dirt."

"So you didn't send your date screaming into the night?"

"No."

"Do you plan on seeing her again?" This time from Donovan, the traitor.

He shot him a dark look. "Why all this sudden interest in my love life?"

"Well, it is part of our marketing plan. To expand our customer base and get people to show up here when we open, and not in protest."

"And as you saw on Instagram, we're still good on that front. Crisis averted."

Donovan pursed his lips. "True . . ."

August glared. He didn't have time for this bullshit, but he was also a realist. Donovan and Nicholas weren't going to drop this, but he could give it the good ole college try. Go Bruins. "And?"

Nicholas rolled his eyes, while Donovan sighed. "And it's been a while since your divorce, and we're happy to see you getting out there again. We wanted to make sure you were okay."

Nicholas moved to stand next to Donovan. "Yeah, that. And also because it's funny that you have groupies who call themselves SugarBaebies. I need to know how a date with a SugarBaeby went."

August side-eyed him. "I appreciate your concern, but it was fine. I'm fine."

Donovan nodded. "You still didn't answer my question."

August gave a momentary thought to playing dumb but dismissed it just as quickly. That wasn't his way. Never had been, never would be. "No, we're not compatible, as our social media accounts reported already. Which I know you checked, because you've been keeping tabs on Sloane's progress and the neighborhood watch group."

Clearly unrepentant, Donovan shrugged. "I had to come see for myself."

August held out his hands. "As you both can see, I'm here doing just fine."

Donovan exchanged a glance with Nicholas before replying. "We don't mean to pry, but are you open to continuing to date other people, now that you've gotten your feet wet?"

They did mean to pry, but August understood. His divorce had fucked him up, even if he rarely spoke about it. He hadn't gotten married with the idea that he'd fail at it. He'd wanted that forever with someone, that partnership, that unconditional support he'd never received from his father after his mother passed away. He'd thought he'd found that with someone he'd known and loved for years. But the marriage had ended anyway.

He'd spent years questioning himself. Had he done enough? What could he have done differently? And in the darkness of night when he had nothing but his thoughts to keep him company in the quiet—was he loveable?

Donovan and Nicholas had been there for him through it all, even if that meant simply stopping by his place with his favorite whiskey and playing dominoes while August did everything but talk about his marriage and how he'd never felt lonelier while roaming through the eerily quiet rooms of his house.

Nicholas had coaxed him out to a club once. August had hated every second of it. He gave zero fucks about the VIP lounge or bottle service or women drawn to men in the VIP area. After that disaster, Donovan had told him about someone who was interested in a blind date. August had politely declined.

But last night, on the date that wasn't a date with Sloane, that situation had felt different. Good different. Natural. He wanted that feeling again. He wanted her. And she wanted him, too, even if she'd run away.

Years ago, the first time they'd kissed, hadn't been their time. But now, now was different.

Donovan and Nicholas were still staring at him, waiting for a response.

"I'm fine. When I put my mind to it, I do know how to speak to a woman."

Donovan's eyes narrowed for a second, then he nodded. "Good to hear."

Nicholas whistled. "Soooo . . . you're not heartbroken that you're not going to see her again?"

August glared at his nosy-ass friend.

Nicholas spread his hands wide. "I had to ask."

"I thought you were up on your social media. Sloane already set up my next date on Tuesday night." Desiree had wasted no time throwing her hat in the ring, sending a direct message through Instagram. Sloane had texted to ask if it was okay for her to accept. He'd agreed because . . . shit, he didn't know why. Probably because he was annoyed Sloane could toss away their connection so quickly. Pride really was a motherfucker.

"You sound less than enthused."

August shrugged. "I've met her. There was no chemistry."

Nicholas crossed his arms over his chest. "So you're cool with dating, but not with this woman?"

Yes, that was it. So simple. Sloane had captured all his attention—long ago, and even more now. If he was going to go through the whole rigmarole of dating, shouldn't he do it with someone he was actually interested in?

Nicholas narrowed his eyes. The gossip hound was on the scent. "Wait. Is there someone you *are* interested in?"

Yes. Absolutely. August shrugged. "Possibly."

Donovan lifted a finger. "That's a yes."

Nicholas's brow furrowed in confusion. "But you're going out with someone else?"

August sighed. "Yeah, because that's what I signed up for. To help the shop. To step out of my comfort zone." What went unsaid was that he always met his obligations.

Oh, shit. That wasn't technically true.

He had agreed to a date, but he could date whoever the hell he wanted to. There were no rules that said he couldn't. This whole premise was about stepping out of his comfort zone and taking chances. This was his opportunity, and not just in a roundabout "hey, we're friends" kind of way. Time to lay it all out on the table.

Opening his dating life up to scrutiny wasn't his idea of a good time, but he'd put himself in this situation. He'd give Sloane the content that would lead to her professional dreams coming true while hopefully making his personal dreams come true. To be with Sloane. To love her with his whole heart like he'd longed to do for too long.

And it was up to him to do it. Years ago, she'd put herself on the line and he'd hurt her. He'd inadvertently rejected her again a few days ago. It wasn't fair to expect her to do it again. This was all on him. Time for him to make a move that couldn't be misinterpreted or ignored or waved away. Yes. Calmness and certainty swept through his pores.

"Okay, change of plans. Yes, I'm going out with someone, the person I'm interested in. If she'll have me."

"Why wouldn't she have you?" Nicholas asked.

"We . . . have history."

Nicholas nodded in understanding. "You fucked up."

Weren't best friends *awesome*? "I've made some mistakes, and I don't think she thinks I'm for real." Who could blame her? Rejecting her all those years ago and telling her their recent kiss was a mistake. Yeah, he'd fucked up.

"You gotta change her mind. Wine and dine her," Nicholas added, ever so helpful.

August held up a hand. He didn't need any help from a member of the peanut gallery, even one with as illustrious a history as Nicholas's. His stomach pitched. Except he did. He hadn't put in effort for a date in way too many years. And when he'd been in the dating stage, he'd been a college kid more concerned with making sure he got to football practice on time. Shit, he hadn't dated in years, forget seriously dated someone with the hope of a future. What was he going to do?

"No need to panic. We got your back," Nicholas said, reading his face.

Oh, God. Nicholas was the king of wining and dining, but never with the intent of really getting to know his date. He kept people at a distance, whether consciously or subconsciously, with his sunny demeanor.

Donovan slapped Nicholas on the back. "I don't think going to the hottest club in town where you can't hear yourself think with a woman you've already silently agreed to sleep with, is August's style."

Nicholas's eyes narrowed. "For your information, we only go to a club if it's her idea. The sleeping together part too. I can't help it that so many women are attracted to me."

Donovan rolled his eyes. "Okay, Pretty Boy Nick. My mistake. Back to August. What do you have planned for this date?"

Sloane had said the date needed to be "aesthetically pleasing" for the 'Gram. She'd also wanted to switch it up from the first dinner date. She'd suggested ziplining. He'd ixnayed that one in a heart-beat. He didn't do heights or flimsy harnesses. Shit, when he flew to away games, he made sure to take sleeping pills during the flight. He also sat in an aisle seat and made sure all the shades were down on all the windows near him.

But he had the perfect idea. He quickly explained.

"Sounds dope," Donovan said. "You got this."

He hoped so. There was just one more thing.

"In the interests of transparency and the rules of being best friends, I need to tell you I'm talking about Sloane."

Donovan nodded, ever pragmatic. "Yeah, I figured that out. I'm just glad you did."

Nicholas held out his hand toward Donovan. "Gimme my money."

August glared. "You assholes really bet on my love life? You bet on your sister's love life?"

"Yes," Nicholas and Donovan answered simultaneously.

"At least I had faith in you," Nicholas said.

"I wasn't sure you'd get out of your own way," Donovan said, holding up his hands when August glared at him.

"Get out of my store. Both of you."

Nicholas grinned. "We will as soon as Donovan pays up."

Chapter Thirty

Move.

Sloane ignored her insistent inner voice and stared out her car windshield instead.

She'd actually done it. She'd actually driven here of her own accord to chronicle August's date with another woman. Again.

Where was her red rubber nose? This was peak clown behavior. Peak.

She was officially a strong contender for the "Glutton for Punishment" Hall of Fame. Was that a strong enough phrase for the hell she was willingly putting herself through? Maybe "masochist" was a better term.

But she couldn't sit here forever, could she? Well . . . maybe? No, no she couldn't.

Sloane reluctantly opened her car door and trudged across the parking lot toward her destination. Why exactly was she doing this to herself? Oh, yeah, because she'd wanted to help out her brother and the guy she'd had a massive crush on as a teen, and she wanted to land a job, so she could pay her bills and advance her career.

None of those reasons were holding up in the light of day, but here she was. And she hadn't even gotten to the part where she'd tried to climb August like a tree two days ago.

But she was the one who'd pulled away. The one who said she couldn't do this. The one who'd burned rubber to get out of there. And still thought about it a million times a day. A rough estimate. The number was likely higher.

Sloane blew out a breath. Time to pull up her big-girl panties and do what she had no desire to do.

After she'd chickened out for the second day in a row about going in to work, August had texted her earlier with a change of plans. He didn't want to play Putt-Putt golf like she'd suggested after he'd said no to ziplining. He wanted to visit a bookstore instead. The social media visuals will be better, the text read.

Who knew he gave a damn about visuals? Did this mean he was now committed to this whole thing? Was he actually going to try to charm and win over his date and be open to the thought of something more?

Her heart rate tripled and her eyes blurred at the very thought, but that fell under the definition of a me-problem, so she needed to get her shit together and walk into the bookstore. When she was done, she could go home, stuff her face with ice cream, and cry.

But she was here now. Like the adult she was. She would simply not acknowledge the fact that being an adult was clearly overrated.

Sloane inhaled deeply as she stepped into the bookstore. A joyous scent filled her nostrils. She loved the smell of books. Clean and crisp and woodsy and yet not like a man. Sloane's lips quirked.

There weren't many places that ranked above bookstores for her. So many adventures waited on the glorious wooden shelves. She'd have to return one day when she wasn't committed to documenting August's . . . date. Ick.

Sloane came up short. Oh, August was here already, early as usual. *If you're on time, you're late.* That's what his grandfather had always told him, she recalled. But he hadn't seen her yet, so she took the opportunity to ogle.

He sat in an armchair toward the back of the store's café, which meant she shouldn't have spotted him so easily, but her August radar had always been finely tuned.

The armchair was old, its brown leather covered in a dull sheen. It was big enough to fit his large body. He wore jeans and a light green Henley sweater. He was reading a book. She couldn't see the cover from here, but he was engrossed. Which gave her more time to ogle.

His brow was furrowed, his eyes slightly narrowed. He wore reading spectacles. "Glasses" was too common a word to use to describe how fucking fine he looked with the eyewear. Sloane bit her lip to keep an undignified groan from slipping out. He looked like a professor. A really sexy professor.

The crazy thing was no one was paying him any attention. Granted, he'd never been one to seek attention, but still. How could no one notice the hottest thing since habaneros was in their midst?

Sloane glanced at her watch. Where was his date? Well, the hour had just hit. She should do something other than stand in the entryway. She was supposed to be unobtrusively observing the date, not standing there where any—and everyone could see her.

"Sloane!"

She looked up to see August gesturing for her to join him. Her, as in Sloane. Ignoring him and running away wasn't an option. Not this time. She made her way over to him on shaky legs. "Hey."

He jerked his chin up in greeting. "Hey. Seen my date?"

He didn't sound nervous. Not that he ever did, so she needed to chill. He'd clearly forgotten about their last in-person encounter, so she needed to do the same.

"No, but I just got here." She sounded pretty dang close to normal. Points to her. "And I should get out of the way before she shows up."

He nodded. "Have a nonfat mocha latte on me while we wait. I owe you." He pulled a ten out of his wallet.

She snatched it out of his hand before he could change his mind. "You do."

His lips quirked. His finely sculpted lips. Hers spread in agreement. What was she doing? No flirting. No banter. Purely a business, strictly platonic relationship. She wheeled around and headed to the counter and ordered her latte. And she didn't think about the fact that August had her order memorized. Nope. It meant nothing. He was here on a date with another woman. That was the only truth that mattered today.

She settled at a table on the other side of the café that gave her a direct view of August but was far enough away that she wouldn't intrude on his date. August threw another one of his brief, yet dangerous smiles her way that sent her heart galloping before returning his attention to his book.

Sloane tapped her fingers on the table. Now that he knew she was here, she couldn't freely ogle him anymore—well, not until his date showed up and monitoring his every movement officially became work.

She took a sip of the coffee. Okay, yeah, this was the good stuff. The café portion of this bookstore didn't scrimp on ingredients. She definitely needed to make a return appearance soon. Hopefully she wouldn't be bombarded with mental images of August with another woman when she did. Laughing, possibly. Setting up a time for a second date. Proclaiming it was love at first sight. Desiree probably wouldn't run like Usain Bolt if August kissed her. No, she'd probably vault over a table like Simone Biles if August showed any desire to kiss her.

Which was totally fine. And totally a lie. But it would be okay if she put her mind to it. After all, she had no one to blame but herself and her fears.

She should've grabbed a book to distract her, but she didn't want to move in case Desiree showed up while she was browsing. Besides, this view would give her an excellent view of Desiree as she walked in and spotted August. Sloane wanted to capture that moment. It had the potential to be a great photo. Would Desiree's face betray nerves or excitement, feelings everyone going on a first date could sympathize with? Excellent social media content.

Too bad she was going to be sick.

She sipped her latte to distract herself, however momentarily, from obsessing over what could happen. But inevitably, her gaze strayed back to August. He was still reading, glancing up occasionally toward the front door. The sun streaming in from the window nearby gave him an otherworldly glow. He looked like a prince in the oversized armchair. A benevolent, patient prince who only wanted the best for his subjects.

Blech. She needed another diversion. The latte was no longer doing the trick. Being fanciful was so not her. She crusaded. She fought the good fight with a purpose.

Someone had left a *People* magazine on the table next to her. Not her first choice, but whatever. Celebrity gossip could always be counted on to feed the soul. Maybe she'd find some social media inspiration inside.

She flipped through the pages, judging who wore it better—in this instance the acclaimed veteran actress ate up the newest pop star wearing the same Versace dress—and tried not to stare at the man across the café.

She was engrossed in an article about the tennis star who'd opened up about her struggle with depression and had partnered with a company to offer mental health services for teens when the sound of a clearing throat made her lift her head.

August stood before her. How had he moved across the café without her noticing? How could he move so silently? That skill undoubtedly came in handy on the football field.

She looked around. He was standing alone. "Hey, is Desiree here yet?"

He held up his phone. "She's running late."

"Oh. Okay. Well, umm . . ." What was wrong with her? Why did she not have the right words to say? Because, before today, whenever they were together, there were rules. Now things were different. There was no buffer, either in the form of her brother or his date, between them. And, oh yeah, they'd shared the hottest make-out session of her life.

He offered up that brief, devastating smile again. "Want to scope out the shelves while we wait? She said it would probably be another twenty minutes or so. Something about a work emergency she couldn't ignore."

"Yeah. Sure." Time to get her shit together. They were in a bookstore. No need to panic. No need for fanciful flights of imagination. And he'd just given her the best way to pretend everything was okay. She could walk the aisles of a bookstore reading back-cover copy and admiring covers for hours and never get bored.

She checked her phone. No message from Desiree, but Desiree wasn't her date, so it wasn't that strange even if she'd been the one to mainly communicate with her.

Besides, it was only for twenty minutes.

She downed the last swallow of her latte and stood. August didn't move away. He was close, but not obnoxiously so. It didn't matter. He smelled good too. As always. Way better than books.

It would take nothing on her part to press herself against him like she'd done in the parking lot and lift her mouth to his again. He had a world-class mouth, a full bottom lip that begged her to bite and lick it. This close, she could spot the flecks of dark gold in his eyes that just made his eyes a darker, richer brown.

So much for no fanciful flights of imagination.

She moved around him and dropped her empty cup in the trash. "Ready to explore?"

His lips split again. "Absolutely."

He fell into step with her, easily matching his stride to hers, as they exited the café area.

"Where to first?" he asked.

She pointed to the book in his right hand. "What were you reading?"

He held up the book. A spy thriller. "I saw it on the front table when I walked in and was intrigued."

She nodded. "That's a good one. I've read a couple of her other books, but that's probably my fave of hers. Want me to tell you how it ends?"

"Only if you don't want to make it out of this place alive."

Sloane laughed. "The main character, Gina, would approve."

Sloane stopped walking. They'd reached the mystery/thriller section. She took the opportunity to scan the shelves.

"Anything catch your eye?" he asked.

Sloane shook her head. "Not really. I'm more of a fantasy person."

"I thought you liked romance."

He remembered that? Ever since she was a little girl, she'd always been drawn to the genre and its guarantee of a happy ending. Even in movies where the romance could charitably be described as the C story, the brief inclusion of a romance was a determining factor in whether the movie became a favorite. Once upon a time, she'd devoured the genre because of the happily-ever-afters that waited inside. Just because her parents weren't destined for forever didn't mean it didn't happen for other people. Then August broke her heart and her subsequent relationships had never lived up to the hype. She'd drifted away from the genre slowly but surely over the past decade.

She shrugged. "Fantasy is more my speed these days. I like the adventure and badass female characters."

He studied her with those all-seeing eyes for a few seconds but didn't comment further, thankfully.

They turned their attention to the shelves. Or at least Sloane hoped she gave the impression she did. She couldn't help but be aware of the man at her side as he picked up books and read the descriptions on the back. He held one up with a man staring off into the distance, hands on hips. "What about this one?"

Sloane wrinkled her nose. "Oh, you mean men's fiction? I've read it, but it's not really my thing."

He lifted a brow. "Men's fiction?"

"You know how they have women's fiction because it could only be of interest to women? The same thing happens with men. But they don't call it men's fiction. It's just fiction, because of course both men and women, and all genders alike, are always enthralled by whatever men are doing as they seek to find themselves and the true meaning of life."

"Sexism, in literature, you mean."

"Yes!" Argh, why did he have to be so smart and with it? It would be so much easier not to be attracted to him if he wasn't aware of the world around him.

His smile spread. "I knew you wouldn't like that book. I just wanted to see your face."

Sloane's eyebrows lifted. "Oh, really? You think you have me figured out."

"I know I do."

Four syllables should *not* sound so sexy. And yet . . . and yet, nothing. He was here for a date with another woman. They were friends. Pals. Or something equally unsatisfying. Time to act like it. Maybe she'd remember if she tattooed it on her forehead.

"Okay, Mr. Smarty Pants, you think you know me better than I know you?"

"I know I do." How he managed to look confident and sure without crossing over into cocky territory she did not know. She didn't appreciate how attractive a quality it was. She didn't appreciate how attractive he was.

"Care to prove it?"

"Sure."

"Okay, it's on," she challenged. "Let's pick out a book for each other."

"All right."

Sloane narrowed her eyes, her competitive instincts rising to the fore. "But that's not all. Whoever does the best job wins bragging rights. And you have to be honest. If you love—*when* you love—what I pick out, you have to admit it."

"You're on." August's smile widened, like he knew exactly what she was thinking and feeling and still planned on beating the tail off her. It was probably the same smile he gave his opponents on the football field right before the ball was snapped and he blocked them back into next week. No matter. She wasn't a pro athlete, but she'd never backed down from a fight and she wasn't about to start now.

Which was also the reason she was on a not-a-date with a man who was supposed to be on a date with another woman, which would lead to Sloane getting a job. Great. She wasn't going to think about any of that right now. He was giving her the opportunity to run around a bookstore and drool over books *and* win a bet at the same time? Who could ask for anything more? Best date ever. Which was supposed to be for another woman. *Not thinking about that.*

"You have fifteen minutes," she said. "We'll meet back here."

He snapped a sharp salute. "Aye, aye, Captain."

Sloane took off like a rocket until she garnered a disapproving frown from an employee. *Sorry,* Sloane mouthed, skidding to a stop.

"Causing trouble?" an amused voice murmured in her ear.

"Don't worry about it," she answered with a smirk, turning toward him. His chuckle warmed her all over and made her want to draw closer to him. A dangerous, alluring thought. She took an immediate left down the next aisle in a desperate attempt to escape her thoughts.

Thankfully, the books provided a fun distraction. As she perused the shelves, she paused a time or two or three to snap a photo of August, purely for the sake of the 'Gram. Yep, that was it. If her camera loved him, then so be it. It wasn't her fault. She was simply doing what needed to be done.

She also had a bet to win. She returned to her mission, skimming her index finger across the pretty, pretty book spines.

No, not that one. Or that one. She turned the corner and came to an abrupt stop, her breath catching in surprise. Oh, wow. Before her was a table filled with multiple copies of a book, but not just any book. The book penned by MDJ, August's ex-wife. In the center of the table a poster was set up advertising MDJ's upcoming book signing. At this bookstore. Next week.

With trembling fingers, she picked up the book.

"Find something interesting?"

Sloane jerked around and hid the book behind her back like she was tall or wide enough to hide his view of the table. "Oh. No."

His brow furrowed. "Sloane, what's going on? You're being weird."

He was a grown man. He could handle the truth. Without a word, she stepped aside.

As he took in the display, his expression blanked. "Oh. We're still in the middle of our contest, and I'm still looking." He turned on his heel and headed down the next aisle.

Sloane gave a moment's thought to following him, but his stiff back made it clear any sympathy would be unwelcomed. So she honored his wishes and went back to book hunting, though she couldn't help looking back several times to make sure he was okay.

A few minutes later, Sloane's eyes widened. She picked up the book and turned it over in her hands. Ooh.

She bit her lip. Was the book a little too on the nose? Should she go with something a little less obvious? But her gut was screaming that this was the one, and she listened to her gut, even if it did lead to trouble sometimes. She clutched the tome to her chest as a sense of rightness coursed through her. Yes, this was the one.

She raised her wrist to eye level. Crap. Only one minute left. She hustled back to their meeting spot, where August was already waiting.

"Ready to lose?" she asked with a playful curl of her lip.

"Not going to happen." His rumbly, confident tone slid through her like fine wine. Had he ever sounded sexier?

"Let's exchange books at the same time," she said.

He nodded. They quickly made the switch, but she didn't look down. She wanted to witness his reaction to her selection. Had she chosen well?

His face didn't give anything away. It never did. He skimmed the cover with the tips of his fingers, then flipped the book over to read the description.

Sloane struggled not to squirm. She wasn't the type to squirm, but she wanted him to like it, and not because she wanted to win a bet. She wanted to please him. Make him happy. Show him how important he'd been to her all those years ago and was starting to be again.

He looked up. His voice was soft. "Thank you. I love it."

The words were great. The look on his face was more than she could have asked for. Genuine pleasure.

Elation swept through her.

She'd chosen *Conversations with August Wilson,* a book of the playwright's interviews.

"I wasn't sure if you owned it already, but I took a chance."

"I don't. It's absolutely perfect." He jerked his chin downward.

Oh yeah, she still held his choice for her. She looked down. For a second, her thoughts swirled as her brain tried to decide which emotion was going to win out. Disappointment that she was about to lose their bet. Or joy that he knew her so well. In the end, it was no contest. Joy consumed her. No doubt her pearly whites were blinding him. Thank God for braces and teeth cleanings.

The book was *Minion,* the first book in L. A. Banks's Vampire Huntress Legend series, a fantasy romance she'd considered reading countless times over the past few years. The reviews all said the action was great, but the romance would make readers swoon, even those who claimed not to like romance.

How did he know that she picked it up every time she found herself in a bookstore?

"Thank you," she said. "I love it."

His head ducked down for a moment like he was embarrassed by the compliment. Why did she find everything he did so adorable?

It wasn't fair. She was a strong woman guided by her principles. Someone who learned from her mistakes, but right now, if she had zero self-respect, she would find herself describing herself as "a girl standing in front of a boy asking him to love her." She was not Julia Roberts. This was not a romcom. They were not going to be the Black version of *Notting Hill*. No, ma'am. No, sir.

But would it be so bad if they were?

He smiled that crooked smile. "So who wins?"

"I'm a sore loser, so I'm tempted to say I did, but . . . ?"

"But what?"

"But . . . you did. This was the perfect choice."

"How hard was it for you to say that?"

She would not smile. She would not. "Very."

He looked down at her choice again. "I say we both won."

"We did." It took her several seconds to realize she was, contrary to what she'd told herself not to do, grinning like a kid tasting cake for the first time. She composed herself. "Looks like your date stood you up."

He blew out a breath. "Yeah. Oh well. Can't win them all." His head tilted to the side. "Or any of them. I'm officially zero for two."

"Yeah, but at least you got to hang out with me."

"Exactly."

Okay, so what she wasn't going to do was look into that statement more than it deserved. Even though it hadn't been explicitly said, they were friendly. Committed to a fresh start. As friends. "At least we got some pics out of the deal and a couple of books to recommend to the Sugar Blitz audience. I'll make sure everything gets posted. Did you have any other plans for the day?" She was just being friendly. Asking friendly questions. No more, no less.

"If the coffee portion of the date had gone well, I was gonna ask her to join me at the zoo."

He was? Why did her heart hurt at the notion that he'd thought that far ahead, that he'd planned a date she'd told him to plan and that it happened to be at one of her favorite spots in San Diego? "Oh, that was thoughtful of you."

He shrugged. "I still plan on going. Why not? It's a beautiful day, and I have nothing else to do. Want to join me?"

She liked the zoo. Who didn't like the zoo? And if joy was coursing through her veins because she got to spend more time with him, so what? "Sure. Why not?"

It was all totally casual. Totally friendly. Totally.

Chapter Thirty-One

Sloane squealed as she crowded closer to the glass enclosure. "Oh, it's a red panda. I love pandas!"

August side-eyed her. "You've said that about every animal we've seen."

"Because it's the truth. Aww, it's stuck behind this little glass wall. Do you think it wants to be stuck there?"

"It's the only home it knows."

"Yeah," she said dispiritedly. "At least he has room to roam and gets fed on a regular basis. He just has to bear the indignity of all us humans staring at him. And it's hot here in San Diego. Maybe we should break him out and return him to his homeland."

He stared at her.

Sloane scrunched up her shoulders. "What? It's a good idea. I mean, it's not, but I think about it every time I come here. I just want them to be happy and live their best lives."

His lips quirked slightly at the corner, like he was amused by her. Okay, fine. She could admit it to herself—but absolutely no one else—that she lived for that little quirk. That sign that he was really paying attention to and seeing her. That maybe she wanted to see the quirk more often. Maybe after this temporary assignment was over. Maybe as he leaned closer to kiss her lips.

But what if she was alone in these feelings? The threat of rejection never really went away. He'd done it once—hell, twice—before. Who said he wouldn't do it again? Did she really want to put her happiness in the hands of someone else? But what if . . .

What if that other person made her happier than she'd ever been?

And she hadn't addressed the other issue. Yes, she was fairly confident he was attracted to her, but he was supposed to be on a date with another woman. He'd volunteered for the opportunity.

Sloane pressed a hand to her forehead as a wave of dizziness hit her.

"You okay?" August asked.

"Yeah. I'm just a little warm." Maybe she was officially overthinking things.

"It's not that hot today. Want some ice cream?" August stopped and pointed to a concession stand selling the frozen treats.

"Yes!" Absolutely. Anything to distract her from the spin cycle of her brain.

His eyes narrowed for a second, his head tilting to the side, like he was concerned about her way-too-exuberant agreement. She sighed in relief when he asked for her preferred flavor instead of asking why she was acting so strange.

"Butter pecan."

He nodded and stepped up to the cashier.

"I can pay for it," she said. "You already paid for our admission."

He turned. "I know, but I got it this time."

Right. He wasn't trying to control her. He believed in her need to be independent and had never told her she was being silly for not accepting financial help from her millionaire brother. Another reason it was absolutely amazing she hadn't jumped the man's bones yet. Okay, except for one or two or three times.

She was confronted with reason number 853 after they settled at a nearby table. August knew how to lick an ice-cream cone. Her mind could head straight to the gutter as quickly as anyone else's. It took up permanent residency there as she forgot about her ice cream and watched him enjoy his own.

Slow and steady with little licks. In no hurry. Savoring every bite. The concentration on his face. She wasn't made of stone. As the ice cream melted, his swipes got longer and faster. He was so, so talented. His tongue was masterful.

The heat between her legs intensified.

"You okay?" he asked, jerking his chin toward her half-eaten cone.

"Yeah, yeah. Just enjoying the scenery. I love this place," she added quickly, in case he inferred, quite correctly, that she was talking about him. "Can I ask you a question? It's really personal, so feel free to say no."

"I trust you. Shoot."

"At the bookstore, you kinda had no reaction to seeing that your ex-wife is coming to town. Are you okay?"

He shrugged. "Yeah. It was a shock. Hell, the whole divorce was a shock. That's what I had a hard time getting past. I didn't see it coming."

"Do you mind if I ask what happened?"

"I came home one day from practice. She was waiting, with her bags packed, and said the marriage wasn't working anymore. She was on a plane to New York later that night."

"Oh, August. I'm so sorry."

"Thank you." He offered up a small smile. "I'm okay, I promise. The marriage is done. The only thing I ever wonder about is if she ever regrets hurting me."

"August." He truly was the kindest, most genuine man she'd ever met.

"It's okay." He jerked his chin toward her cone. "Your ice cream is melting."

Sloane looked down. Oh, crap, it was. She took a few swipes to mop up the ice cream sliding down the cone. "Mmm," she moaned as the nutty flavor melted on her tongue.

He cleared his throat and shifted in his chair. "Did you have fun today?"

"Uh, yeah! This is the best day ever."

And he'd planned it all for another woman. Sloane came up short. Right? Visiting bookstores and the zoo were all activities she enjoyed. But surely that was a coincidence. Right? Who didn't enjoy wandering aimlessly through a bookstore picking up any book that caught her attention? Going to the zoo that was, yes, a crowded tourist attraction, but had cute animals like red pandas she had to fight through a throng of people to catch a glimpse of?

Sloane blinked as the truth hit her like a sledgehammer. Plenty of people didn't enjoy those things, especially the crowded part. Like August. But he had been so patient the entire time and joined in on the fun at every opportunity.

What was going on? Was this a date? She liked to think of herself as a fairly intelligent person, but she was so confused right now. Was she being conceited to think this was an honest-to-God *date*? She ate some ice cream to give her brain something else to concentrate on.

Suddenly, her stomach cramped, but not with indecision. She groaned and pressed a hand to her abdomen. "I need to get out of here."

August's brow furrowed. He jumped up from his chair and rushed around the table to her side. "What's wrong?"

Oh, no. She puked all over his shoes.

* * *

Sloane opened her front door and staggered inside. Was her place an acceptable form of everyday mess or did it look like a cyclone had swept through? She couldn't remember. Could barely concentrate on the question. Her stomach hated her with the fire of a thousand suns.

"No need," she mumbled as August swept her into his arms. He ignored her half-hearted protest and carried her down the hall. She pointed with a listless hand toward her bedroom.

August strode through the entryway and gently settled her on her bed.

"Go away." She pushed his hand away when he reached toward her forehead.

He smiled. "Don't be stubborn."

"It's the only way I know to be," she mumbled.

"I know." He crouched down next to her. "How are you feeling?"

"Like shit." Food poisoning tended to do that to you.

"Yeah, I know. I'm sorry." He ran a gentle finger down her cheek, concern swimming in his gorgeous eyes.

He'd rushed her to the first aid clinic at the zoo. She didn't have any food allergies that she knew of, so they'd ruled that out quickly. Her symptoms were consistent with food poisoning. Maybe that grocery-store sushi she'd had for dinner last night wasn't the best choice.

Groaning, Sloane covered her stomach again as its contents roiled again. Not that there was much left inside.

He ran into her en suite bathroom and returned with a trash

can. "Just in case." He set it down on the floor and rushed out of the bedroom again. A few seconds later, he returned with a bottle of ginger ale she kept in her refrigerator. "Here."

Thankful, she guzzled the liquid. And then flopped back on the bed, all her energy drained from that simple act. She hated relying on anyone, but she didn't have the strength or the energy or the desire really to protest when he slipped her shoes off, swung her legs onto the bed, and tucked her in. Or when he pressed a cold cloth to her brow. She could barely keep her eyes open, so she didn't see the point in trying.

"Please get better," she thought she heard him say as she dozed off. A light pressure on her forehead reminiscent of a kiss accompanied the murmur, but she wasn't sure.

Throughout the night, a bucket magically appeared underneath her chin when she needed to throw up even though there was nothing left. A glass of water was there when her mouth ran dry. A cool towel was pressed to her forehead when she felt overheated.

Magic was the best, she thought as she drifted off to sleep again.

* * *

Sloane's eyes flew open. Pee. She needed to pee. Now.

Feeling and no doubt looking like the baby giraffe she'd mooned over at the zoo, she stumbled on unsteady legs to the bathroom. She sighed in abject relief when she got to the toilet in time to relieve her bladder. "Whew."

Then her stomach rumbled. "No, not again." She dropped to her knees and puked up bile, the only remaining remnants in her stomach. A hand rubbed her back and cooed reassurances at her in a deep, heavenly voice. The angel then wiped her mouth, helped her to her feet, and tucked her back into bed.

"Thanks," she mumbled as she drifted off to sleep.

When she woke again, sunlight peeked through the window. Sloane blinked and determinedly pushed herself upright against the headboard with heavy limbs that weren't really interested in cooperating.

What time was it? What *day* was it? Why was she in her bed, feeling like a truck ran over her?

It all came back to her in a rush. She groaned and dropped her head into her hands. "Ugh."

She'd thrown up all over August's Js. Not her finest moment. But today was a new day. She had a job to do. Reputations to save. Her stomach growled. A tummy to fill. But first a shower.

Twenty minutes later, she felt marginally more human. A hot shower, toothpaste, and mouthwash could do that for a gal. She donned an old loose-fitting Knights T-shirt she'd stolen from her brother years ago that was three times too big, because who needed tight clothing when you felt like crap?

Grr. Smiling, Sloane placed her hands over her stomach. That was a good growl, not a there's-terrible-stuff-in-here-that-we-want-out-now growl. Food was next on her to-do list.

When she made the turn into her living room, she screamed. Someone was lurking in the dark. The person flipped the light switch. She slapped a hand over her galloping chest. Not a person. August. And he'd scared the shit out of her. "What are you doing here in the dark?"

The corner of his mouth lifted. "I wasn't in the dark. I was coming back from the kitchen. And hello to you too."

Right. She was being an ass. He'd obviously stayed to take care of her. It hadn't been a figment of her always overactive imagination. "Sorry."

"Don't worry about it. You hungry?"

She nodded.

"I'll make you something." He turned, like that was the end of it. She hurried to keep up with him.

August was in her apartment. Her tiny apartment. She'd always thought it was a decent size, but he took up so much space. So much air, leaving her breathless.

He pointed to one of the stools on the other side of the countertop.

She sat. "Ooh, it's like I'm at a roadside diner in the movies. Can I have hash browns, a triple stack of pancakes, and bacon, extra crispy?"

"No."

Sloane gasped. "What do you mean 'no'? I'm the sick person here!"

"Exactly. You don't need all that grease after what you just went through. Toast and scrambled eggs it is."

Damn the kindhearted man. Sloane snorted to hide how touched she was that he cared about her well-being. "You're no fun."

His lips, still lickable, still biteable, twitched again. "You'll live."

A few minutes later, he slid a plate in front of her. Eggs and toast, like he'd promised. She looked up at him with a grimace. "Seriously, this is it?"

"Eat."

"You're so bossy," she muttered.

"What was that?" he called out from the refrigerator where he was grabbing a carton of orange juice.

"Nothing." She hastily picked up her fork and took a bite of eggs. They were great. Not that she was surprised. They looked good—fluffy and yellow. She just liked to give August shit. She took a bite of the toast—a light brown like she liked. Another winner. "Thank you for taking care of me."

He leaned his back against the counter. "You're welcome."

Sloane set the toast on her plate. "Why?"

"Why what?"

"Why did you take care of me?"

"You wanted me to drop-kick you out of my car as I barely slowed down on my way home?"

Sloane shot him a look. He was being deliberately obtuse. "No. You know what I mean. You could've called my mom or my brother or sister."

"I was already here."

Right. Damn the man and his uncanny ability to say a whole lot of nothing when he wanted to. She finished her meal and held up the empty plate.

"Good girl."

A pleasurable shiver slid down her spine. Okay, time to get out of here. She slid off the stool, circled around to the living room, and settled on the couch. She tried not to be happy when he followed her a minute later. She failed. He held something behind his back. She tilted her head to the side. "What's going on?"

"How are you feeling, really?"

"Better. But I'm still hungry. *Someone* wouldn't let me eat a huge, greasy meal."

"Awful. Diabolical." He paused. "I'm probably not being a good nurse, but I got you something."

He pulled a distinctive teal box from behind his back. A Sugar Blitz cupcake.

Sloane squealed in delight and clapped her hands. "Gimme."

He held the box close to his chest. "Any nausea?"

"No. Pinkie promise."

He sat next to her on the couch and handed the box to her. Sloane's mouth watered at the delightful smells emanating from inside. She wasted no time in ripping the container open and taking out the lemon meringue cupcake. She moaned as the flavor burst on her tongue. "Oh, my God, this is so good. Nicholas is the best baker ever."

A clearing throat interrupted her fawning spiel.

Sloane beamed at him. "And you are the absolute best for getting it for me. Did you go out and get this?"

"And leave you alone? No, I had it delivered. I thought about making them, but you have nothing but eggs, leftover fried rice, juice, and ginger ale in your fridge."

"All I need in this life of sin."

She was rewarded with his beautiful, crooked smile. She dropped her gaze to the cupcake. "This is exactly what I needed. It's so beautiful."

"Agreed."

She looked up. Her breath caught in her throat. "You're staring at me."

He shrugged. He didn't stop.

Sloane's lips curved with pure joy as her heart picked up pace to a gallop. "Is this the part where you tell me I look beautiful even though I'm in a ratty T-shirt and have bags under my eyes after a night of puking?"

"No. You looked terrible last night. Still do."

Sloane gasped. "Get out!" She pointed to the front door.

"No. This is the part where I say I'm happy you're feeling better after you took a couple of years off my life. I was worried sick about you. I'll raise holy hell if you ignore what your body is telling you like that again."

Sloane's heart melted. "Thank you."

"You already said that."

"I know, but thank you for everything. Yesterday. Wait. It was yesterday, right? I haven't lost a week of my life to food poisoning, have I?"

His lips quirked. "No."

God, she wanted to bite that bottom lip. Suck on it.

"Good. Thanks for yesterday. It was the perfect day until I got sick."

"Agreed."

Sloane dropped her eyes to the cupcake. Did she have the guts to put her heart on the line and risk heartbreak? Risk not being able to control the future? Yes. Time to go for broke and lay it all out there. No more guessing and assuming. She lifted her head. He was still watching her. Always watching her. "Did you plan it for me?"

"Yes." Said with the quiet intensity that never failed to mesmerize her. Said so simply, like there had been no other choice. Maybe there hadn't been.

Her heart stuttered once. Twice. Not that she'd expected him to lie, but she'd thought he'd be a little more reticent, hesitant to put it all out there. But why? This was August. He always spoke the truth. He was always honorable.

Yes, she'd thought the probability that she was right was fairly high, but still she hadn't let herself truly believe, because what if . . . She looked up into his eyes. Yes, what if? What if she went after everything she'd wanted for twelve years?

She caressed his jaw, rough with stubble.

"Was Desiree ever going to show up?"

"No. I canceled."

Wow.

"Why did you plan those specific activities?"

"Because I knew you'd enjoy them." He reached for her hand and traced the lines in her palm. "Because I wanted to go out on a date with you, and if I asked you directly, I knew the odds were pretty good you'd freak out."

Because he knew her. If he'd asked, she would've overthought the whole situation and worried about things not working out. Freaked out, in other words. She felt his eyes on her mouth as she took another bite of cupcake and tried to adjust to this new reality. As her heart practically burst with happiness. "So you planned a sneaky date."

"I did."

"Thank you. I loved it. Well, before the puking, anyway."

That special smile spread across his face. "Anytime."

She held up the dessert. "Wanna try it?"

"Sure."

She pinched off a piece of the ridiculously fresh cupcake and pressed it to his mouth until his lips parted. She gasped at the quick flick of his tongue against her thumb. He chewed slowly, his eyes never leaving hers.

"What do you think?"

"It's sweet."

"Hmm, let me try." She gently pressed her lips to the left corner of his mouth, then the opposite side. Her pulse accelerated at his quick inhalation of breath.

"Sloane. Are you trying to seduce me?" His hand landed on her leg and squeezed.

"Yes," she answered breathlessly.

"Your stomach—"

"Is fine. I'm fine. Now, hush and let me complete my mission."

Chapter Thirty-Two

*Y*our wish is my command." The words came straight from his gut. Everything he'd ever wanted was here for the taking and there was no way he was messing it up or letting it go.

"August." The look in her eyes dazzled him.

"Say it again. My name."

"August." Her voice. So captivating. She sounded like all his dreams come true.

Every millimeter of doubt he'd harbored for so many years disappeared like a puff of smoke.

He didn't remember acting. All he remembered was the taste of her lips. The feel of her body pressed against his. The beam of sunlight through the window warming them and silently giving its approval.

Better. She tasted better than he remembered. And he'd done all he could over the years to remember what she tasted like. Like sunshine and sugar and Sloane.

Her lips were works of art. He could linger over them for the rest of his life. He needed nothing else to sustain him. He wanted her closer. Needed her closer. Unfortunately, there was a fragrant barrier between them getting crushed in Sloane's hand.

"Give me that."

"Yes." She leaned in closer.

He chuckled. "No, not that. Well, yes that, but after that." He gestured to the half-eaten cupcake in her hand. She took one last bite, then dropped the dessert on the coffee table like a hot potato.

August could only laugh. How had he denied himself the joy she brought to his life for so long? She cut off his laughter with her mouth. The cream and taste of lemon still lingered on her tongue. So damned sweet. Sweeter than pure honey.

She swept her tongue across his bottom lip, silently seeking permission to enter. He happily complied. Their tongues met, hungrily curling around each other. It wasn't a battle so much as a consummation of all they'd felt and never said. A simultaneous moan rent the air.

Greed surged through him. How had he managed to deny himself for so long? He wanted all of her now. Forever. Always.

She was straddling him now, her T-shirt riding up, and he couldn't be happier. He was already hard, and then she ground against him, her lust clear and equal to his.

"Yes, right there," she moaned when he circled his hips and bumped the ridge of his erection between her legs. Her uninhibited response spurred him to repeat the action. Her pleasure would always be paramount.

His mouth sought the curve of her neck. A hint of honey teased his nose. How often he'd dreamed of kissing her there. The curve of her neck, her jaw, her lovely cheekbones, the gentle sweep of her forehead. There wasn't an inch of her he didn't want to taste and kiss.

There wasn't an inch of her he *wouldn't* taste and kiss. Over and over again, if he had his way.

She lifted her chin, giving him much-appreciated better access. He swept his lips across the soft expanse of skin.

He was rewarded with the sweetest moan. "Oh, my God, that feels so good."

Music to his ears. He wanted to give her more pleasure than she could handle. August skimmed his lips down the smooth silkiness of her neck till he reached the base. Her pulse throbbed under his seeking tongue. Her deep, ragged breaths in his ear spurred him on.

More. He wanted to give her more. He wanted to give her everything.

His hands tightened on the back of her legs. The urge to ravage her drummed inside him, but he beat it back. Not yet. Not this time. He slipped a hand between her legs, her panties offering very little resistance.

"Oh, shit," he mumbled.

She was so fucking wet. He wanted to be inside her more than he wanted his next breath.

Her head dropped to his shoulder. She was panting. "August. Touch me. Please."

"Your wish is my command."

Anything she wanted. Any time.

He slid a finger down her folds. Her panting increased in volume. Her hip movements increased in pace as she chased his finger. He found her clit and circled it with his thumb, as he pushed inside her with his middle finger. Her inner walls clasped tightly on to the digit. He groaned at the heavenly sensation. He dragged his finger in and out, savoring the feeling. Her hips moved in tandem with the movement of his finger.

Her hold on his shirt tightened when he rubbed against a spot high inside her. Her hips bucked forward. A tiny moan slipped from between her lips before she pressed her mouth shut. Not on his watch. He wanted it all.

"Don't hold back. Tell me," he demanded.

"Feels so good," she whimpered, the fucking sexiest sound he'd ever heard.

"I can make it better."

He wedged another finger inside her. And pressed gently against her clit.

He swallowed her scream with his mouth. The kiss was wild, greedy. Lips, tongue, teeth sliding, clinging, giving, demanding pleasure. She tasted like heaven, offering all the sustenance he would ever need.

Her hips picked up speed. She was so fucking tight wrapped around his fingers. How good would his dick feel inside her? Incredibly, he got even harder. As if sensing the direction of his thoughts, her hands landed on the front of his jeans. She squeezed once, twice.

He almost detonated. "Sloane. Sweetness. Please."

She didn't heed his plea. Instead, she pulled his zipper down and slipped her fingers inside. He didn't have the willpower to stop her. Her hand wrapped around his dick was so fucking good. She pulled up and down, exerting the perfect amount of pressure to have him gasping as pleasure sang through his veins.

No, this was supposed to be about her. About making sure she was taken care of and wanted for nothing. August summoned a will he didn't know he possessed and pulled away from her exhilarating touch.

He scrambled to sweep her T-shirt up and over her head. But it wouldn't cooperate, so he jerked down until the shirt was nothing but two pieces of material in his hand. He tossed it aside. Greed consumed him. He stared at her beautiful breasts. Earlier, he'd tried—unsuccessfully—not to notice she wasn't wearing a bra. Her breasts were perfect. She was perfect. He wanted to taste those pretty little nipples. His mouth watered as they puckered under his watchful gaze.

She twisted to look at the shirt that now lay on the floor in pieces. She gasped. "You ripped it."

"I'll buy you another one."

She mock gasped. "It's a family heirloom."

He grinned. "You're full of shit."

Laughing, they fell into another kiss. He filled his hands with her breasts and rolled the nipples between this thumbs and index fingers. Her groan let him know she approved of his actions.

Then her hands snuck under the hem of his shirt, touching him everywhere she could, leaving him breathless.

"Take it off," she whispered in his ear.

He took it off.

"Nice." She unabashedly ogled him.

As much as he appreciated her approval, he had other concerns at the moment. Like tasting every inch of her body.

Sloane mewled in protest when he lifted her. He wasn't deterred. Her pleasure was his top priority and he wouldn't stop until she was satisfied.

He laid her back on the couch. Her smile dazzled him. He wanted to take and take, but he forced himself to go slow. To savor. To fully satisfy. He'd waited a long time for this. There was no way in hell he was going to rush.

He started at her temples, trailing his lips across her forehead, to her nose, and her lips. He grasped her hands and kissed the pulse points at her wrists. Yes, this is where he was meant to be.

* * *

"August."

Sloane was caught up in a web of sensation. Every touch of his lips and hands ensnared her more.

First, he skimmed her arms with a barely there touch, followed immediately by a whisper of lips and tongue. Then a soft kiss, barely there, landed on her parted lips. She'd never thought of the spot behind her ear as being particularly erogenous. How wrong she'd been. She gasped as he took the skin there between his teeth and tugged slightly, following the sting with a quick swipe of his tongue. He repeated the action on her neck, then her collarbone.

Her breath quickened as he drew closer to her breasts. She wanted his touch on her aching flesh. But he detoured. A kiss to each of her trembling fingers, then each palm, followed.

She was drowning, and there was nothing she could do to stop it. Nothing she wanted to do to stop it. Her eyes drifted open. His, so fierce, so intent, were locked on her. To her every response.

She gathered the last vestiges of her strength and reached for his hands. Never taking her eyes from his, she raised his palms to her breasts. She inhaled sharply when he made contact with her sensitive skin. Finally, she lowered her gaze. His large hands covering her naked flesh was an erotic sight she'd remember for the rest of her life.

She arched her back, wanting more of his touch. Greedy for it. But he seemed content to take his time, to learn the shape and feel of her. What made her gasp. What made her moan. Her nipples, already tight, beaded into impossibly sharp points. He kept his eyes on her, weighing her reactions. A slight scrape of a fingernail across the sensitive flesh had her pushing her chest upward. A slight pinch of her other nipple had her crying out his name. Lust arrowed straight between her legs with each act.

Then his mouth descended, and thinking was no longer an

option. His tongue swirled around and around her areola before finally scraping across her nipple. His eyes lifted. "Do you like that?"

"Yes. More." Her voice came out broken, gasping.

His teeth scraped across her nipple, back and forth, before tugging at the mound of flesh. Sloane cried out as the orgasm rolled through her out of nowhere, leaving her quivering and shaking as ecstasy consumed her body.

When her eyes fluttered open, she found his dark, glittering eyes watching her every move. Silently waiting for permission to continue.

At her nod, he continued his journey, his lips skimming her quivering stomach muscles. He pulled her to the edge of the couch. Her panties were whisked away. Then a nip on her outer thigh caught her attention. His magical hands swept up and down her legs. Again, his lips and tongue followed his hands, tasting her like she was the ice cream she'd been so jealous of at the zoo. Another nip to her other thigh sent a wave of sensation cascading through her. Then he drew her legs over his massive shoulders.

"August?" She sounded nervous, uncertain even to her own ears.

"I got you."

She lifted on her elbows. His shoulders corded with muscle. His mouth between her legs. A portrait that belonged in the Louvre. A quick flick of his tongue had her seeing stars. Then, a slower swipe had her wishing for more. Sloane's mouth dried.

He alternated between faster and slower swipes, taking his cues from her. He nibbled, then bit. Faster when the movement of her hips slowed. Slower when she came perilously close to the edge. Beautiful torture. His mouth on her was a million times better than she'd ever imagined. He was a certified master with his tongue. When he found her clit, her whimpers ramped up to full-on cries.

She bucked, begging him for more. Demanding more. Sweat

slickened her skin. Her hands slipped on the sofa cushions, searching for purchase.

Through it all, he was there. August and his wonderful tongue. Her eyes squeezed shut as delicious sensations bombarded her from every direction.

Then his fingers, long and immeasurably talented, joined in the action between her legs. He was so slow and deliberate, going at his own pace, despite her demands. And she fucking loved every second of it.

He held his tongue tight against her clit as he sank three fingers inside her. In and out. The sensations inside her twisted tighter and tighter, pushing her higher and higher.

Until she broke, splintering into a million jagged pieces.

As she floated back to earth, she was barely aware of him maneuvering her to lie on her side on the sofa. He joined her bringing their chests together. She languidly lifted her leg over his hard thigh. "You took your pants off," she murmured.

"I did," he said with a chuckle.

"Thank you."

He answered with a soft, lingering kiss that quickly caught aflame. The long, drugging kiss rattled her senses. When the need for air became too much, she broke away to lay quick, hungry kisses to his neck, his Adam's apple, his strong shoulders, his biceps. Anywhere she could touch.

It wasn't enough.

She rocked against his hard length and wiggled her hand between them to grasp him. Hard, thick, and long. She took immense satisfaction in his low groan and the shudder that rocked his whole body as she pulled upward. She affected him as much as he affected her. This was meant to be.

But then her concentration was shot to hell when his hand

landed between her legs. He pleasured her with his fingers, scraping across her clit just the way she craved before sliding two fingers inside her. Sensations rocked through her.

Another quick orgasm claimed her, shocking her. She'd never been this responsive to, this hungry for, a man's touch.

He gripped her thigh hard enough to leave a bruise and lifted it higher on his thigh. His intent soon became clear. He rubbed the tip of his dick against her clit. As a scream drew in her throat, she sank her teeth into the vein in his neck and sucked. His fingers continued their magical maneuvering as he worked his erection against her. It was almost too much. But not enough.

She wanted more.

She was going to die if he wasn't inside of her in the next thirty seconds.

Vague recollections of condoms in her bathroom flittered through her head, but she didn't have the strength to get that out or to tell August to stop to procure them. Not when another bolt of lightning hit her when he touched her in the most brilliant way.

She dug her nails into his shoulders. "Please tell me you have protection."

A foil packet appeared in front of her eyes. Oh, thank God. She didn't give a damn where it came from as long as it was there. She watched as he ripped the package open and rolled the condom down his erection. Then he was at her entrance, pressing inside.

Sloane gasped at the amazing sensation. At the stretch and pull. Had anything felt so good in the history of ever? Their eyes met when he was fully inside. He felt it too. How perfect this all was.

Then they were kissing again as August slid in and out of her in a slow, perfect rhythm. His fingers rubbed against her clit. She was so close. So close.

But the couch's width only allowed a certain amount of movement. She needed more. She hummed her frustration. Her hum increased in volume when he slid out of her without returning.

"Shh," he murmured. Then, before she could blink, she was draped over the arm of the couch and he was thrusting into her from behind.

Oh, wow. This was better. She hadn't thought that was possible, but she was thrilled to be proven wrong. This angle allowed him to go deeper. Fill her completely. He twisted his hips, changing the angle slightly. It was too much. Perfect. Unyielding.

She turned her head for another wild, incandescent kiss. He filled his hands with her breasts, alternatively massaging and pinching her nipples. Through it all, his hips never stopped their magical motion. Sensations were bombarding her from every angle, leaving her gasping for air.

"Touch yourself," he commanded in her ear. It didn't occur to her to argue. Even as he continued to thrust in and out of her, she eagerly slid her fingers between her slick folds, coating her digits in her wetness.

Pleasuring herself was nothing new. Men were often temporary, but vibrators were forever. But this, being with August while she saw to her own pleasure, was amazing. Her clit, now so sensitive, sent bolts of feeling through her as she rubbed it the way she'd mastered over the years.

"That's right. Get yourself off while you ride my dick." His low, deep voice in her ear spurred her on as he twisted her right nipple, sending a jolt of pleasure-pain through her body. She cried out in ecstasy as she moved in tandem with him, pushing her hips down as he thrust inside her. She wanted to give him all that he was giving her. His tortured groan was everything she wanted to hear.

"My dick loves how wet you are. Give me your fingers."

Without hesitation, she held them up to his mouth. He licked them dry, his tongue sliding in between and around her fingers. He moaned in appreciation.

"Give me some more." He accompanied the demand with another intoxicating roll of his hips and scrape of his nails against her nipples. Sloane was on the edge of delirium, her vision blurry, her mind fuzzy. Relying solely on instinct, she dropped her hand again. But this time, his hand joined hers. Mesmerized, Sloane watched the tandem action of their fingers, his thicker and longer, as they moved in and around each other. Lifting her hand, he licked the juices off his fingers, then hers.

"Sloane, Sloane," August groaned over and over. It was more like pleading. Her name had never sounded so soulful, so necessary. So magical. His hips picked up speed, pressing her deeper into the couch. He found her clit again, rubbing, scraping. Sloane held on for dear life as she hurtled toward the cliff. Still, nothing prepared her for tumbling into a dark, wide-open abyss that didn't seem to have a bottom with August's guttural groan of completion in her ear.

Chapter Thirty-Three

Sloane bit her lip to stop a *very* undignified protest from slipping past her lips as August disentangled their limbs and slid out of her. She felt adrift without his body pressing into hers. Without him offering her warmth and comfort. Without his voice whispering the sweetest, dirtiest commands into her ear.

On unsteady legs, she stood to face him. He tugged her closer, until once again, his warmth seeped into her body. Peace, a sense of homecoming, settled into her.

"Hey," August whispered, his voice extra gravelly.

"Hey," Sloane answered, her voice equally hoarse.

"You are the most beautiful person I've ever seen." He pressed a soft kiss to her forehead and smoothed a braid away from her face. To her amazement, heat rose in her face. She, who'd always claimed she would let no man penetrate the armor around her heart, was unbearably touched.

She turned her face away. A finger under her chin didn't let her get very far.

"Hey, you okay?" His dark eyes penetrated hers, determined to wrest all her secrets. He sounded ready to fight whoever, whatever had made her potentially not okay. To right whatever wrong had been done to her, even if he were the perpetrator.

She nodded quickly, a little too close to tears for comfort.

"Are *we* okay?"

She nodded again. She didn't know how to explain it to him. She didn't know how to explain it to herself. She'd just experienced something she'd longed for as a teen. And even as a horny seventeen-year-old with an overactive imagination, she'd never imagined such a mind-blowing, soul-altering encounter.

Everything she'd always wanted was finally in her grasp, and she was scared as fuck. She didn't want to mess it up. She didn't know how to fully grab everything she'd ever wanted with both hands when she'd spent more than a decade trying to convince herself it was everything she didn't want.

"Sloane."

The worry in his voice had her lifting her head to meet his eyes. She wanted to give him the truth. He deserved the truth.

"Yes, we're okay."

His eyes narrowed. "But . . ."

She shook her head. "No but. It's just that I'm having a hard time wrapping my head around the fact that we're . . ."

"Us."

"Yeah." She rubbed her arms. Being naked in a room with the A/C blasting while having an existential crisis after having the best sex of your life with the guy she'd crushed on forever made one cold. Who knew? Twisting around, she tried to locate a throw that usually resided along the back of the couch, but surprise surprise, it had slipped to the floor.

Seeing the direction of her gaze, August reached down and handed it to her.

"Thank you." She draped the chenille around her body. Her gaze shifted back to the sofa. "We debased the couch."

His eyes flickered in surprise at the abrupt change in topic, but after a beat, he snorted and nodded solemnly. "We debased the couch."

"I'm not sure I'll ever be able to look it in the eye again."

"It had to learn about the birds and the bees sometime."

Sloane's laughter turned into a yelp of surprise when August scooped her up in his arms like she was the size of your average kindergartner. She hastily wrapped her arm around his neck. She didn't think he'd drop her, but being in a vulnerable position always freaked her out. "What are you doing?"

"You're cold. We should shower."

Sloane sniffed. "I had a shower an hour ago."

August strode out of the living room. "And then you had sex."

She considered his response for a second. "This is true."

"Great sex."

"This is also true."

"Stupendous sex."

"True once again."

"With a certified sex master."

"Now, sir." Sloane slapped him on the shoulder and then decided to linger, because good Lord, he was ripped. Hot skin covered muscles that rippled for days.

"Girl, you know it's true," he sang in a horribly off-key voice.

Sloane gasped lightheartedly. She loved seeing this side of August. The lighter side he rarely showed anyone. "Did you just quote a Milli Vanilli lyric? Are you eighty?"

He grinned down at her. "Only if you are. I mean, you knew what I was referencing."

Sloane sniffed. "I can't help that I grew up in a house where we cleaned every Saturday morning, and my mother made the playlist that consisted of nothing but R&B hits of the '80s and '90s. And you know this, because you weren't exempt when you came home with Donovan."

They shared a smile as they entered the bathroom at the collective memory. The tension knotting the muscles in her shoulders eased a bit. Getting back to their natural rapport felt good. She could relax with him. Be herself.

Still juggling her in his arms, August turned on the shower tap. She would not be impressed. She was not that impressionable. She would not swoon like Cinderella did the first time she saw Prince Charming. She was a grown-ass woman, not a girl who believed in fairy tales anymore.

"Shower cap, or no?" he asked.

"Yeah, I'm not trying to go through my hair routine today," she said, grabbing the shower cap she kept on a hook next to the shower and donning it.

"Okay, in you go." He lowered her into the shower and stepped in behind her. The small space was not meant for two people, especially when one of them was a buff pro football player. But she had no intention of telling him to get out. Not with his hard chest pressed to her back. She soaped up a washcloth and handed it to him over her shoulder.

"Thanks," he said. "I haven't forgotten what you said. When we were in the living room."

Sloane swallowed hard. She should've known he wouldn't let her get away with changing the topic of conversation for long. He saw through the bullshit and beneath the surface to the unvarnished truth better than anyone she'd ever met. Instead of answering, she stared straight ahead through the streaming water to the tiled wall. Swirling, chaotic thoughts were spinning through her head.

"Okay." He dropped a kiss to her shoulder. "Let me start. You're concerned about the turn in our relationship, what it means, and where we go from here."

She made a small sound of agreement.

As if sensing she wasn't ready to face him yet, he spoke directly into her ear as he made lazy circles with the washcloth across her back. "Sloane, I want you. I want to be with you. The wanting only gets more intense the more time I spend with you. I would do anything to make you happy." He took a deep breath. "Even date other women."

She almost broke her neck, slipping and sliding on the wet tub floor, turning at that last confession. "Wait. What are you talking about?"

His face was resolute. "I saw that list you made after you had that Zoom meeting. I figured I'd make your life easier if I did what needed to be done to get you that job."

She poked him in the chest. "No, you made my life miserable, you jackass! Did you think I liked sitting there while you were on a date?" She poked his very impressive chest again. She closed her eyes. She would not be distracted by perfection in all its hot, wet glory. "Or that you agreed to another one?"

"You know you can stop poking me, right?"

Her eyes flew open. "No, I don't!" She poked him again. "You should have told me that." Poke. "And although what you did is really sweet in a twisted, nonsensical 'the road to hell is paved with good intentions' kind of way, don't ever try to rescue me again." She paused to catch her breath. "Still . . . thank you for trying to look out for me."

"Will I get poked again if I say 'you're welcome'?"

"Yes!"

He smiled. "Okay, how about this? I'm sorry I hurt you back in the day."

They were going there? Oh. Okay. The air backed up in her lungs.

"I've never forgiven myself for putting that look on your face."

Entranced, Sloane stared at him. The look on his face now. Nothing but pure sincerity. The pain he'd suffered back then was easy to see. All this time, she'd believed that hurt belonged solely to her. How incredibly wrong she'd been. Resisting him, even remotely— not that she'd done a good job of doing that, if she wanted to keep it real—was proving to be futile.

She shook her head. "No. It wasn't your fault. I knew you had a girlfriend. I thought I was sooo irresistible and that you couldn't possibly feel as strongly about her as you did about me. My ego led me astray."

August reached for her hands. "Hey, don't do that. Try to put it all on you. You thought we had a connection. And we did. You thought you were smart? I thought I was smarter. If I said you were just a friend, then I wouldn't have to examine my feelings too closely."

She peeked up at him. "Where does that leave us? Well, besides naked in the shower?"

His lips curved up, but his eyes were still a little shy. A little uncertain. "I want to be with you. Only you. Please say you feel the same."

It wasn't a declaration of love, but would she have been ready if it was? Probably not.

It was past time to move past the past. To move past her misgivings about what could go wrong and what it meant to make herself vulnerable. Continuing to deny herself, to deny him, what they both wanted, was no longer an option. "I do."

His smile blossomed to a full-blown grin. "Good. Because this water is getting cold. And I have more sex master moves to show you."

* * *

"I want to apologize," Sloane said later that night while they were eating dinner. Mexican this time. They'd ordered in due to the dire contents of her fridge.

August tilted his head to the side as he set down his fork. "For what?"

"For pushing you into all of this. I know you're not really comfortable with the SugarBae stuff. I get very passionate about things I believe in, and act without thinking about how my actions might affect others. Sugar Blitz is so great, and I love my brother, and I want all of you to be successful. And seeing an opportunity to help make that happen that would also land me a new job . . . Well, I just ran with it. You wouldn't have gone through all this if it wasn't for me."

His lips quirked. "Appreciate the apology, but no one makes me do anything I don't want to do."

Her eyebrows lifted in disbelief. "You wanted to go on blind dates and have the spectacles broadcast to anyone with access to Instagram?"

He chuckled. "No, but remember, I'm the one who agreed to becoming a social media star. Well, before I changed my mind. I knew—okay, kinda knew—what I was getting myself into."

Sloane studied him. "Why did you agree? Really? You can tell me."

"I know." He went silent for a second, then sighed. "You ever feel like you're not enough? That you're not doing enough?"

"Oh, August, of course I have." Sloane covered his hand with hers and squeezed. "But you're more than enough just as you are."

He shrugged, his eyes darkening with the clearly painful memories. "I haven't always felt that way."

Was he talking about his dad? His ex-wife? "It's the truth."

"Thanks. In any case, I was having one of those moments." He chuckled and wiggled his shoulders like he was trying to shake off the heavy mood. "The next thing I knew I was on TV."

She wanted to press for more, but clearly he wasn't in the mood to share yet, and she would respect that. He wasn't one to automatically spill his guts and would only do so when ready. Time to lighten the mood.

"So here's the thing. Now that we're a thing, I can't have you dating other women, just so we're clear. I know you told me you did it for me, but if you ever get any thoughts about dating other women for real, it ain't happening."

The corner of his mouth quirked in genuine humor this time. She'd never get tired of seeing it. "Really? Why not?"

"Because there's a good chance I'd rip their hair out and/or yours the first time they smiled at you or you looked at them with that patented August intensity."

His eyebrows lifted. "Patented August intensity?"

"Like you're really paying attention to them and really hearing them, like we all dream of having in our partner. If you did that, I wouldn't be responsible for my actions. And then I'd end up in jail."

August took a bite of his beef enchilada and swallowed. "Can't have that, now, can we?"

Her smile bloomed. "No. Ending up in jail was basically what I wrote as one of the cons for you dating Paige before I scratched it out because I didn't have any claims on you."

"But now you do."

"Yeah." And she couldn't be happier. "So, are you still up for the social media campaign?"

"Yes." Again, his face and voice backed up the truth in his words. "Cynthia is still leading her merry band of protestors against us. I want the location to be successful. And I can admit I've had a wee bit of fun with all this, so I'm willing to continue to put myself on the forefront of the effort."

Sloane shimmied her shoulders in a little victory dance. "Fantastic. Then, we're on to plan B. Or maybe C. I've lost count."

He looked at her in that way that always made her heart flip and remember why she used to believe in love and romance so much. Like he believed in her and was awed by her. "You already have a plan."

Her heart melted. The look. His belief in her. His willingness to believe in her expertise. Damn, she was stronger than she'd ever given herself credit for. How had she resisted throwing herself at him again all these years since his divorce? She nodded. "I do."

He spread his hands wide. "Let's hear it."

"We need to play to your strengths, not your weaknesses," she said, leaning forward, the familiar buzz strumming through her veins. She truly loved this. Creating a plan that showcased her client's strengths and would help get them the results they wanted. That would help them genuinely connect to their target audience. Yes, they might be trying to sell a product, but it was because they believed in it and the good it could do, the good it could provide the community.

August studied her. "What are my weaknesses?"

Of course he asked that. It wasn't vanity. He wasn't being flippant. His curiosity about himself, about the world around him, was unmatched. He wanted to be a better, more aware person.

"They're weaknesses in the sense of what we're trying to accomplish here. You're not an attention seeker. You're not someone content to casually date a bunch of women."

He nodded in agreement. "And my strengths?"

Too many to count. "You're someone who cares, who listens. You see the whole picture and underneath the surface to the heart of the matter. You're truthful, yet kind."

His head ducked for a moment like he was embarrassed. "Thank you."

Why was he so unbelievably adorable?

"You're welcome. It's the truth." She sighed. "Here's some more truth. I've been trying to turn you into someone you're not, and that's not the path to success."

"So, what's your idea? Do you want to talk about our relationship, since people are way too invested in my love life?"

Even as he said it, her gut screamed in protest.

They looked at each other and shook their heads simultaneously.

"No," they said in unison.

Sloane didn't need words to know what he was thinking.

What was happening between them was special. Rare. And she didn't want to share it with the world quite yet. If ever. Which should have gone against everything she stood for as a social media manager, but she didn't care. She'd always believed you should only share what you were comfortable with.

"Y'all want to be a part of the community, right? To give back?" At his nod, Sloane settled back in her chair. "Trust me. I've got a great idea. A couple of them, actually. But first we need to talk to Donovan and Nicholas. No, I didn't forget about our delayed meeting."

Chapter Thirty-Four

*F*amiliar nerves danced in August's stomach, but he was ready. "Excited" was going a little far, but Sloane had come up with a good plan. No more dating his "fans." No more IG Lives, at least for the near future. He'd promised to stay open to the possibility if a really cool idea came up. Like he could ever say no to her. She'd looked at him with her soulful eyes and he'd been toast. Happily.

"Remember, be yourself," Sloane said.

Right. That was the plan.

"I believe in you." She followed that up with a soft kiss. He nearly groaned when the short embrace ended. He'd never tire of tasting her lips, of inhaling her scent, of luxuriating in her presence. He was in love with her. But he sensed a reserve in her that hadn't entirely gone away after their talk in her shower.

So he'd go slow.

She'd closed her heart years ago, and to expect her to simply open it because he was the awesomest guy in the world was ridiculous. But he was only human. She had her reservations, but so did he. Would she want to stick by his side through good and bad, through thick and thin, or would she retreat like his dad and his ex-wife had?

But torturing himself like that solved nothing. It's not like he'd told her the full truth about why he'd decided to pursue social media stardom, so he needed to chill. Being a hypocrite was not the move. They were together now, and if he had anything to say about it, they'd be together for the rest of their lives.

But first, a podcast. Good Lord, he was doing a podcast.

"We should do a podcast and use it as neighborhood outreach," she'd said. "We'll help the community at large and the business at the same time. It's perfect."

Her excitement was infectious. "Can I ask you something?" At her nod, he finally gave voice to a question that had been plaguing him for days. "You really seem to be happy doing what you're doing. Do you really want to work for that other company?"

She looked at him like he'd grown another head. "Yes! It's a dream job, and I won't be riding my brother's coattails."

The look on her face made it clear the subject was closed, so he simply nodded and changed the subject. That was yesterday. Today was today.

He looked at all the equipment Sloane had purchased and set up. She'd had a lot of fun using the company credit card. He had no clue what everything did. Wires and speakers and little black boxes were everywhere.

"Trust me. I got it," Sloane had assured him as they unpacked the boxes. And she did. Apparently, being a sound engineer was in her bag of tricks as a social media manager. It was sexy as hell.

She slipped on a shiny new pair of professional-looking black headphones. "Ready?"

He adjusted his own headphones and nodded. "Yes."

"Excellent. Recording begins in three, two, one." She injected a light tone into her voice. "Welcome to *Sugar Blitz Talk* with Sugar-Bae, August Hodges."

"What's up, Sloane?" he said. He sounded normal. The key, as always, was to focus on her. They were just talking like they always did. He never felt more comfortable, more himself, than when he was speaking with her.

"I'm excited to be here and to talk about issues that are close to both of our hearts."

He reached for her hand and squeezed. "Exactly. We want to highlight unsung women in society, and the work they do to make their communities better."

Sloane's eyes gleamed. "As you know, I'm ridiculously excited about this. Every week, we'll talk to a different woman from communities all across the US. If you want to nominate one of these special women, please hit us up in our inbox. We're starting with a local hero right here in San Diego."

That was his cue. "Our first guest ever on this podcast is Cynthia Franklin."

"For those of you not in the know, August and his partners are planning to open a second location of their cupcake shop, but some residents aren't happy about it."

"That's right," Cynthia interjected, looking him up and down disapprovingly. "We're not."

August exchanged an amused glance with Sloane. Cynthia still wasn't sure if they were setting her up, but she hadn't been able to resist the allure of telling her side of the story.

Sloane spoke. "She's been a community organizer for decades, heavily involved in making San Diego a better, more equitable place. She's organized fundraisers for the local library, civil rights sit-ins at city hall, and tons of other things."

Cynthia's frown showed no signs of abating. "I know your date with my daughter didn't go well. Is this your way of buttering me up so I don't kick your behind?"

A burst of genuine laughter bubbled from August's chest. "Only if it works."

Cynthia's lips pursed. "The only reason I didn't hang up when you called is because my daughter said you were very nice, checking in on her after your date. You can't be all bad."

August covered his heart with his hand while he struggled not to laugh. Look at that. He was, dare he say, *having fun*. "Thank you. I think."

Sloane laughed. "Tell us why you're concerned about the shop."

The expression on Cynthia's face turned serious. "It's not just the shop. It's what you plan to do after the shop opens. Open up more businesses, jack up the rent, push out residents who've been here for decades."

"We have no plans to do that," August said.

She let out a joyless laugh. "I've heard that before from people who probably meant it, but then the allure of money becomes too much to ignore, and all those so-called principles go right out the window."

"I don't doubt it, but all we can do is continue to be us and show you who we are. If you'll let us."

Cynthia harrumphed. "We'll see."

"Yes, we will," Sloane said. "That's one of the reasons we invited you onto the podcast. We wanted you to be the first to hear the news."

"What news?" Cynthia's suspicion had ramped up to Level 533. It took everything in August not to wilt under her glare.

Donovan and Nicholas, who'd been hiding in the hallway, entered the room.

"What is this?" Cynthia hissed. "What's going on here?"

"Everyone, Nicholas Connors and Donovan Dell, the other co-owners of Sugar Blitz, are joining us," Sloane said. Donovan and Nicholas slipped on headphones and sat.

"Happy to have you here, fellas," August said.

"We're happy to be here," Donovan said.

"Some might even say *thrilled*," Nicholas, ever the showman, added.

"I'm not one of them," Cynthia said.

August laughed. "Give it a minute. Maybe you will be."

"All three of us wanted to be here to share the news with you, Cynthia. While we can't say we loved having picketers outside our business, you did make us think," Donovan said. He nodded at Nicholas.

"As you know, we own several buildings on this block," Nicholas added with a charming smile.

"Yes, I know," Cynthia said, clearly uncharmed.

Nicholas laughed and nodded at August. As a group, they'd decided August would be the one to share, since this was "his" podcast after all.

August leaned toward his mic. "In addition to committing to hiring people from this neighborhood, we've decided to turn one of the buildings into a multipurpose community center."

Cynthia's mouth dropped open. "Wait. What?"

August's smile spread. "It's true. The community center will be a place for people to gather, but we are also committed to making it a place where people can get job and skills training as well as rental and housing assistance. Kids can get help with their homework and play sports while they wait for their parents to get off work."

Sloane had laid out the idea to him and his partners. They'd all come onboard quickly because it was brilliant. Sloane was brilliant. And she was his. And he was hers.

Sniffling brought him back to the present. Tears had started to slide down Cynthia's cheeks. "Are you serious?" she asked.

August looked across at Sloane. She, too, was crying. Okay, yeah, this was a cool moment.

"Yes, we are," he said.

"The plans are still in development, but it's absolutely happening," Sloane said.

Cynthia clasped her hands together. "Oh, my goodness. I can't wait to tell my husband."

Sloane leaped from her chair. "Why don't you call him? Do you mind if we listen in on the call?"

"No, after that announcement, you can do whatever you want." Cynthia dialed her phone and set it on the table. Sloane set up a microphone next to it to catch the output from the speaker.

"Hello," Ben said. His voice came through loud and clear. August looked across at Sloane, who was beaming. She was pleased with that development. He grinned. Always with her eye on the social media prize.

"Ben, honey, we did it, Ben! We did it," Cynthia said, practically kicking her heels.

"Did what?" Ben asked. "Are they treating you well? Do I need to come down there?"

"Yes. No. I mean, yes, they're treating me well. No, you don't need to come down here."

"You sound worked up. What's going on?"

A couple who was suspicious together stayed together, apparently. August looked at Sloane again. Her lips were twitching.

Cynthia quickly explained.

"Yes, ma'am!" Ben exclaimed when she was done. "I knew you would get those young'uns to see the errors of their ways. My wife is the baddest woman on the planet."

The call ended, and, as planned, Nicholas and Donovan took their leave with high fives all around. After a five-minute break, they resumed taping.

"Your husband's support was very sweet," Sloane said.

"Thank you," Cynthia said with a proud smile. "Ben is with me every step of the way."

"But you're the leader," August said.

"I am, and my husband has always supported me in my causes. He never tries to steal my shine. He's there to support me, never to talk over me."

"That's great that you have such a supportive partner," Sloane said.

"It is," August said. "You're lucky."

Cynthia gave a wise, all-knowing nod. "And don't I know it. I've seen a lot in my day. Partners not being partners to their spouses. Not supporting them when they need it most."

"Yeah, my mother never got the credit she deserved." August stilled. Shit. He hadn't meant to say that out loud.

Sloane sat up straight and reached for his hand. "August, are you okay?"

Yeah, this was not the direction this episode was supposed to go in. He searched for an answer. No, he wasn't okay. Not when it came to his mom.

"Why don't you tell us about her?" Cynthia said quietly, reaching for his other hand. "You look like you have a lot on your mind. Like I always tell my daughter, the healing can only start after you acknowledge the feelings."

August shook his head. "We're supposed to be talking about you."

"We can do that after you say what you need to say." Her eyes, once so suspicious, now offered only kindness and sympathy. Understanding.

August's eyes fluttered shut as memories bombarded him. "She was a chef. Self-taught. There wasn't any money to send her to culinary school, but she didn't let that stop her. She was always trying new recipes, studying the techniques of world-renowned chefs to get better. She fed the neighborhood. Anybody who needed some good home cooking with a twist knew they could stop by our house at dinnertime, and she'd feed them. And they'd leave with the best dessert they'd ever had in their entire lives."

"Sounds like an incredible woman," Sloane said.

"She was, and then she got sick. She passed away when I was young. It wasn't until I was in high school that I found out my father had built his success on her recipes."

A lifetime of weight lifted from his shoulders as he told the unfiltered truth for the first time in his life. He may not ever be comfortable speaking in front of a crowd, but speaking the truth would always be his calling.

"Your father?" Cynthia asked.

"Yes, he's Dale Hodges."

"The chef."

"Yes."

Telling the truth had never felt so good.

Chapter Thirty-Five

"What the hell is this?" His dad shoved a page against August's chest and pushed past him into August's house.

With a sigh, August caught the paper before it drifted to the floor and followed him inside. It was too early in the morning for this. "Nice to see you too, Father."

"Don't try that sarcastic bullshit with me, son." His father puffed up his chest and glared. August guessed he was supposed to find the look intimidating. Not long ago, he might have. But he was a different person than he was two weeks ago.

"You have some explaining to do." His father jerked his chin at the paper still crumpled in August's hand. August smoothed it out and quickly perused it. Sloane's PR efforts were really taking off. That woman was damned good at her job. Not that he would say that out loud right now. His father's face was already an unhealthy shade of red, an impressive feat given his deep brown skin tone. The article, printed from the internet, highlighted their plans for the community center and the podcast, including a section on the inaugural episode. August didn't have to guess what part had pissed his dad off.

"You made me look like a fool!"

August gritted his teeth. "I told the truth."

His father sniffed. "How would you know what the truth is?"

"I found Mama's journals. The ones she wrote in every night."

His father jerked back in obvious surprise. "What are you talking about?"

"She talked about her love of cooking. How it was a joy she shared with her husband. She was a little annoyed that her husband was getting all the credit, but that would change soon, he reassured her. They just needed to get the family name off the ground. Ringing a bell?"

When his dad remained silent, August kept talking. "Imagine my surprise when I stumbled upon the recipes she was working on, tweaks she planned to try. Imagine my even greater surprise when it dawned on me that her chicken cacciatore was the exact same dish that catapulted you to stardom. She loved you—that too was evident in her journals—which is why I've kept silent until now.

"I didn't mean to put you on blast like that, but I'm not upset about it either. I've protected you for far too long, thinking that maybe if I was just a little more perfect, one day my dad would love me." August shook his head in disgust. "But to get you to show up at my house, I had to put a dent in your precious reputation, because at the end of the day, that's all you care about."

At the end of his tirade, August's chest heaved with exertion. Damn, that was the second time he'd gone off on someone in the past month. At least no one was there to record it and put it on social media this time.

Stilted, tense silence filled his living room. But he refused to break it. He'd said what he had to say. It was his father's turn.

A muscle jerked in his father's jaw as he glared at his only child. "Do you know everything I've been through?" he ground out.

That was his father's response? Fuck not saying anything more.

A lifetime of pent-up emotion came spewing out. "Of course I do. You tell anyone who's willing to listen. Yes, being a Black chef in a white-dominated field was challenging, but you know who had it even rougher? My Black female mother, who wanted nothing more than to be a pastry chef. Yes, Dad, I opened a cupcake shop because my mother loved to bake, and I'll never apologize for it."

"How dare you?" his dad raged.

"How dare I? How dare I tell the truth? How dare I make the great Dale Hodges feel bad? I'm so fucking done. Mama put your feelings above hers. I've done the same thing since I was a *child*. But I'm done doing it. I'm done waiting for my father to show he loves me. I'm a good person. I do have people in my life who love me, who have my back. I don't have to settle for the little breadcrumbs you throw out when it's convenient for you. I let my father's lack of love eat at me my whole life. How great could I be if my own father didn't have time for me? If I was nothing more than a nuisance to him? But no more. No fucking more."

His father's face remained impassive. The only sign he might have been affected by August's torrent of words came in his slightly downcast eyes. Finally, he lifted his head.

"I am Dale Hodges. I will not apologize for who I am or my life's work. I am a damned good chef. Yes, I was jealous that innovation in the kitchen came so much easier to your mother than it did for me. I got tired of being turned down for jobs. Tired of laboring in kitchens waiting for my big break. When someone at a festival asked if one of her dishes was mine, I said yes, and I was hired. It was cowardly, but I felt I had no other choice than to keep going if I wanted to keep my job and advance in my career." He paused, worked his jaw side to side. "She told me it was okay. I told myself no one was getting hurt in the process. And then she was gone and no one else knew. And I buried myself in work."

Dale walked over to the fireplace and picked up a photo of August's mother. It was August's favorite and how he chose to remember her—her head thrown back in pure and unadulterated laughter. A brief smile cracked Dale's lips. "She was so beautiful. So smart and clever."

He returned the frame to the mantel and took the few steps to August's side. August kept silent, steeling himself for whatever his father would say next.

Dale's voice came out as a whisper. "Despite all of her accomplishments, what I admired about her was her ability to show everyone, especially you, how much she loved them."

For the first time, August was reminded that his father was not the young man in his mid-thirties August always visualized him as. There was a slight stoop in his shoulders, more gray in his hair than black, lines around his mouth.

But then Dale lifted his head. His eyes were as resolute as ever. "I'm sorry I was never the father you deserved. Then, in my grief, I became even worse and never recovered. I told myself you were better off with your grandfather. That he was there for you while I was busy. I'm sorry."

Stunned, August stumbled back, his father's words reverberating through his head. That was more raw, unfiltered emotion out of his father than he could ever remember.

Silence, that familiar foe that always arrived and overstayed its welcome when he and his father found themselves in the same room, made an appearance once again. But he couldn't let it win. Not this time. He had to speak. To bridge the gap that had always existed between father and son. "Thank you for being honest and apologizing. It means a lot to me."

Dale scrubbed his face with shaky hands. "I'm so sorry. I miss her so much. That's not an excuse, but it is the truth."

August stepped forward. His father fell into his arms. For the first time ever, August saw his father cry. He dropped his head as tears welled in his eyes, as well. Maybe, just maybe, they could heal together instead of separately.

* * *

"You okay?" Sloane asked from the driver's side of her car. They were driving to August's place after a day at Sugar Blitz Two.

August shrugged. "Sure. Why wouldn't I be?"

She gripped the steering wheel harder. "Oh, I don't know. Maybe because you had a deeply emotional talk with your father after you talked about him in such an open, honest way on your podcast."

A wry chuckle filled the air. "Oh. Yeah. It was rough, but it had to be done. Sugarcoating got us nowhere. I just told the truth."

"It was still brave." She pulled to a stop at the red light and pressed a kiss to his cheek. "For what it's worth, I'm proud of you. I'm in awe of you. You deserve everything nice in the world."

"Thanks," he said absentmindedly.

Whatever had him so enthralled had nothing to do with her. Sloane glanced down at the phone in his hands. She sucked in a breath. He'd been scrolling through Instagram and stopped at an ad promoting his ex-wife's San Diego bookstore appearance.

"Can I ask you something?" she asked. Something had been bothering her since their first incognito date at the bookstore.

He dropped the phone to his lap. "Sure. What's up?"

Sloane sucked in a breath and clenched her stomach muscles like that could stop the butterflies rampaging inside her. "Is she why you're doing all of this—to prove something to her, especially since she's coming back to town? Did you decide to pursue something with me to prove you've moved on?"

He sighed. "Yes. And no."

Sloane tried to hold her heart together, but a tiny fissure appeared in the tissue anyway, and there was nothing she could do to stop it. Luckily, August spoke before she was forced to test out her voice.

"She's been giving interviews promoting her new book. Before I agreed to all of this, I saw one where she talked about how our relationship held her back. How I held her back. I admit I did feel some type of way about it. And it did push me to act, to take on a more active role in Sugar Blitz's success. But hear me when I say this. I'm not trying to prove anything to her, or anyone else for that matter, by being with you."

She sighed, happy she had the road to concentrate on while she spilled her guts. "I was so young. You chose her over me. I know why, and I get it. I don't begrudge you for it, but I guess a small part of me is still hurt by it."

August vehemently shook his head. "Hey, listen to me. What we have has nothing to do with her or anyone else. The only two people in this relationship are you and me."

Sloane glanced at the phone lying so innocently on his lap. Melinda smiled confidently at her. She believed him, but she also knew things were rarely that simple. Old insecurities and wounds were hard to let go or recover from. For her and August.

Chapter Thirty-Six

he Sugar Blitz owners are fully on their way to successfully launching their second location. Social media engagement has increased by fifty percent across all platforms. August Hodges, one of the owners, has launched a successful podcast. Early buzz has made it clear that he's found his audience, who hunger for more, literally and figuratively. With continued investment in their social media, Sugar Blitz will place themselves in a prime position to be successful for a long time to come."

Sloane ended her spiel with a confident smile. Her presentation had been fantastic. She had the stats, the posts, and the comments to prove how effective her efforts had been over the past few weeks, even through all the ups and downs. No one could take that away from her, not a boss or a competitor for a job or another woman who wanted her man for herself. Her hard work had paid off. Hopefully, she would be reaping the rewards soon.

Emily nodded. "That was very impressive, Sloane."

Sloane nodded. "Thank you."

"You've accomplished a ton in a short amount of time. You had roadblocks thrown in your way, but you persevered. If I wasn't convinced already, you are a strong contender for this position. However, I still have Preston's presentation to go. But I am very, very impressed. Expect to hear from me very soon."

Sloane floated out of the office. She hadn't left with a job offer, but she had the next best thing. Nothing but positive feedback.

Sloane came up short as she exited the elevator. What if Preston's presentation was better than hers? She violently shook her head. No, none of that negative thinking. It added nothing positive to her psyche. Besides, being confident was way better. That job was hers. It was only a matter of time.

Sloane nodded briskly to herself. Yep. That was the positive vibe she wanted to put out into the universe. And she knew exactly how to celebrate. And with whom.

* * *

After opening his front door, August only had a second to brace himself before a whirling dervish launched herself into his arms. He stumbled back into his foyer as Sloane wrapped her legs around his waist and rained kisses all across his face. He chased her wandering lips until he finally caught them beneath his. He willfully sank into the embrace.

Sweetness. Desire. Their lips melded together, tongues contouring together. He delved deep, seeking more, needing more. Groaning with desire when she met his every thrust with a parry of her own, just as hungry as he was. Kissing her would never get old. It was a new, revelatory experience every time.

"I'm pretty sure I got the job, and I have you to thank," she said when the need for air became too much to ignore.

Joy surged within him. "That's amazing, sweetness. But this was all you."

Her beautiful eyes narrowed. "Stop arguing with me when I'm trying to give you a compliment."

He grinned. "Yes, ma'am."

She tightened her legs around his waist. "Let's put those lips to better use."

"Yes, ma'am."

He made his way, by instinct and bumping into various walls, to his bedroom, while Sloane did her best to distract him with kisses to his mouth, his neck, his ear.

"Hurry," she moaned against his mouth. She backed up the command by cupping him through his pants. His eyes damn near crossed with lust.

"Shit, Sloane."

"Want me to stop?" she purred into his ear as she squeezed his diamond-hard erection.

"Fuck, no." Walking was no longer possible as lust rampaged through his system, so he leaned back against the nearest wall and concentrated on tasting her sweet lips and trying not to lose his mind thanks to her nimble fingers. His zipper was perilously close to bursting open.

When she tore her mouth away from him, he swallowed his growl of disappointment. But then his eyes landed on her pretty, smooth neck. He dropped his head to the enticing spot where her shoulder met her neck. Nipped the soft skin with his teeth. Her breathy moan sent a shiver of desire down his spine. Yes. Now. Always.

But first they needed a flat surface, so he could explore to his heart's content. Then, her hand landed on his dick again and he damn near forgot his own name.

Only sheer determination saw him through. He would make this so fucking good for her.

He tripped over some shoes, obviously put there by the devil, and sent Sloane and him tumbling. Mid-air, he twisted his body, so his back would hit first. As her laughter rang in his ears, they landed on his bed and bounced once. He blinked up at her. "I'm usually much more suave than this."

She shook her head. "No, you're not."

"No, I'm not."

He swallowed her laughter with his lips and fell into the embrace again. Their mutual mirth flittered away into something hotter and much more essential to his immediate well-being.

It had been less than twenty-four hours since they'd been to-gether. An eternity. He needed her now. Now wasn't the time for slow and steady.

She scrambled to her knees and straddled him. "Ooh, I like this position."

He cocked an eyebrow. "You do?"

"Oh yeah." Her hands went seeking, slipping under his T-shirt.

Her delicate, nimble fingers stroked across his stomach muscles. He sucked in a breath, words deserting him. She pushed his shirt up his chest, her hands immediately going back to sweeping across his stomach, sending heat streaking through him.

"Ooh, someone's been working out. You feel so good," she mur-mured. "I bet you taste even better."

"Sloane." Instead of the semi-warning tone he was going for, his voice broke off in a quiver as she lowered her mouth.

The first touch of her lips on his abdomen sent his pulse sky-rocketing. "I was right. You taste so good." She lifted her glittering eyes. "Let me play."

This was her party. She was feeling good. He wanted to flip their bodies and taste every inch of her body, but she wanted this. And he wanted whatever she wanted. He nodded, since talking was beyond him at the moment. He sat up to whip his shirt over his head, then returned to his prone position. He was immediately rewarded with her mouth on his neck.

"You have the best Adam's apple," she murmured. "I've lusted after it for over a decade."

His laughter turned into a moan when her lips and hands continued exploring. "The veins in your forearms turn me on," she whispered. "I command you to wear dress shirts every day and then as soon as you see me, roll up your sleeves very slowly, so I can lust after them in public."

"Got it."

Her little nibbles and licks were driving him out of his mind. But he would lie here and endure for eternity if she commanded it. Whatever she wanted, whenever she wanted. Her lips swept along both his shoulders as her fingers skimmed his arms, leaving goose bumps in their wake. Then, she lingered across his chest. Her soft hands would be the death of him sooner rather than later. He would have no regrets.

She flicked his nipples. They immediately drew into tight beads. Her tongue peeked out of her red lips. He held his breath as her head lowered. Still, he wasn't prepared for the bliss that zoomed through his entire body when her lips landed on his nipple. She hummed against his chest. Then her tongue joined the party as she sucked and licked one nipple while rolling the other between her fingers. The dual sensations traveled through his body right to his dick, which pressed against his zipper, begging to be let free. But he wouldn't move until she gave him some clue that that's what she wanted.

Today was all about Sloane.

"How does that feel, August?" She captured his gaze. Not that he had any intention of looking away. "Tell me."

"The best." The absolute truth. When her smile bloomed across her face, he felt like he could slay any dragons that crossed their paths. Anything for her.

"Good." Her fingers had never stopped moving, making it hard to keep up with the conversation, but he did his damnedest. "This happy trail is so enthralling. The places it leads . . ."

Her breath tickled the hair on his chest. She murmured against his skin, her tongue coming out to play. His stomach muscles tightened in anticipation. He grabbed the comforter with both hands to keep from reaching for her and rolling her underneath him. Of seeking the sweetness between her legs. But he couldn't. He wouldn't. Not yet.

Sloane's show, Sloane's show, he chanted silently.

"Problem?" Sloane whispered, ever the temptress, clearly sensing and reveling in his distress. Her hand had landed on his waistband, so close, but not close enough to where he needed her touch.

"Touch me. Please," he added when her eyebrows quirked at his demanding tone.

"Since you asked so nicely." She carefully pulled the zipper down and reached inside. Her fingers wrapped around his dick. She pumped up and down hard, the way he loved. Breathing became mission impossible. His skin buzzed. He'd have it no other way. He lifted his hips and she tugged his pants and underwear away.

Her lips skimmed across his legs. "These thighs. So biteable."

"Thank you," he said after swallowing hard and gathering his faculties to speak.

"My pleasure, trust me."

He reached for her. She scooted away. "Nope. I didn't say you could touch."

He swallowed hard. "I'd really like to see you."

Her eyebrow cocked. "You mean like this?" She slowly unclasped the top button of her shirt.

He propped up on his elbow. "Yes. Hurry." This game was going to kill him. And he'd have it no other way.

Her lips curved in a tempting, teasing grin. "A little bossy. Too bad we're playing by my rules."

His mouth dried as he followed the movements of her fingers. One more button slipped free, offering a teasing glimpse of her brown flesh. It wasn't enough. He curled his hands at his sides to keep from ripping the shirt off her. He wanted to taste her flesh more than he'd wanted anything in his life.

Her hand slipped inside her shirt, inside her bra. Her soft gasp went straight to his dick.

"What are you doing, sweetness? Touching your nipple?" She nodded, her eyes glazing over.

"Show me," he demanded. She nodded. He'd never been so happy to see a red shirt disappear. She rose off the bed and stood before him in a sexy black lace bra, her pretty breasts spilling over the top. "If I'd known that was under your shirt, I would've it ripped it off you."

"Oh, really? Why?" Her fingers skimmed across her collarbone. He tracked every millimeter of movement with greedy eyes.

"You know why. Touch yourself." He sounded like a fucking Neanderthal. Luckily, she didn't seem to mind. If anything, her eyes darkened and her breath quickened.

"Whatever you say, August." Maintaining eye contact with him, she slipped two fingers inside the cup. She cupped the mound and massaged. Then her nimble fingers moved to the nipple. She squeezed the tight flesh between two fingers. His mouth watered. He knew the sensation of pinching her nipples. He knew how they felt against his tongue. Like heaven. He wanted that again. Almost as much as he wanted to continue watching her please herself. Her lips parted on a silent gasp as she squeezed.

Her fingers skimmed the curve of her right breast. She pulled the cups of the bra down, allowing her luscious breasts to fully slip out. They were the most perfect breasts in the entire world. They were so close to his mouth and yet so far.

She rolled both nipples between her fingers, alternating between lighter touches and harder squeezes. Her breathy moans accompanied the movements. He was going to lose his fucking mind.

"Come here," he demanded. He swung his legs to the side of the bed. He could be docile no longer.

"Since you've been such a good boy . . ."

He murmured his approval when she stepped in between his thighs. She crawled onto the bed, straddling his hips, a position that put her tempting breasts at mouth level. He wasted no time, sliding his tongue around her right areola. She tasted like sunshine and the purest honey. He tugged on her nipple with his lips and teeth, just the way she liked. The way he loved. Her quickly drawn-in breath was his reward.

But he wanted more. Always more.

He delved underneath her underwear, straight to her clit. Her forehead fell to his right shoulder as she dug into his opposing shoulder with sharp nails. He loved the sting. He loved how her breath quickened, how she shivered under his touch. Her scent surrounded him. He would and could happily stay drunk off it for the rest of his life. He varied the pace of his fingers against the small bit of flesh based on her reactions. Slow to start off. Mid-tempo when her breath quickened. Faster when she bit him. Slower to prolong her stay on the knife's edge of desire. Her hips moved, back and forth, chasing the movement of his hand.

Being inside her was his second priority. His first? Making her come so hard against his fingers she'd feel the aftershocks for days.

August slipped a finger inside her. Her hips' movement quickened.

"Just like that, August." Her moan acted as rocket fuel to his lust. He added another finger, sliding in and out of her. His plan had been to go slow, but shit, she was so tight and so fucking wet and it felt so damned good. She squeezed her inner muscles around him. He bent his fingers, rubbing against the spot inside her that made her go wild. With his other hand, he rubbed circles around her clit.

"Shit, Sloane," he gritted out when her hand wrapped around his dick. This was supposed to be all about her.

"Two can play this game," she whispered in his ear. "I bet I can make you come before you make me come."

He was a professional athlete. Competitiveness flowed through his veins. "You're on."

Two minutes later, he was questioning his life's choices. He'd been so sure he could win this bet. Why? His hubris was going to be the death of him, but what a way to go. Her fingers were magical.

"Shit," he moaned when she rubbed some of her wetness along the head of his dick and then up and down his length. Just following the movement of her fingers nearly short-circuited his brain. Her fingers moved a little easier, up and down with one hand and squeezing with the other. She knew he didn't like a gentle hand. He was fucking close. But not yet. Not yet. Not until he'd given her all the pleasure he could. Not until he made her feel more than she'd ever felt.

They fell into a decadent rhythm, fully intuned to the other. She moved her hand up and down his length at the same tempo he slid his fingers in and out of her, just like they would if she was riding his dick. He was so fucking close. August ground his teeth into dust. In due time.

Back to work he went. He sought out her mouth. His tongue teased the seam of her lips until she let him in. His tongue happily reacquainted itself with hers. How wonderful she tasted. He needed to savor. To memorize the taste and shape of her lips. That was his intention, anyway. The slow, sensual languid slide lasted for only a few seconds before the kiss became hungry and voracious.

She pressed against him, the thrust of her hips no longer moving in a measured circular motion, but a jagged, erratic, desperate motion. She was near the edge.

"August, August," she repeated over and over like she was in a trance. He twisted his fingers inside her and ground the palm of his hand against her, right against her clit. He pinched her nipple with his other hand.

Her back arched as she came against his fingers, her body shaking, her eyes dazed with wonder and joy as a loud, prolonged cry spilled from her lips. Watching Sloane come was one of the top highlights of his life.

But they weren't done.

Once again, he turned their bodies. This time, Sloane landed underneath him. He hastily procured a condom from the nightstand drawer, donned it, and covered Sloane's warm, tempting body in less than ten seconds. She welcomed him back with open arms. He wasted no time, thrusting inside her in one smooth glide. He burrowed his head in her shoulder as his skin buzzed with lust. How had he denied himself for this long? Being with her like this left nirvana in the dust. Then she twined her legs around his waist and lifted her hips.

"Oh, shit." How was it possible that this position felt even better? "August, please. Move."

"Yes, ma'am." Her wish would always be his command. Her cries of harder, faster urged him on. She liked hard, long strokes. He could do this for the rest of his life if that's what she wanted. Each time she whimpered when he retreated, only to cry out in ecstasy when he returned, made his heart soar. Made his determination to make it even better for her soar.

The tingle started at the base of his spine and spread to his extremities. He wouldn't last much longer. But not without her. Never without her. He kissed her again and found her clit. When she got close, she liked him to press hard against the bundle of nerves.

With her cries ringing in his ears, he came, stars shooting across his eyes, shaking with the intensity of the orgasm.

When he came to his senses, he whispered, "I win."

Sloane's beautiful laughter filled the room. "I hate you."

"I love you."

Chapter Thirty-Seven

Sloane blinked rapidly as her heart slammed against her chest. Her voice came out faint and unsteady. "You . . . love . . . me?"

"Yes, Sloane Renee Dell, I love you." Unlike her, he sounded sure and confident. He sighed. "And you're not ready to hear that yet."

Her heart bloomed with joy, while her head, always so hesitant, nervous, and wary when it came to love and the necessity of trust and vulnerability that came with it, struggled to keep up. "I—I . . . just . . ."

He reached for her hands. "Hey, it's okay. What we have is new. I sprung that on you. I can see you're struggling, trying to figure out whether to believe me and what it means if you do. And yeah. I'll be patient."

Sloane's eyes squeezed shut for a second. "August . . ."

"No, it's okay."

She wasn't sure. His mouth was saying all the right things, but the mask he usually reserved for strangers and those he didn't trust had slipped over his face. She hated it. When he let down his guard, it was a beautiful sight to see. Her heart never felt more full than in those moments.

She had to make him understand. "I've been hurt before. Opening my heart to that type of hurt again is scary. But I do want to be with you."

"You're just not sure you want all of me."

Damn it, he had a way of getting to the core of the matter every single time. It was one of the many reasons she . . . cared about him. Sloane sighed. What the hell was wrong with her? He was everything she'd always wanted, and she wasn't grabbing him with both hands and jumping in feetfirst. And she'd put that look on his face.

Her phone rang. Damn, she didn't have time for whoever it was. But it wouldn't stop ringing.

"Go ahead."

Sloane wrapped a bedsheet around herself and slipped off the bed. She stumbled out of the bedroom and located her purse, where she'd dropped it in the hall. She dug the phone out and almost lost her grip when she saw who was calling. Her heart picked up pace again. She let out a little squeak.

"What? Who is it?" August barked out from behind her.

"It's SDT," she whispered like the woman on the other end of the call could hear her talking about her.

"Answer it," he whispered back, inadvertently picking up on her neuroses.

"Right." She cleared her throat. Her hands were still shaking, but she got it together enough to stab at the screen to answer the call. This was it. "Hello."

Points to her for sounding halfway normal.

"Hi, Sloane. This is Emily Chan."

Sloane listened intently. A few minutes later, she said, "Okay. Thank you. I'll let you know." She ended the call with an unsteady finger.

"Let her know what? When you can start?" August said.

She turned to him, the man who had always been in her corner. Even now, despite the fact that she hadn't returned his declaration of love. "No, not that."

His brow furrowed in confusion. "Then what? You did get the job, right?"

"Not exactly."

"What do you mean, not exactly? You've busted your ass the past few weeks."

Sloane swallowed, still struggling to process the one-sided conversation with Emily. Her emotions and thoughts were on a seesaw that showed no signs of slowing down. "She thinks I've done a great job, but she also learned that MDJ—*Melinda*—is coming to town and thinks it would be the biggest get if I could get her to do something with Sugar Blitz. Possibly come on the podcast or IG Live. Show I'm really committed to the cause of generating buzz and presumably sales. That's what they're looking for, for their position—someone to go that extra mile, apparently, even if it means relying on and hyping up gossip."

His face, his voice remained stoic. "Do it, and the job is yours?"

Sloane forced the answer out. "Yes."

He was silent for a few seconds, the longest three seconds of her life. "Then you have to do it."

She jerked back in shock. "You want me to put all your business out in the street? *Exploit* you?"

The mask remained in place. "That's what we've been doing this whole time. I know what this job means to you. You're so close. It would be a shame to quit now. You were made for this job. You'll be fantastic."

Then why didn't she feel fantastic?

* * *

"To what do I owe the pleasure of your company?" Donovan asked as he opened his front door.

"Can't a gal come hang out with her big brother?" Sloane asked as she swept by him into his home.

"Sure, but I know you. You always have an ulterior motive," he said, following her down the hall to the kitchen.

"Love you, too, Donny," she said as she entered the kitchen. "But you're right. I actually came to see my soon-to-be sister-in-law." She stepped into a hug with the always fashionable, always welcoming Jada. She looked over her shoulder. "And you always have food, so it's a win-win for me. Besides, you invited me, remember?"

Donovan shot her a look. "If I recall correctly, you called, asked what we were having for dinner, said 'ooh' when I said chicken parmigiana, and asked if you could stop by."

Sloane waved her hand. "Details, schmetails."

As annoying as he could be in that big-brother-knows-best way, Donovan could always be counted on to offer good advice. And who knew August better than he did? But she wasn't ready to spill her guts just yet. She was still in denial that spillage was necessary.

"Well, you know I'm always happy to see you, Sloane, no matter the reason," Jada said. She was dressed "down" in the cutest jumpsuit Sloane had seen in a minute and black strappy sandals.

"Likewise," Sloane said. "You're too good for my brother, you know that, right?"

Donovan rolled his eyes, but went into big-brother mode anyway, grabbing her a Coke, her fave, from the refrigerator and handing it to her. She took a seat on a stool at the massive quartz countertop and observed her brother and his love finish preparing dinner, which mostly consisted of warming up and then plating the food Donovan's personal chef had already prepared. But they laughed and joked through it all, sneaking kisses and light touches as they passed by each other.

If Sloane didn't love them both dearly, she'd find it sickening.

She stayed out of the way, sipping the ice-cold soda while they brought the food to the dining room table. In companionable silence, they passed the dishes around and served themselves. The pasta dish smelled heavenly, but her appetite had deserted her. She took one bite and that was more than enough. Instead of eating, she cut the chicken into smaller and smaller pieces. Donovan kept sending curious looks her way and sharing concerned glances with his fiancée, but knew enough not to push her until she was ready.

She wasn't ready yet. "Jada, how's the business going?"

"Great, actually. The grand opening for Sugar Blitz Two is right around the corner, which is keeping me super busy," Jada said. "It's going to be fab."

"Awesome." Sloane went back to picking at her food.

"Sloane, what's going on?" Jada asked. "You don't look so great."

"Honey," Donovan hissed.

Sloane laughed, far from being offended. Jada's commitment to speaking her mind was one of the things Sloane loved about her the most. It felt good to laugh and release some of the tension that had filled every muscle in her body since leaving August's house yesterday.

"Chill, Donovan." Sloane set her fork down. "How do you two make it work? Y'all are complete opposites, and yet it works."

Donovan and Jada exchanged another glance, silently communicating with each other. Sloane tried not to be jealous. She failed miserably. She wanted what they had, but . . . but. Wasn't that the crux of her problem? She couldn't let go of the "but."

Donovan's hand landed on Jada's where it rested on the table. "We love each other."

"But we're not perfect. It took us time to get here," Jada said.

Sighing, Sloane nodded and forced down another bite of chicken. The undoubtedly excellent sauce might as well have been sawdust.

"Sloane, what's going on? Jada was right. You look terrible."

Jada slapped his hand. "I said 'not good,' not 'terrible.' I have tact."

Sloane offered up a small smile when Jada winked at her, then quickly explained the new job offer requirement and her subsequent conversation with August. "Why would he think I'd choose a job over him?"

Her brother shrugged. "Because everything you've done the past few weeks has been with the goal of getting a job?"

Sloane quickly shook her head. "But this is different. I'd never put him in a bad position if I can help it."

"Did you tell him that?"

"Well . . . no. I was in too much shock that he said he'd do it."

"But should you have been?"

Recalling the conversation, Sloane groaned, loud and extra-long. "No. He said he loved me."

"You said it back, yes?" Jada prodded.

Sloane groaned again and buried her face in her hands. "No."

"Oh, Sloane." Donovan rose and rounded the table. He sat in the empty chair next to her. "What's going on?"

She lifted her head and searched his face. "How did you get past it—the hurt that Dad caused, the rejection you felt when, sorry, Jada broke up with you—to trust that she wouldn't hurt you again and that your love will last?"

"I ended things, temporarily I might add, because I was scared," Jada said.

Donovan's look at his fiancée was full of love. "Once I understood that, the hurt melted away. I realized my life sucked without Jada and I didn't want to continue living that way. I knew I wanted to be there for her in the future whenever she got scared. People aren't perfect, Sloane. Once you understand that, it makes accepting their shortcomings and mistakes a little easier."

Wise, wise words from her brother. And maybe one of her shortcomings was not being able to let go of the past. August hadn't handled that situation long ago perfectly. Lord knew she hadn't either. "And the hurt Dad caused?"

He sighed and sat back. "It wasn't easy, but I finally came to grips with the fact that I'm not Dad. Yes, I've been shaped by him and Mama, but ultimately I'm my own person with my own life and thoughts, and I have to grab what I want and live the life I want to live. I'm my own person."

"And August is his own person. He's not our father." He wasn't the college kid who'd broken her heart. He'd shown her over and over how much he cared about her, his partners, and what they were trying to build with Sugar Blitz. He cared deeply about the people around him and always supported them. Wasn't that everything she'd always wanted?

Donovan nodded. "Right. He has his own shit to deal with when it comes to his dad and Melinda. Maybe that's why he so easily believed you'd choose your job over him."

Damn, damn, damn. She'd royally screwed everything up. Instead of being supportive, she'd hurt the man she loved with all her heart. But all was not lost. She wouldn't let it be. This was her newest and most important mission.

"I have to make this right." She leaped up from her seat. "I know what I have to do."

Chapter Thirty-Eight

"*G*et your head together," August muttered to himself as he stood on a ladder. "How many brain cells does it take to screw in a light bulb?" Apparently, more than he possessed, because it took three attempts before he managed to get the bulb into the opening. No surprise. He couldn't do shit right today. Not with his mind about fifteen miles away, still stuck in the hall outside his bedroom.

Why the fuck had he told Sloane he loved her? She wasn't ready for that. He knew that. Who the fuck knew when she would be?

She was understandably skittish. Had closed her heart after so many letdowns, starting with him. Yes, they were building something special now, but that took time.

August reached for his scalp with both hands and squeezed as hard as he could.

Hell, maybe she never would love him. After all, things never worked out for him. Not when it came to the people in his life loving him the way he loved them.

Is that why he'd told Sloane to do whatever it took to get the job? In some masochistic attempt to prove his theory that he wasn't worth loving? Wasn't worth fighting for?

That doubt—that no one would ever truly love him—had crept into his brain as soon as she pulled away when he confessed his feelings. It had burrowed its way into his psyche even more after that phone call. And it was still there, settling in for a long stay. It had found its dream destination with a king-size bed, unlimited food and beverage, and a beach just outside the window.

August climbed down the ladder and turned in a circle, taking in his surroundings with unseeing eyes. He was at Sugar Blitz Two, because where else would he be? Home was no longer a sanctuary. He needed some peace and quiet, and hey, no one was outside protesting. Cynthia had officially given her blessing after the community center announcement. Speaking so lovingly about his mother had really sealed the deal, she'd told him. So all in all, things were going great. Except he felt like shit and couldn't concentrate on anything.

He moved the ladder a few feet and grabbed another bulb. As he placed a foot on the first rung, the light fixture slipped out of his hand and crashed against the floor, splintering into jagged pieces. Shit. What the fuck was he doing? He blew out a breath and trudged to the supply closet for a broom. Thankfully, he found his way there with no more mishaps and returned to the storefront shortly.

He swept the shards into the dustpan. He squinted to make sure he hadn't missed any errant slivers, because that would be just like him to think everything was hunky-dory and then slip and fall and cut his hand.

The door creaked open behind him. One day he'd learn to keep the door locked. But residents seemed to like stopping in to check out their progress and offer up suggestions for local heroes for the podcast. So instead of yelling that they were closed, he forced the corners of his lips upward and turned. "Hi. How—"

The rest of his statement frittered away.

"Hello, August," Melinda said.

Somehow, someway, he found his voice, though shock was ricocheting through his body like a ball in a pinball arcade game. "Hi."

"You look surprised to see me."

"That's because I am."

She looked the same. They hadn't been in the same room for five years, since she told him there was no point in fighting for their marriage because it would never work. As he'd noticed the night she was on cable news, her hair was longer. But other than that, she looked the same. She wore a long, bright red sundress that complemented her brown skin. Her ever-present turquoise earrings dangled from her lobes.

Once upon a time, his heart would lighten every time she stepped into a room. Now, not so much. He'd always have fond memories of the time they spent together, but that's all it was. That love, that clinging to what they were, was gone forever. His heart truly belonged to another. Would Sloane ever return his feelings? He didn't know, but he couldn't think about that right now.

Melinda stepped farther into the building and took a look around the store. "I don't think I have to tell you I was surprised to hear that you and the other triplets started a cupcake shop. Now you're opening up another location."

"I'll let Donovan and Nicholas know you say hi."

She threw a sarcastic smile his way. "You do that. I'm sure they'll love hearing from me."

He shrugged. His friends cared about him. Had been there for him when he was going through a painful divorce. She wasn't their favorite person. Oh well. She sauntered over to him in that slow, steady way of hers. Something else that hadn't changed.

August slipped his hands into his pockets. "Why are you here, Melinda? We haven't spoken in years."

Her brow creased. "Sloane didn't tell you? She sent me."

As his knees gave out in shock, August reached blindly behind him for a chair and plopped down. "*Sloane* told you to come see me? Why?"

She casually sat across from him like she hadn't shocked ten years off his life. "She said we should talk."

Oh, right. Because he was the one who'd told Sloane she should exploit his relationship with his ex-wife for her career gain. "You're here about the interview. You want to get our stories straight before we start recording."

Her brow creased even more. "Interview? What interview?"

"The interview Sloane wants us to do to get more publicity for Sugar Blitz, which will also help her get a job."

Her mouth dropped open. "Okay. Wow. That sounds like that would be a hot mess. I'm sure everyone on social media would eat it up like ice cream, but no. Sloane never mentioned anything about an interview."

August blinked rapidly and shook his head. He didn't think he could take any more shocks to his system. "She didn't?"

She shook her head. "No, she didn't." A considering light entered her eyes. "And now things make a lot more sense."

That made one of them. "Then why are you here? What did Sloane say?"

She peered at him closely. "She said we should talk. That we should clear the air."

Another shock. "We're divorced. Is there any more air that has to be cleared?"

"She felt like there was. I have to admit I've known she was right for years, which is why I agreed to come."

August blew out a breath. "What do you want?"

"I want to say what I couldn't say five years ago. What, if you're honest with yourself, you weren't ready to hear."

August scrubbed a hand across his face. She was right. He was in a better place than he'd been in five years ago. He wasn't sure she had anything valuable or necessary to say, but at least he'd listen. That was more than he was able to give five years ago, when hurt and anger consumed him. He sucked in a lungful of air. "Okay. Have at it."

Melinda slapped her hands on her thighs. "Wow. I'm nervous. I've given speeches in front of thousands of people, been on national TV plenty of times, but this is weird."

"Now that you're done enumerating your accomplishments, why don't you get on with it?"

She shot him a look. "How I've missed that caustic wit." She held up a hand when he opened his mouth. "We used to be so close. I hurt you. I knew I was hurting you, and I did it anyway. I'm sorry. That's the most important thing I have to say. About Sloane . . ."

"What about Sloane?" He would protect her with every fiber of his being, whenever, however she needed it.

"I knew you felt more for her than friendship freshman year." He started to rise, but stopped when she shook her head. "I also knew you would never cheat on me, which is one of the reasons I married you. But duty cannot be the sole reason for a marriage."

"I loved you."

She nodded and reached for his hand. No shivers ran up his arm like they did whenever Sloane was in the same zip code. She squeezed, and stared at him with beseeching eyes. "And I loved you. How could I not? You were my support system when I thought I would never be okay again. You were the best friend I could always count on. And I hope I provided the same for you."

He stared at their joined hands before lifting his gaze. "You did, which is why it hurt like hell when you said you wanted a divorce."

"I know, but I felt stuck. All I knew was that I had to get out."

"You felt stuck with me. You had to get away from me."

"No. Yes." She raked her free hand through her hair. "With life. You would never let me down or turn your back on me. But we were so young when we started hanging out and then we started dating when we were fifteen."

"We were there for each other."

"Yes, and I'll be forever grateful for that. And if I'm being completely honest, I still miss it. But it was the right thing to do. When I got that opportunity to move to New York, I knew I had to take it. And that I wanted to go on that adventure alone. To figure out who I truly was."

"Without your crutch holding you back." He'd accepted that truth long ago.

"Oh, August, it was never about you. It was about me. You were always the good in my life. I couldn't put it into words, but I needed to be by myself for a while to figure out who I was. I didn't remember who I was before I was 'Melinda-and-August.' Hell, I was a kid before then."

"You didn't love me anymore."

"No, never believe that. I'll always love you. But I wasn't in love with you. I don't know if I ever was. You were my rock. Back then, as time went on, I started to realize what we had was a great friendship only. We bonded over trauma, but that deep, huge once-in-a-lifetime love was missing. We were together because we felt a duty to be there, not because of a connection that could never be replicated or bested with someone else." Melinda sighed. "To be perfectly honest, I didn't see that spark in your eye that I saw in my friends' eyes when they talked about their partners. It was missing with us. I tried to tell myself I was being silly. That people spend their whole lives looking for a partner as decent as you."

He'd always been able to read her like a book. "You've found that with someone?"

"Yeah, I think I have. Her name is Toni." When he nodded, she continued. "At our best, we were best friends. At our worst, we were each other's roadblocks. We couldn't explore the world and what it could offer us if we were tied together at the hip."

"So I did hold you back." Even as he was willing to accept that, a small part of him hurt.

"But no more than I held you back." She turned in her chair, holding out her hands. "Look at this. Look at what you've built. What you plan on building. The old August never would have done any of this. Starting a cupcake shop. Becoming a social media darling. I've been following your exploits. It's been quite amusing."

"Thanks. I think."

"I'll always feel bad about hurting you. You are the most honest, honorable man I will ever know."

He accepted the compliment with a stiff nod and sigh. "You're right. That spark was missing with us. I can admit that now. But it still hurt like hell when you walked out."

"I know, and I'll be forever sorry." She paused. "But if I'm not mistaken, you've found that feeling with someone else."

August shrugged as his present-day problems returned to his mind like a force field. "Have I? I don't know. Telling you this probably qualifies as weird, but you were my best friend once upon a time and you showed up here uninvited, so you get to hear my ramblings. I told her I loved her, and I got a thanks in return, basically. Can you blame me if I'm wondering if anyone is capable of feeling that kind of love for me?"

Melinda crossed her legs and leaned forward. "Look, I'm not going to pretend that Sloane and I are BFFs now, but I do know she was worried about you. Extremely worried."

He shrugged, unwilling to attach meaning to Sloane's actions. Too scared to.

She grasped his hand again. "Do you think she would've encouraged me to come see you if she didn't see a future with you? If she wasn't concerned about you? If she didn't realize you were still carrying some hurt from the past? I would say she knows you pretty damn well. She doesn't even have to see or talk to you to know you're beating yourself up. And back to your earlier point, she never once mentioned anything about a job or interview to me. That doesn't sound like a woman who's putting her career above a relationship to me. I saw her when she came to my book signing. She looked devastated. She kept asking me if I thought you'd be okay. She was concerned she'd hurt you."

Hope began to unfurl in his chest, but he kept quiet, not fully trusting it yet.

Clearly sensing his hesitancy, Melinda nodded. "It's not every day a girlfriend reaches out to an ex-wife. Are you sure she doesn't love you?"

No, he wasn't. And it was the best damned feeling in the world. Hope had turned into certainty. Letting go of the past was the only way to move forward into the future. He bounded up and rushed toward the exit. At the door, he turned back. "Thank you for coming today."

Melinda walked into his waiting arms. "I believe this is known as closure."

He smiled. "I believe you're right."

"You know I actually talk about that in my book. About what we, as Black people, need in order to reconcile our place in this country and achieve closure with the past. I've been told it's very insightful."

"Melinda."

"Right, right. Not the time."

Chapter Thirty-Nine

August settled on the chair he'd put together with his own two hands and leaned forward to press the red button on his phone. He took a deep, calming breath during the countdown. That did nothing to stop his leg from jiggling with nerves, but luckily, the table hid his limb.

But no time for that now. He stared at the image of himself on his phone screen.

"Thanks for tuning in. The first thing I want to say is I'm very, very nervous. This is the first time I'm doing a Live by myself. It's the first time in my life I'm intentionally seeking attention for myself. If you're watching this, you've probably joined me on quite the journey over the past few weeks. A journey that had a lot of ups and downs. I wanted to talk about that and give an unvarnished take on what I've been through."

A sense of calm settled through him. His voice came out stronger. More sure. "My name is August Hodges. Not SugarBae. Not pro athlete. As someone much wiser than I once told me, that's what I do, not who I am. I'm a real human being who bleeds when

I'm cut. I hurt, I live, I love just like you. A lot of you discovered me when I gave a little impromptu speech a few weeks ago. What I said resonated with you. I hope what I'm about to say does the same."

Now for the hardest part—opening up a vein. But he had to do it. Being open and honest had led him to this moment. He couldn't turn back. More importantly, he didn't want to. The only way to move forward was to continue to be open and honest. To continue being himself. "I used to think I was unlovable. My mom died when I was young. I don't have any siblings, at least not the blood kind. My dad and I don't—didn't—have the best relationship. My marriage broke up after a few years. I told myself I was okay with that. But really, I wasn't. I always felt I had to prove myself. I never seemed to be good enough. But I was wrong. Very wrong."

The certainty of what he was saying swept through him.

"If you take one thing from me, let it be this. No one is unlovable. That doesn't mean love is going to land in your lap. You have to be open to it. You have to be honest. You have to be vulnerable. Being vulnerable is the test I failed for so long. Because I didn't want to get hurt. Because I didn't think anyone could love me for me, so why even risk it? People are just going to hurt you in the end, right? In trying to protect myself, I was hurting myself. I wanted love but was too scared to risk being open and hurt to find it.

"But over the course of the past few weeks, I've learned that's no way to live. I didn't realize that until her. I didn't know how to love. Until her."

August chuckled. "Yes, you heard it here first. Straight from my lips. I found love. Not with one of the SugarBaebies, though I'll always be grateful for your support. But maybe she's a SugarBaeby, even if she'll never admit it. All this growth I've experienced has been because of her. She pushed me out of my comfort zone and made me a better person. She made me realize I can't hide. More importantly, I don't want to hide. I learned that we can make a difference in this world if we try hard enough and don't give up. If we don't settle for coasting."

He shrugged. "Y'all have said you wanted to get to know me better. Well, here is me being as real as I can be."

The door opened and Sloane walked in. She stopped in front of the table. August met her eyes. A sense of calmness, the sense of rightness he'd been searching for his whole life, settled around him. She was the one.

He stood. "I'm just a guy who doesn't like talking much, standing in front of a woman, asking her to love me."

"I do. And that's all, folks." Sloane stepped around the table and ended the Live. She slowly turned to face him. "I think we've given them enough."

He nodded. What was said next was only for them. "Hey, sweetness."

"Hey, MOTY. I'm so proud of you. That was beautiful." Her voice shook with emotion.

"Don't cry." He wiped away a tear slipping down her soft cheek.

"I can't help it. What you said was so beautiful. I don't deserve you. I was so focused on getting that job that I never considered the toll all this was taking on you or that I was taking advantage of you. I'm so sorry I made you think I would seriously choose a job over you. No job is worth your well-being or what we have."

He moved closer. Always closer. "Sending my ex-wife was a wild, brave move."

She twisted her hands together and made a face. "Did I overstep? I did, didn't I?"

He reached for her hands and squeezed. "No. Even though I didn't know it beforehand, talking to Melinda was exactly what I needed to finally let go of the past and look forward to the future."

"So, y'all are good?"

August chuckled. "As good as you can be with an ex-spouse. It was good to clear the air."

Relief settled on her face. "I'm happy to hear that."

"You didn't send Melinda to talk me into doing a podcast with her."

Sloane vehemently shook her head. "No. I would never."

"What about the job, though?"

Sloane let out a rueful laugh. "I've been so focused on getting that job, thinking about how it could advance my career, but I never stopped to consider whether it was the right job. And to be perfectly honest, her last request, or command, pissed me all the way off. I thought about showing up at her office and yelling at her, or at least calling to do the same, but I calmed down and thought better of it. I went with a very professional email instead."

He side-eyed her.

"What? It was! Here. Look for yourself." She retrieved her phone from her purse and scrolled through it, then handed it back to him.

While I appreciate the opportunity to work for your company, I do not believe I would be a good fit. While I love social media, I don't believe in using it to exploit people. If used properly and responsibly, social media can be a place devoted to change, community, and goodwill.

August smiled. "Good job. You didn't burn the place down."

"I know, right! I even edited it before pressing send, because I am the new and improved Sloane. The email originally said 'exploit people for shits and giggles.'"

His lips twitched. "I'm so proud of you." His eyebrows lifted. "You cc'd that dude you hate."

Sloane shrugged. "If he wants to work there, the job is his. I'm done chasing what I think I should want."

"At the risk of sounding crass, how are you going to pay your bills? I know you were, understandably, very worried about that." Despite his interest in her answers to his questions, he couldn't hold out any longer. He had to touch her. Hold her. He wrapped his arms around her waist. Grinned like a besotted fool when she mirrored his actions.

Her smile warmed every part of his previously frozen heart. "Funny you should ask. As it so happens, I've accepted another position. You are looking at Sugar Blitz's newest director of social media *and* community outreach. I've fussed at you about making sure you don't gentrify the neighborhood. Now I'm in a position to make sure it doesn't happen."

He lowered his forehead to hers. She was the most brilliant person he knew. "It's perfect for you, but . . ."

"But why did I accept after saying, incessantly, that I didn't want to rely on my brother or any man?"

"Yeah. That."

Sloane laughed. "My brother gives pretty decent advice when he isn't trying to run my life. He made me see that I was my own worst enemy, too scared to reach out and take what was absolutely perfect for me. I don't want to be scared. Or at least I don't want to let the fear win. Working for Sugar Blitz doesn't make me less than, especially if it's work that I love. And I do. This is the most fun I've had at a job ever. How many people can say that? Why run from it? And let's be real. I did an amazing job. Plus, I came up with the job title and description. I don't want him getting too much credit. He already thinks he knows everything."

"Very true. I'm absolutely thrilled for you and Sugar Blitz." He drew her closer. "Speaking of love, can I get you to repeat what you said earlier?"

"You mean about loving my job? Oh, yeah, I do." She grinned when he growled. "Oh, that's not what you're talking about? How about this? I love you with all of my heart, and I'm so sorry I gave you cause to believe otherwise. You are my world. You're everything I've ever wanted and more."

"That's better." He cradled her cheeks between his hands. "I love you, sweetness."

Her blinding smile melted his heart. "I'm totally a SugarBaeby."

"I know. Now kiss me."

"Your wish is my command."

August drew her flush against him and met her halfway for the most extraordinary kiss of all time. Sweet and loving. He poured all his love for her into the embrace. How had he managed to make it through the last few days without holding her, touching her, kissing her? Her mouth was heaven. Being with her was better.

Eventually, he became aware of a noise. Reluctantly, he pulled away and turned toward the commotion. A large crowd had gathered outside. Thankfully, he'd finally remembered to lock the front door. The group, led by Cynthia and Ben Franklin, were chanting something. Beside him, Sloane started giggling.

He cocked his head to the side. "Are they—"

"Chanting *SugarBae, SugarBae*? Oh, yeah. You're so going viral again."

He drew her back into his arms and lowered his head. "No, *we* are."

Acknowledgments

To all the readers who read *Fake It Till You Bake It*, thank you for giving it a chance and for letting me know how much you enjoyed it. Authors want to bring readers joy, and it's the best feeling in the world when you let us know we've accomplished our goal. Thank you so much for your infinite patience and kindness as *Legend* was delayed.

To my mother and my family, I love you always.

Thank you to my agent, Sara Megibow, for your continued help.

To my editor, Tiffany Shelton, thank you for taking me on and being patient with me. I know I don't make it easy.

To everyone at St. Martin's Griffin—including Marissa Sangiacomo, Sara La Cotti, and Kejana Ayala—who had a hand in shepherding this book into the world, thank you so much for loving books and doing what you do. I am forever grateful.

Thank you, Olga Grlic and Alex Cabal, for designing and illustrating the best covers ever! I gasp in sheer delight each time I see what you've created for me.

Author friends are the best. Destin Divas, I love ya.

About the Author

Kim Campbell

Jamie Wesley has been reading romance novels since she was about twelve years old, when her mother left a romance novel that a friend had given her on the nightstand. Jamie read it instead, and the rest is history. When she's not writing or reading romance, Jamie can be found watching TV, rooting for her favorite sports teams, and/or planning her next trip to Walt Disney World.